NINE LIVES

Peter Swanson's novels include *The Girl With a Clock for a Heart*, nominated for an *LA Times* book award; *The Kind Worth Killing*, a Richard and Judy pick and the iBooks store's thriller of the year; *Rules for Perfect Murders*, the 2020 Richard and Judy Pick; and most recently *Every Vow You Break*. He lives with his wife and cat on the north coast of Massachusetts.

What readers are saying:

'It **gripped** me from start to finish.'

'Prepare to be **blown away**.'

'Another **fast-paced** edge of your seat masterclass.'

'What an absolutely **wild ride**.'

'Best Peter Swanson murder mystery I've read.'

'An absolute winner . . . A **must-read** for lovers of a good thriller.'

Also by Peter Swanson

EVERY VOW YOU BREAK
RULES FOR PERFECT MURDERS
BEFORE SHE KNEW HIM
ALL THE BEAUTIFUL LIES
HER EVERY FEAR
THE KIND WORTH KILLING
THE GIRL WITH A CLOCK FOR A HEART

PETER SWANSON

NINE LIVES

faber

First published in the UK 2022
by Faber & Faber Limited
Bloomsbury House, 74–77 Great Russell Street
London WC1B 3DA

First published in the USA in 2022
by William Morrow, an imprint of HarperCollins Publishers,
195 Broadway, New York, NY 10007

This paperback edition first published in 2023

Typeset by Typo•glyphix, Burton-upon-Trent, DE14 3HE
Printed and bound by CPI Group (UK) Ltd, Croydon, CR0 4YY

A CIP record for this book
is available from the British Library

ISBN 978-0-571-35857-1

2 4 6 8 10 9 7 5 3 1

For John Merrill Swanson

Balled up in pain
and without a flashlight in the dark:
eighty-three, sooner or later.

Those who are just:
quite a few, thirty-five.

But if it takes effort to understand:
three.

Worthy of empathy:
ninety-nine.

Mortal:
one hundred out of one hundred—
a figure that has never varied yet.

— Wisława Szymborska, "A Word on Statistics"

MATTHEW BEAUMONT—a suburban father stressed by the complexities of family life in Dartford, Massachusetts.

JAY COATES—an aspiring actor in Los Angeles, California.

ETHAN DART—a singer songwriter in Austin, Texas.

CAROLINE GEDDES—an English professor at the University of Michigan, lives in Ann Arbor with two cats.

FRANK HOPKINS—a longtime resident of Kennewick, Maine, owns the Windward Resort.

ALISON HORNE—currently living off the largesse of a married man in New York City.

ARTHUR KRUSE—an oncology nurse grieving the loss of his husband, in Northampton, Massachusetts.

JACK RADEBAUGH—a retired businessman, recently divorced, who has moved back into his childhood home in West Hartford, Connecticut.

JESSICA WINSLOW—an FBI agent in the Albany, New York, field office.

NINE LIVES

NINE

Matthew Beaumont

Jay Coates

Ethan Dart

Caroline Geddes

Frank Hopkins

Alison Horne

Arthur Kruse

Jack Radebaugh

Jessica Winslow

I

WEDNESDAY, SEPTEMBER 14, 5:13 P. M.

Jonathan Grant, unless he let her know ahead of time that he couldn't make it, always visited on Wednesday evening. His wife had a standing "girls' night out" on Wednesdays—occasionally in the city, but usually in New Jersey—so Jonathan would leave the office by five and be at Alison's one-bedroom apartment in Gramercy Park by five-thirty at the latest.

Alison Horne was ready when the doorman buzzed up to let her know Jonathan was on his way.

She met him at the door, and he presented her with a bottle of Sancerre, a Bulgari scarf she didn't think she'd ever wear, and that day's mail that he'd picked up from the doorman. She started to flip through the mail, but he stopped her and led her to the bedroom. She was in a white satin robe—it was how he liked to be greeted—and she slid back onto her bed while he undressed. He looked great for a man in his early seventies, full head of hair, fairly trim, but the muscles in his chest and arms were beginning to sag. He slid next to her on the bed, already erect, and with the red mottled skin on his face and neck that was a telltale sign he'd taken some kind of ED pill as soon as he left the office. Sometimes he took it just after he arrived, in which case they'd drink the bottle of wine first while the pill kicked in.

Afterward, while Jonathan dozed, Alison took her second shower of the day, then dressed as though they were going to go out for dinner later, although that hadn't been confirmed. She opened the wine and poured herself a glass, then looked through her mail. Two catalogues, an Amex bill, and an envelope with no return address. She opened it, curious, and pulled out a single folded sheet of paper, and stared at a list of names.

Matthew Beaumont
Jay Coates
Ethan Dart
Caroline Geddes
Frank Hopkins
Alison Horne
Arthur Kruse
Jack Radebaugh
Jessica Winslow

She frowned and pressed the sheet of paper flat onto the coffee table, telling herself that she'd show it to Jonathan. A shiver went over her skin, and she shook out her limbs to make it stop. There was something vaguely threatening about receiving a list of names with no explanation. It occurred to her that it just might have something to do with Jonathan. Although she knew relatively little about him, considering the time they spent together, she did know that he had a lot of money. And people who have money usually have enemies. It made her wonder if he would recognize any of the names on the list, besides hers.

He emerged from the bedroom fully dressed, accepted a glass of wine, then looked at the sheet of paper Alison handed to him. "This mean anything to you?" she asked.

He shook his head. "What is it?"

"I just got it, in the mail."

"Was this all?"

"Yeah. Strange, huh?"

"Strange."

He handed the list back to Alison. She asked: "We going to dinner?"

"I would if I could, but I got roped into dinner uptown with some hedge fund guys. Sorry, Al."

She shrugged. When they'd first begun this relationship— a year and a half ago—she used to make a fuss when he had to leave her. She did it for him, mostly, till she realized that he didn't need those kinds of reassurances. He was in it for the sex and the company, and she was in it for the money, and, she supposed, the sex. Before he left, he gave her a prepaid Visa card, telling her it was an anniversary gift, in case she didn't like the scarf.

"How much is on it?" she asked. Again, something she would never have asked when they were first together.

"I'll let you be surprised. Don't try to buy a car with it, though."

After he left, Alison Horne called her best friend, Doug, and asked if he'd like to have dinner that night. On her.

2

It was the most interesting piece of mail that Arthur Kruse, having just returned from physical therapy, received that morning.

He opened the envelope, not expecting anything of note, and was surprised to find a short list of names, including his. He didn't recognize any of the other people on the list.

There were three hours in the day before Arthur was due for his shift as an oncology nurse at Cooley Dickinson Hospital in Northampton. He'd just begun reading *A World Lit Only by Fire* by William Manchester. Since reading *A Distant Mirror* over the summer, he'd found he didn't want to leave the Middle Ages. Something about those past lives, the constant suffering, the search for God, acted as the only balm to Arthur's state of mind since the car accident, nearly a year ago, that took the life of his husband, Richard, their cocker spaniel, Misty, and most of the function of Arthur's left leg. He couldn't quite believe it had been a whole year. Joan, his minister—and Arthur's closest friend—told him it would be at least two years until he began to feel some semblance of normality, of happiness, of a return to his life, but Arthur wondered. The past endless year felt like it was just going to be repeated ad infinitum. Nothing helped. That wasn't entirely true. Medieval history helped. He gingerly slid into his reading chair and picked up where he'd left off in Manchester's book, not nearly as good as Tuchman's. He read two pages, then drifted off, waking an hour before he had to be at the hospital.

His leg was always at its worst after midday napping, and he found himself limping to the kitchen to put on hot water for a cup of tea. While waiting for the water to boil, he looked out the window over his sink and caught a glimpse of the fox—the one he'd named Reynard—skirting the edge of his property. It was moving fast, and just before it ducked into the trees, it turned its head and Arthur thought he saw something—a small rodent maybe—in its jaws. It inexplicably made Arthur happy for the moment. The last time he'd seen Reynard he'd been worried about how skinny and ragged he looked.

The day was overcast, and the willow tree down by the brook had just begun to exhibit a yellowish cast. He drank the tea at his computer and thought of the list he'd gotten in the mail. What had it meant? Some strange automatic mailing, a computer screwing up somewhere in the middle of the country and sending out some random names. It was a possibility. Ever since Richard's passing he'd taken to giving small amounts of money to multiple charities, ensuring that his name was on about a hundred different mailing lists, probably specified as an "easy touch." That was okay. There were worse things to be, and getting mail was actually something he looked forward to. He'd been one of those children who sent away for catalogues just to receive them, until his father found out and put a stop to it.

He finished his tea, returned an email to Joan to let her know he was available to do the flowers for church that Sunday, and prepared to go to work.

3

THURSDAY, SEPTEMBER 15, 11:00 A. M.

Ethan Dart heard the mail flop through the slot in his apartment door. He spotted the mysterious-looking envelope right away, and opened it instantly, hoping that it was a response from an agent. He'd recently gone through a period of unprecedented productivity and sent his demo tapes out to about a dozen agents who represented songwriters. It was a stab in the dark, he knew, but he figured it couldn't hurt. Inside the envelope (the postmark was from New York City, and that was promising) was just a single sheet of paper with a list of names, nine in all, including his. He wondered if it had been sent to him by mistake, possibly because he'd made some sort of short list for representation.

He took the list, plus his mug of coffee, back to his bedroom and fired up his laptop. Ethan punched in the first name from the list—Matthew Beaumont—along with "songwriter" to narrow the results. Nothing came up, at least nothing that indicated Matthew Beaumont was another songwriter seeking representation. He tried a few more names, but lost interest. It clearly wasn't a list of other songwriters or artists. It sparked an idea for a song, though, the chorus something like, "I want to be the last one on your list." He grabbed a pencil, flipped over the sheet of paper, and began jotting down lyrics for a country song. *List* was both a great rhyming word—so many options—and a crappy one since the options were all clichés. *Missed. Kissed. Insist.* Still, he wrote three verses, and even began to hear the melody in his head. He got another cup of coffee and his guitar, and, after smoking the day's first bowl of weed, began to work it out.

He didn't think again about the list of names until much later that night, when he was sitting at the bar at Casino el Camino on 6th Street in Austin, trying to come up with something clever to say to Hannah Scharfenberg, who'd been sitting with him for the past hour.

"I got a list in the mail today. Eight names I didn't know, plus mine."

"What do you mean?"

Ethan took a foamy sip from his just-cracked bottle of Lone Star. "Just like I said. I got an envelope addressed to me. Inside was a sheet of paper with nine typed names on it, in alphabetical order. And mine was one of them."

"They were typed?"

"No, not typed, but not handwritten. They were printed. From a computer."

"Strange."

"I guess so. Good thing was I got a song out of it. 'Last on Your List.' Wrote the whole thing in about an hour. Kind of an Eric Church thing."

Hannah, a pharmacist and a rabid Longhorns fan, did not have a whole lot of interest in Ethan's songwriting hopes and dreams, and he watched her eyes glaze over at the mention of his song. He bought her, and himself, a shot of George Dickel, then talked her into letting him walk her home. Ashley, her housemate, was away visiting her parents in Dallas, so Hannah invited him in. They smoked some pot, then watched half of *The Royal Tenenbaums* before having sex on the futon couch.

"We have to stop doing this," Hannah said, coming back from the bathroom, wearing one of her old softball jerseys and nothing else.

"Why?"

"Because you're *seeing* Ashley. And I live with her."

"We're not exclusive, at least that's what she tells me."

"No, but I *live* with her, and if she finds out it's going to make life around here very awkward."

"I think I like you more than I like her."

"It doesn't matter."

"It matters to me."

"Trust me, things that matter to you don't matter to anybody else. You haven't learned that yet."

He convinced Hannah to let him stay over. This was after he'd made them both a cheese omelet they ate at the Formica breakfast table in the kitchen. In Hannah's bed—a mattress on the floor, actually—they'd fooled around a little till Hannah told him the Ambien was kicking in and she had to sleep. She curled away from him, and Ethan, his hand still pressed up against her hip, thought about his day, wondering if Hannah was on to something when she told him how the things that mattered to him didn't matter to anybody else. It would explain a lot about his life.

Before finally falling asleep himself, he thought again about the list he'd gotten in the mail. He recited seven of the names to himself—he had a near photographic memory—but couldn't remember the final one, probably because he'd barely looked at it. Then he recited the lyrics to the new song, decided they sucked donkey dick, and fell asleep.

4

THURSDAY, SEPTEMBER 15, 1:44 P. M.

The name that Ethan Dart couldn't remember belonged to Jessica Winslow. On Thursday she received the list of names in an envelope that was addressed to Special Agent Winslow at the Albany field office of the FBI. There was a single Forever stamp in the right-hand corner of the envelope, and the postmark indicated the letter had come from New York City, mailed two days previously.

It was unusual for her to receive any mail at the office, particularly something so cryptic. Just a list of names. She instinctively held the letter at the very edges, then dropped it gingerly onto her desk. She called her immediate supervisor, Aaron Berlin, asking him to swing by her office.

"Do you know the other names?" he asked, five minutes later, peering at the letter from over Jessica's shoulder.

Even though she'd read the names on the list several times, she reread them silently to herself one more time.

"Arthur Kruse is the only name that's familiar to me, but only because my dad used to mention a friend of his named Art Kruse, or maybe I'm imagining it. I always assumed the last name was spelled Cruise, like Tom Cruise, though."

"You never met him?"

"No, my dad just talked about him. Whenever anyone mentioned a lake house, or living on a lake, my dad would always say something like, 'Back in college I spent a summer at Art Kruse's lake house.' We used to make fun of him for it, and that's why I think I remember."

"It's an unusual name."

"What, Kruse? Not really. Not if you're German. I've already looked it up on Google and I found some Arthur Kruses but they were all German. Germans from Germany."

"Hmm."

Jessica swiveled in her chair to look up at Aaron. She'd never really seen him from that angle and noticed how much dark hair he had in his nostrils.

"What do you think?" she said.

He shrugged. "Get it analyzed if you want. Could be nothing. Could be some computer glitch somewhere spewing out junk mail."

"Could be."

After Aaron left, she put the envelope and the letter in separate plastic bags, then moved them to her out-box. She went back to studying the file on the William Brundy murder trial she'd been called to testify at the following week. She kept waiting to hear from the prosecution that it was going to be settled before heading to trial, but now it looked like that wasn't going to happen. William Brundy was a patrol officer in Stark, New York, who had killed his ex-wife by staging a break-in at her split-level ranch.

Blood evidence and crime scene photographs had been forwarded to their office and Jessica had been given the job of lead investigator. She didn't particularly mind testifying at trials, but Brundy's defense attorney was a dickwad named Elliot Skenderian who always somehow managed to get under Jessica's skin. If she owned a dartboard, she'd put a picture of Skenderian's face on it.

Before leaving the office at just after five o'clock, she took another look at the mysterious list of names and wrote them down using the Notes app on her smartphone. Maybe that night she'd catch up on *The Good Wife* while doing some more googling. If there was a connection between her and these people, she'd find it. The internet liked to give up its secrets.

She wasn't surprised to see Aaron Berlin at the Club Room after work, but she *was* surprised that he wasn't alone. He was sitting at a booth with Roger Johnson, the outgoing special agent in charge. Roger spotted her entering the bar and asked her to join them.

"I'm going to have dinner with Anthony at the bar, but thanks, anyway."

Anthony, the bartender, had a glass of Pinot Noir already poured and waiting for her when she slid onto the padded leather stool. She wondered briefly if it looked bad that she'd shunned her colleagues in favor of eating alone at the bar, then shrugged it off. Johnson was moving to the Schenectady office, and Berlin, well, fuck him.

She drank her wine slowly, doing the *Times* crossword,

Anthony helping her out when he wasn't busy. She asked for a second glass plus a half order of penne with puttanesca sauce and a garden salad on the side. When she'd finished the crossword, only unsure about one of the answers, she slid the folded newspaper back into her purse, paid the bill, and prepared to leave.

"Two Belvederes please, Anthony. On the rocks." Aaron deposited himself onto the stool next to her.

"Uh, no thanks, Aaron. I was about to go home." Jessica looked over Aaron's shoulder and saw Roger making his way to the exit.

"One drink, Jess. Please."

She agreed, and, surprisingly, he asked her several questions about her recent life before starting in on his favorite topic: their affair and why it had ended.

"You're married," she said.

"Sort of. Not really. My wife has affairs. I know she does."

"That's not really the point."

"Then what's the point?"

"Honestly, I don't even know if I want to be in a relationship, but if I did want to be in one, it would be with someone closer to my age, someone unattached, someone without kids, someone I don't work with, someone who isn't a narcissist . . ."

"I already don't trust this guy."

Jessica smiled, even though his attempt at humor was the type of thing she had grown to dislike about him.

When they'd first gotten involved, there had been a real intensity between them. Aaron was a little bit of a jerk—she'd always known that—but he took his job seriously, he had empathy, and there had been a week early on when she thought they might be falling in love. She sipped at her vodka with slightly numb lips and knew she'd made a mistake by agreeing to one more drink. She decided to change the subject. "You really didn't think there was anything strange about that list I got in the mail?"

Aaron was signaling Anthony with just his eyes, trying to get two more drinks. "What? That list of names? That bothered you?"

"It didn't bother me. I was just interested. It was unusual."

"I guess so. If you want, I'll get Rick to cross-reference them in the database. Maybe there is a connection. Maybe you all won three free days at a timeshare in Fort Myers."

"Maybe you're right. Just some glitch in some mass mailing system."

Two more vodkas arrived, and Jessica eyed the glass, knowing that the difference between drinking it and not drinking it was the difference between a full night's sleep and Aaron winding up in her bed tonight.

She slid off the stool and began to put on her coat. "Sorry, Aaron. I need an early night."

He pursed his lips, but said, "Okay. Lunch soon?"

"Sure."

Anthony glanced over at Jessica, and she thought she

saw a little bit of approval in his eyes. Although he'd never said it out loud, Anthony was not a huge fan of Aaron. "You leaving so soon?" the bartender asked, a crooked smile on his face.

"I am, Anthony. Thanks again, and tell Maria that I loved the penne."

Anthony was reaching for the extra vodka on the bar when Aaron stopped him. "That's okay, T, we'll keep it." He poured her drink into his as Jessica knotted her scarf around her neck. She turned and left before she changed her mind. She really did need an early night.

5

Thursdays were Caroline Geddes's office hours, two hours that she had begun to rely on as quiet writing time, due to the low number of students who stopped by to see her. That Thursday there was only one, Elaine Cheong, who dropped by unannounced, while two students who had previously arranged meetings didn't show up. Caroline had taught long enough—a dozen years now—to see how email had transformed the student–teacher relationship. Today's students went out of their way to do everything via email, or via the wiki she'd set up for some of her larger courses. They sent their late papers, their excuses, and even their grade-grubbing compliments, all via email. One of her male students from last year might even have sent a sexual proposition to her, although, despite twenty years spent parsing text, she still wasn't sure what he'd meant by "Wish you were my teacher aide, know what I mean? jk." It took her half a day to realize that *jk* stood for " just kidding."

Elaine, with tears in her eyes, explained to Caroline that she was late for the second class of the semester because of a problem with a faulty alarm clock and that was why she'd missed the pop quiz. "It's not fair that I can't make it up," she said, for the second time.

"It was a pop quiz. It'll be a very small part of your final grade."

"I need to get an A in this class."

"Tell you what, Elaine, I'll give you a new pop quiz right now."

Caroline pulled a piece of paper out of one of her notebooks and quickly jotted down three new questions on one of the Wordsworth poems that they hadn't gone over in class that morning but which had been assigned. Caroline pushed the sheet of paper across to her student and told her she had ten minutes.

"This isn't the same quiz," Elaine said, two distinct lines appearing on her otherwise flawless forehead.

"No, it's a new pop quiz."

Caroline pulled out a book and pretended to read it while watching the girl bite at her lower lip so hard that she left little teeth impressions in it. "I didn't know we were supposed to memorize dates."

"Just do your best, and at least you'll get better than a zero."

Elaine hunched herself over the paper and scrawled some answers, and just before Caroline was going to announce that time was up, she pushed the paper across the desk. "I still don't think it's fair," she said, but almost so low that Caroline couldn't hear it.

"I'll see you in class next week," Caroline said, and Elaine left in a huff, her phone already in her hand. Caroline imagined she was texting someone about what a bitch her English professor was. It didn't matter; there were twenty minutes left in her office hours. She glanced at her emails and there was nothing pressing to respond to, so she opened the email she'd received two weeks earlier from David Latour, the professor from McGill University whom Caroline had met when she'd delivered her lecture on Joanna Baillie at the Scholarly Theories Conference in Toronto over the summer.

He'd written to say how much he'd enjoyed her talk, but also to share a poem he thought she might enjoy by Louis MacNeice, called "Wolves." Its opening line was "I do not want to be reflective anymore," and Caroline had had that particular line trapped in her head ever since she'd read it. She reread the poem now, nearly wrote David to tell him again how much she loved it but stopped herself. It was enough that she'd written him once, and enough to think she might see him again at some further date and be able to tell him in person.

Her office hours over, she crossed the campus to where her Prius was parked, then drove to her two-bedroom cottage in the Water Hill section of Ann Arbor. She'd left Fable, her adventurous cat, out all day, and was relieved to see him waiting on the front porch for her, relieved also that he hadn't caught and killed a bird and left it on her doormat. He followed her in, pinned his gray ears back, and bolted toward the food bowl in the kitchen. Estrella, her shy orange tabby, leaped up onto the dining room table to greet her. Caroline flipped through the mail she'd received, pulling out a white envelope, her address printed out on a mailing label in Courier font. A single Forever stamp with the American flag was in the right-hand corner. There was no return address.

Something about it seemed personal somehow, even though there wasn't anything remotely personal about it. She set aside the excise tax bill, the solicitation letters from any one of the animal welfare nonprofits she got—Pet Smart had *clearly* sold her address to some sort of mailing list—and slit open the envelope with an unvarnished thumbnail.

Inside was a single piece of paper, computer printed, the font Courier, like the mailing label.

Matthew Beaumont
Jay Coates
Ethan Dart
Caroline Geddes
Frank Hopkins
Alison Horne
Arthur Kruse
Jack Radebaugh
Jessica Winslow

Caroline looked into the envelope to see if there was anything else, but there wasn't. Just the single sheet of paper with the list of names, none of which was familiar to her, except for her own, of course.

Estrella tried to rub her cheek against the edge of the paper, and Fable loudly mewled from the kitchen, waiting for food. A horrible thought went through Caroline's mind: *It is a list of death. Someone has marked us for death.* She thought this automatically, in the same way that she automatically thought that every time her phone rang it was news of some unspeakable tragedy. She read the list again, then laughed internally at how morbid she'd been. Of course, if it was a list of living people, they were all marked for death, sooner or later. It was eerie, no matter what, and reminded her of that Muriel Spark book, *Memento Mori*. Of course, she was reading too much into what was probably a list of no consequence. But that was what she did with her life, that was her profession—she read into things.

"'I do not want to be reflective anymore,'" she recited to herself, "'envying and despising unreflective things.'" MacNeice was onto something there, even though he'd probably been talking about the political situation in Germany right before World War II and not about a tendency to overanalyze. But in her own life, though not necessarily in her class, she allowed for personal interpretations of literary works. What was the next line in the poem? Was it *"I do not want to be a tragic or a philosophic chorus,"* then something, something, then *"And after that let the sea flow over us"*? Maybe tonight she'd memorize the whole poem. It was the one good thing that her mother had taught her to do. Memorize and recite poetry.

Caroline rubbed Estrella beneath the chin, feeling the vibrations of her purr against her fingers. Then she went into the kitchen to feed Fable.

6

THURSDAY, SEPTEMBER 15, 12:33 P. M.

He glanced through the list, didn't think much of it, and threw it into the kitchen wastebasket. Jay Coates had a callback for a commercial that day and was feeling halfway bullish about his prospects. It was an ad for instant rice, and he would be playing the elitist chef won over by the crappy processed rice in a box. His meeting was at three that afternoon in Burbank, so that gave him two hours before he'd need to be in the Beemer and on his way.

Even though he'd gone for a short run right after he'd gotten up, he pulled out the rowing machine and did a solid hour on it, finally watching the *NCIS* episode that his friend Madison was in. It had been on his DVR for weeks, and she'd been asking if he'd watched it yet, hoping for notes. *Notes. Jesus.* It was *NCIS*. She had two scenes, and a total of three lines of dialogue. She played a personal trainer at a gym, and the director made sure her tits—he probably thought they were real—were prominently framed in both of her scenes. After watching the whole episode, Jay was relieved that a) it was a crappy role, and b) Madison was crappy in it. The real reason he'd delayed watching her big break was the fear she might have nailed it, and that it might lead to more work for her, and *that* was something he couldn't handle right now.

After parking in one of the guest spots outside of the single-story office park where Buchman Creative was housed, Jay did two quick lines of the coke he'd been saving up for just this occasion, then walked across the gluey asphalt in the near ninety-degree heat, hoping he wouldn't start sweating before the meeting. He was ushered straight in by the doughy receptionist, who had some sort of Midwestern accent, turned down the offer of a bottled water, and asked for tap. Madison had suggested the tap-water move—made you seem down to earth, she'd said. He ran his lines again in front of the two ad writers, creeps who might be younger than he was, although he was not a hundred percent sure, plus Amy Buchman, head of the agency, who swung by because she'd just found five free minutes in the day. When he left, Jay spotted Dan Sweden in the waiting room. They both pretended not to see each other.

His manager called an hour later to tell him that they'd passed, but that Amy was impressed, and if anything else came up, etcetera. The call came while he'd been walking through the Brentwood Country Mart, considering buying some new sneakers at James Perse. Instead, he went and got onion rings at Barney's Burgers, sat at a table, and, seething, began to look for a good prospect. It took twenty-five minutes but just as he was finishing his rings, he saw her. She was perfect: late twenties, yoga pants, not quite as pretty as she'd been told she was, and all alone. He followed her, knowing exactly how to blend in, not be noticed, but always keeping her in his peripheral vision. He followed her into Christian Louboutin, where she was pretending she could afford a pair of shoes, and asked the woman behind the desk if Tracy still worked there. She looked confused, then finally asked, "Do you mean Theresa?"

"Right," Jay said.

"She works on the weekends."

"Thanks," Jay said and left the store just as the blonde did.

He trailed her to the parking lot, where she got into a silvery blue Honda Civic, probably purchased by her father when she turned twenty-five. "It's a very reliable car, sweetie," he'd undoubtedly said, then she'd kissed him on the cheek and told him in her little girl's voice how much she loved her daddy.

After she got into her car and pulled straight out of her parking spot, Jay trotted to his Beemer, managing to find her again on San Vicente heading east. He followed her all the way to Koreatown, memorizing her license plate number. She parked in front of a two-story stucco apartment building and entered through the plate-glass doors using a key on the same chain as her car key. This was where she lived. Jay pulled into the strip mall across the street, parked so that he could keep an eye on the building, and lit one of the two Parliament cigarettes he allowed himself per day. He got on his phone, and went to Instagram, punching in #brentwoodcountrymart, not really expecting to get a hit, but not entirely surprised when the most recent image, a close-up of some latte foam swirled into a heart, was posted by an abbybritell. Her pictures, mostly selfies, confirmed it was the blonde he'd been following. She called herself an actress, writer, and tai chi instructor.

And like that, he owned her. Her name. Her personal photos. He knew where she lived, what she drove. And Jay knew, without a doubt, that he could murder her in the next twenty-four hours. And no one would ever catch him. There was zero connection between Jay Coates from West Hollywood and Abby Britell from Koreatown. He could imagine the headlines already. A pretty white girl murdered in Hollywood. It would be *everywhere*. He started to fantasize about how it would play out but stopped himself. There'd be time for that later, and, right now, just the fact that he'd learned her name and where she lived was giving him a hot buzz of adrenaline. He felt better as he pulled the car out of the lot and drove toward home. He thought he'd feel good the entire drive, but he didn't, not really. It had been way too easy tracking that woman, and maybe what he really needed to do was to up the game, actually hurt one of those smug bitches, and then see how he felt.

That night, after doing a hundred push-ups, then his

facial routine, he called Madison to let her know he'd watched her *NCIS*.

"Oh, finally. So?"

"It was so, so good. Your tits . . ."

"I know. They looked great. And can you believe I got three lines?"

"Technically two."

"I guess so. You're right."

"But it was all great. It's a solid credit, Mads, you should be pleased."

"Yay. Thank you, Jay."

He didn't tell her about the callback, but before they hung up, he did say, "And, Jesus, good makeup there at *NCIS*, huh?"

"What do you mean?"

"You were worried, remember? You had that outbreak. You could barely tell. I mean, *I* could tell, but that was because I was looking for it. The makeup really covered it all up."

"It did," she said. "They did a good job."

Jay could hear the insecurity creeping into her voice, and he quickly ended the call, got under the covers. He fell asleep wondering what it would be like if he had the courage to go visit Abby Britell, or some other wannabe just like her, and actually do the things to her that he dreamed of doing. Really show her who was boss. He reached down and allowed himself to wrap his hand around his dick, hard as a piece of rebar now, but didn't allow himself to do anything more than touch it. He thought some more about Abby Britell but then he was thinking about Amy Buchman ("Amy passed, Jay, but she *was* really impressed"), and how he'd like to tie her up and take an actual piece of rebar and make her choke on it. It was this thought that finally calmed him down enough to allow him to sleep.

7

On his ride home from work—forty minutes of solitude that went way too fast—Matthew Beaumont recited the facts of his life. It was a daily routine, a way of remembering what was good, and reminding himself about the things that needed work.

Today he told himself that Emma, his oldest daughter, was a lovely seventh grader who was beginning to show noticeable signs of insecurity and anxiety, just like her mother. But she was so compulsively good, such a people pleaser, that she was easy to forget about in the chaos of their daily lives. Pay attention to her, he told himself, make sure she knows that things turn out okay in the end. Alex, about to turn eight, had finally, and formally, been diagnosed as not only having ADHD, but also oppositional defiant disorder, which explained some of the behavior issues. Not *all*, as Nancy insisted. But, still, getting the diagnosis was the right first step, and would help the school system in crafting his educational plan. Joshua, his youngest, was fine except for the persistent sinus infections. He needed to have another conversation about alternative medicines with Nancy, who just kept wanting to throw antibiotics into him. Tonight was probably not the night, but this weekend, maybe, depending on her mood.

He turned on to Trail Ridge Way, the long, sparsely populated road that culminated in a cul-de-sac anchored by three brand-new mansions, each in distinctly different styles. His was the Italianate one, at least it was Italianate on the outside, although distinctly Palladian, if that was the correct word, on the inside. Thinking of the house, his mind turned to Nancy. Was she better, or worse, lately? He wasn't even sure anymore, although in the past few weeks her obsessive thoughts had been mostly about Alex, and the latest tests to determine his disorder, and less about Matthew's "affair" with his new executive assistant. She was wrong about the affair, of course; Matthew, except for an occasional fantasy he allowed himself, usually about Ellen Matthiessen, the head of legal, had been faithful for all fifteen years of his marriage. It was true that he'd gone out for drinks with his team back in July, and had ended up walking Jada Washington back to her apartment in the South End before returning to the Back Bay to get his car, but Jada, who mostly talked that night about her obsession with The Mortal Instruments books, had reminded him more of his own daughter than any potential object of desire. His mistake had been that he told Nancy about the evening, thinking she'd be amused that his "executive assistant" had so much in common with their twelve-year-old daughter. She hadn't been amused. She'd kept him up all that night accusing him of infidelity. He managed to convince her that nothing had happened, and spent the remainder of the summer trying to convince her that he hadn't *wanted* anything to happen. But she'd been quiet about the subject for over a week now, and possibly, just possibly, it was over.

He pulled his Lexus into the four-car garage, then sat for a moment, listening to a few more minutes of his Foo Fighters mix before heading through the vestibule into the kitchen, where Nancy, leaning against the island, was holding up a piece of paper for him to see as he entered.

"What's wrong?" he asked.

"You tell me," she said.

He approached her tentatively, just as Alex came racing into the room, wearing the ninja outfit, complete with plastic samurai sword, that he'd already picked out for Halloween. Matthew fended off Alex's repeated attacks, as he took the sheet of paper from Nancy. It was a list of half a dozen or so names, including his. None of the other names on the list was familiar.

"What is this?" he asked his wife, then, turning to his son, yelled "Alex! Enough!"

"I don't know what it is. It came for you in the mail today, and I'm sure I wasn't supposed to see it, and I wish I hadn't, but now that I have, I'd like to know what it's all about. Some sort of code."

"I have no idea. *Alex, that's enough.* Go find Joshie, and see if he wants to play. Nance, why are you making that face? What do you mean, some sort of code?"

"Well, I don't understand what it is, that's all."

"I don't understand it either. It's probably nothing, just some mistake. What was on the envelope?"

Nancy turned and retrieved the envelope from the pile of mail on the granite countertop. Emma came into the kitchen and hugged Matthew as Alex careened off to look for his younger brother, hiding probably, since Joshua was the only six-year-old in the country who didn't like play fighting.

"There's nothing on it. That's why I was suspicious."

Emma took the sheet of paper from her father and began to read it.

"Honestly, Nance, I have *no* idea."

"There's an Abby Horne in my school but I don't think there's an Alison Horne," Emma said.

"Never mind," Nancy said, pouring herself a glass of wine now. "It just looked suspicious. I overanalyzed."

"What did you think it was, Mom?" Emma asked, her voice verging on disdainful. Matthew had noticed that as Emma had gotten older she'd become more and more critical of her mother, as though she were starting to recognize some of the more erratic nuances of Nancy's personality. It was not a comforting thought.

Joshua entered the kitchen, crying, a pink welt raising up along his cheek. Matthew went to look for Alex. The samurai sword had been a huge mistake.

8

FRIDAY, SEPTEMBER 16, 7:00 A. M.

Early September was the best time of year, by far. It was still summer, the normally cold Atlantic Ocean was at its warmest, and the tourists—the ones with brats, anyway—had gone for good. The stretch of sandy beach that led from the Windward Resort up to the stone jetty was practically unoccupied (one lone figure crouched near the tide pools) as Frank Hopkins took his morning walk about half an hour after sunrise. The sky was the sickly color of fish chowder, and there was mist hovering above the sand. He wore shorts and topsiders but had pulled an old cotton sweater on over his polo shirt. Unless he was mistaken, mornings had been a little bit cold lately. Or maybe his bones were getting cold. *Getting old and getting cold,* he rhymed to himself, then stopped for a moment to have a coughing fit.

After he was moving again, he nearly stepped on the carcass of a seagull half covered by the shifting sand. There was part of a wing, an exposed spine, what looked like its beak, open slightly as though it were cawing. His stomach flipped a little, which probably had more to do with that glass of brandy he'd drunk in his room last night after closing time. He'd known it was a mistake but couldn't help himself, propped up in his bed on four or five pillows, trying to remember what it was that Shelly had told him in the lounge, something about her husband wanting to move to Florida. She wasn't happy about it, that much he knew, but the sound system in the lounge was getting louder and louder these days and he didn't catch everything she'd said. He hoped that Shelly, who'd been tending bar at the Windward for over a decade, wouldn't leave, but he supposed it was inevitable. Bartenders come and go. Just like wives, and just like the years. Still, losing Shelly would hurt. Spending every evening with her—even from opposite sides of a bar—was the best part of his day.

He looked up to see how close he was to the jetty, where he would turn around and walk back. Even though the sun was hidden behind an expanse of hazy cloud cover, he found himself squinting at the brightness of the sky. He stumbled slightly. What had he just been thinking about? Shelly leaving him? Or had he been thinking about Gloria, his second wife, and how when she'd left him she'd done it by simply driving away one morning and never coming back? Lately, his memories were increasingly jumbled; events that happened in his childhood suddenly popped into his mind as though they'd happened the day before, and things that were happening now, like the stalled renovations on the veranda, seemed like they were taking place in some hazy past life that he couldn't quite remember.

How had he gotten so old so fast? He really needed to cut down on his drinking. Tonight he'd tell Gloria that for every drink he had—every real drink—he'd also drink a seltzer water. That would be a good thing. Then maybe he wouldn't wake up in the middle of the night, his mouth so dry that his tongue felt like an unused sponge. Yeah, tonight he'd start drinking more seltzer water. And no brandy while he lay in bed. And he'd get whatever the daily fish was instead of the cheeseburger. That would impress Gloria—no, not Gloria, Shelly!—and maybe she wouldn't leave him after all. He liked the way she lowered her voice when she talked with him—it was very intimate, even though he didn't always understand what it was she was saying to him.

He was nearly at the jetty when the disk of the sun appeared in the sky, the mist starting to burn off. His eye went to the barnacled rock he always superstitiously touched before turning back. The shape of the rock made him think of a child curled into herself, her head tucked between her thighs, her hair the black seaweed that clung to the rock at the high-tide line. The rock, like the beach, had stayed virtually unchanged in Frank's long life. What was surprising on this particular morning was the presence of a single white envelope resting at the top of the rock. The envelope was held in place by a perfectly round gray stone, ringed in white. Frank picked the envelope up, holding it at just the right length from his failing eyes so that he could read the mailing label. It had his name and address on it.

A strange sense of unreality passed over him. Why was there a letter for him at the jetty? Was he dreaming? If so, it would make sense. He dreamed the same dreams over and over, and they often took place on this very beach, near this very jetty. He blinked rapidly, as though to prove that he was still in reality, then looked down to see that the damp envelope remained in his grip. With trembling hands he opened it, pulling out a single sheet of paper that he unfolded. He didn't exactly know what he'd been expecting but it wasn't the simple list of names he was presented with. He ran his eyes over the names, noticing his own, and not immediately recognizing the others.

He was about to turn to see if he could spot who'd left the envelope on the rock when he felt the tight grip of someone's hands around his ankles, then he was yanked violently, so that he pitched forward and landed face-down on the damp sand. His head had partially struck the edge of his turn-around rock, and there were sudden tears in his eyes, a sharp wet pain on his temple. Whoever had attacked him hoisted him by his belt and moved him a foot forward along the sand so that his face landed in a shallow divot filled with seawater. He tried to get up, but his arms felt weak, and he yelled out for help instead. The person on his back pushed his face violently into the pool of water. Frank's nose stung with terrible pain, and his mouth filled with sand and water.

"Do you know why you're going to die?" came a voice in his ear.

Frank coughed, and now he could taste warm salty blood mixed in with the sand clogging his mouth. "No," he said, although part of him *did* know why he was dying. It had to do with the jetty, didn't it? And the dreams he always had.

The voice spoke again. He could feel breath moving over his skin, and the words that his murderer said made him realize that he had been right. His dreams had been right too. And for a moment he felt something resembling peace, the real world mixing in with his dream world to make just one place, the world of his existence, rapidly coming to an end. The strong hands pressed his face deep into the sand, the water licking at his ears. In the red darkness he saw concentric circles, like tide pools growing and shrinking. And he saw his mother, back in the old kitchen, wearing an apron over a dress. She was turned away from him, doing something at the stove, and he was crying, begging his case, telling her how sorry he was. *I'm sorry, Mommy. I'm sorry*. But she wouldn't turn around. Even the darkness was now shrinking until there was nothing but tide pools, and his mother still not turning back, the world getting smaller, breathing water instead of air.

EIGHT

Matthew Beaumont

Jay Coates

Ethan Dart

Caroline Geddes

Frank Hopkins

Alison Horne

Arthur Kruse

Jack Radebaugh

Jessica Winslow

I

FRIDAY, SEPTEMBER 16, 8:45 A. M.

Detective Sam Hamilton stood about eight feet from the body, attempting to memorize the crime scene, take it all in. The victim was on his stomach, one leg hitched up slightly, as though he were sleeping. His face was submerged in the damp sand so that all you could see of his head was straggling gray hair and a sunburned neck.

"Is it definitely Frank Hopkins?" Lisa Banks, one of Kennewick's patrol officers, was standing next to Hamilton.

"Jim thought so, and so do I. It's his clothes, right? I mean, who needs to see the face?" Frank Hopkins owned the Windward Resort, having inherited the business from his parents, and he was a regular fixture at his own bar. All the year-round residents of Kennewick knew him.

"Yeah, I guess I could tell it was him, as well."

There were about four other members of the Kennewick Police Department in the vicinity of the scene, but no one except for Jim Robichaud, first to arrive, had gotten close to the body. The Maine State Police had been alerted, and their crime scene and forensics people were on the way.

"What's that?" Lisa said.

Sam looked toward where she was pointing. It was a piece of white paper, or maybe an envelope, crumpled up in Frank's left hand.

"I was wondering about that myself," Sam said.

"Should we get it?"

"Better not. It's not going anywhere, and it might be evidence."

"Evidence of what? You think there was a crime here?"

"It does look like someone pushed his head pretty deep into the sand."

"You don't think he just keeled over from a heart attack, and the tide did the rest. I know you're not from around here, but you've been to the beach, right? If you stand at the edge of the water the sand sucks your feet into it."

"No, you're right. It just feels like something else happened here."

As soon as he'd said the words, Sam wondered if he actually was imagining a crime where there was none. Frank Hopkins was not a young man. Not healthy either, judging by how much time he spent drinking at his own bar. The most likely explanation for what had happened was that he'd been on a morning walk and his heart had simply gone out. Sam knew that he was prone to see criminal activity where there was none, and maybe he was doing it again.

Lisa shrugged, then turned back to look toward Micmac Road. She thought she heard a vehicle and she was right. Three metallic-blue SUVs were pulling up along the edge of the road. There was also a local news van arriving from the other direction. "They're here," she said, stretching out the vowels and Sam laughed because she was imitating that little girl from *Poltergeist*. He began to take long strides toward the arriving officers.

It was much later in the day when Sam, back at the station, learned about what had been found in Frank's hand. A torn envelope addressed to Frank. There'd also been a piece of paper, damp from the sea but still legible, and presumably originating from inside the envelope. On that piece of paper was a list of nine names, including Frank's. The letter had been taken directly to State Police headquarters, but Sam saw a photograph and read through the names twice. None were immediately familiar to him. There was also a photograph of the front of the envelope. No stamp, no postmark, just an address label. It was bewildering, a true mystery. Not that it wouldn't have been a mystery had the envelope not been there. The initial, unofficial coroner's report stated that there were bruises on the back of Frank Hopkins's neck indicating that someone had held his face down in the water until he'd drowned. Who would want to kill Frank Hopkins on his morning walk? A mugger? A jilted lover? Both seemed highly unlikely.

Sam, who had been a police detective in Kennewick for fifteen years now, knew Frank Hopkins fairly well. He'd been one of the first citizens Sam had had contact with when he'd moved to Maine from Houma, Louisiana, back in 1999. He'd interviewed for the job on a sunny October weekend, then arrived for it five weeks later in early December, and Kennewick was already encrusted in a grungy layer of hardened snow. His new colleagues told him it was slightly early to feel like Siberia in southern Maine, that they'd just been ambushed by an early nor'easter followed by a long cold snap. There'd been lots of jokes along the lines of "Welcome to paradise," and "I hope you brought your long johns," but, secretly, Sam was thrilled to be greeted by the snowy beauty of New England. He'd spent his first thirty-five years either in Louisiana or Jamaica, where his family was from, and neither truly felt like home to him. He'd longed, for reasons mostly mysterious to him, for somewhere else. And the weathered houses of Kennewick, the low gray skies, had felt right.

His first official act as Kennewick's only police detective had been to visit the Windward Resort to follow up on a suspected theft. He'd been greeted by Frank Hopkins, a man with a Maine accent so thick that it sounded just a little bit fake to Sam's untrained ear. The cash register at the bar of the Windward had been cleared out—no more than a couple of hundred dollars, Frank said—and he suspected a recently terminated employee named Ben Gagnon who'd been working as a busboy in the dining room. Ben, a local kid, had been let go for calling in sick one too many times.

46

"I fired him yesterday," Frank had said, "but Barbara, one of the cleaning women, told me she saw him this morning, and he told her he'd come in for his last pay-check. Anyhoo, he did no such thing because we mail out all the paychecks, and Barbara, another Barbara, the one who works the bar, said that all the paper money was gone from the register."

"Was the cash register locked?"

"Well, yeah. Except that the key to unlock it is hanging off a hook right below the back of the bar, so it wouldn't take a genius to pull off this particular crime. Look, I'm friends with Ben's mother and to tell the truth, I'm not sure I even want to press charges. I'm just worried that if he thinks he got away with it once he might try to get away with it again. Does that make sense to you?"

"It does," Sam said. "Where do you think Ben is now?"

"Probably at Cooley's. It's a bar down the other end of the beach. He'll be spending my money and badmouthing me all at the same time."

Sam had gotten a pretty good description of Ben Gagnon, then gone down to Cooley's and brought him back to the station for questioning, where the kid made a full and weepy confession. Frank hadn't pressed charges, and Ben had returned the money. It had been Sam's first case in Kennewick and that was probably the only reason he'd remembered it. But since then, Sam had regularly gone to the Windward for a scotch and soda on a Friday night. And occasionally, over the years, he went to Cooley's for a beer, despite the fact, or maybe because of the fact, that it was the only place in his new town in which he'd experienced any kind of racism. A very drunk real estate developer from Wells, the next town over, had said to Sam, sometime during his first winter in Kennewick, "Anyone tell you you're the wrong color for Maine?"

"What's your name, son?" Sam had said, aware that he was letting a little of his Jamaican accent slip into the question.

"I don't have to tell you that."

"No, you don't. I'll remember your face. And one of these days I'll arrest you, probably for drunk and disorderly, and when that happens, you'll be glad to know that I forgot you ever said what you just said to me."

The man had looked confused. He'd looked confused, too, when Sam had, in fact, arrested him about two years later after he'd gotten drunk, this time at the Kennewick Harbor Hotel, and reached across the teak bar top to grab the breast of the college girl who'd been working behind the bar. True to his word, Detective Sam Hamilton acted as though he'd never met the real estate agent named Harvey Beach before. It had been the only time anyone had said anything racist to him in the state of Maine. In fact, most people he'd met had been perfectly friendly, despite the reputation New England had for unfriendliness. And that had included Frank Hopkins, ever-present owner of the Windward, who'd been murdered on his morning walk.

Sam thought back and was pretty sure that Frank had been married when he'd first met him. A dark-haired woman who worked at the post office. He thought her name might have been Sheila. She'd left town to move to Florida and had not invited Frank to go with her. That was years ago, and Frank was now a confirmed bachelor and a man of strict habit—the walk on the beach each and every morning unless the wind was just too much, then most likely a half-day spent working on the daunting task of keeping the Windward Resort profitable and running, then a long evening spent in the Windward lounge, quietly nursing a succession of Bud Lights—and as far as Sam knew, there was no room in that schedule for love affairs. Not only that, but Frank did not make enemies. He was an easygoing boss, friendly to everyone. Which meant that what happened to Frank on the beach felt like something else altogether, something, for lack of a better word, *wrong*. If it hadn't been for the letter, Sam would have thought that Frank had been killed by accident, a mugging gone wrong maybe, or, who knows, maybe someone who just wanted to experience how it felt to kill a man, press his face into the sand. But what about the letter? That list of names?

Sam did a search of the other names online, to see if any of them had come up in a murder investigation, but there was nothing. Still, he was just searching through Google. The state police would be looking at their own database. Something—some connection between the names on the list—would come up.

2

FRIDAY, SEPTEMBER 16, 12:30 P. M.

Jessica Winslow almost always went to Cece's for lunch on Fridays, usually with Mary from the accounting department, but Mary was on vacation this week, and Jessica thought she'd try that new lunch place over on Congress Street, the one with the rotisserie chickens in the window.

All the tables were taken but there was a seat at the back counter. She ordered iced tea, a smoked chicken leg with rice and beans, and fried plantains on the side. The old Latino guy behind the counter scanned her face, then asked her one of her least favorite questions. "Where you from, *chica*?"

She hadn't heard this particular question in a while, but she'd heard it enough in her life. That and "What are you?" or, the less rude but just as condescending "Aren't you pretty?"

"Maryland," she answered.

"No, I mean before that."

"Maryland, far as I know."

The old man raised one eyebrow, but gave up, and went down the counter to take another order. Jessica had been adopted, but all her parents knew for sure was that she'd come from Vietnam. There was definitely some Vietnamese in her, but there was also some African blood, and white blood as well. She wasn't certain, but she assumed she was the product of a Vietnamese woman and an African-American soldier. And if that was the case, then it was possible that her mother had been a prostitute. Honestly, she didn't care that much. She never thought about it till some stranger decided they'd love to know all about her ancestral history, as if it were any of their goddamn business. She felt the anger rising up and tamped it down. The old guy was probably harmless, just wanting to figure out if she spoke Spanish. Lots of people took one look at her and assumed she did.

The geezer brought her the chicken leg, and it was much better than she'd been told. Halfway through her lunch, her phone, turned upside down on the counter, buzzed twice, and Jessica ignored it, partly because her fingers were covered in chicken grease, but mostly because she just wanted to enjoy the remainder of her food. But the third time her phone buzzed, she put the chicken leg down, wiped her fingers on her napkin, and looked at the screen. Two of the calls were from Aaron, and one was from Stephanie, the receptionist. There was also a text from Aaron. Where are you?

She was about to text him back but called instead. He picked up right away.

"Where are you?" he asked, some annoyance in his voice.

"Lunch. It's lunchtime."

"You know that list?"

"The one I got yesterday in the mail?"

"Yeah. One of the names on it was Frank Hopkins."

"I remember."

"A Frank Hopkins was murdered this morning in Kennewick, Maine."

"Seriously?"

"Yeah, seriously. Come back to the office, soon as you can."

"I will. I'm on my way."

She thought about bagging up the remainder of her lunch but decided against it. She paid up and left.

Back at the office Aaron intercepted her halfway between reception and her cubicle. She thought he looked pretty ragged and wondered how long he'd stayed at the Club Room last night.

"What's the story?" she asked.

"I sent the list to analysis, and apparently someone there had actually read about the murder of a Frank Hopkins today in Kennewick, Maine. I mean, they would've caught it, anyway, but still."

"What happened to him?"

"To the analyst?"

"No, to Frank Hopkins. In Maine. How're you doing this morning, Aaron?"

"Sorry, I hung out a little too long with Anthony last night."

"No worries. How'd this guy die in Maine?"

"He'd been taking a walk on the beach near where he lived. He was forcibly drowned, his head held in a tide pool or something."

"Who was he?"

"I don't know. No one. I know you saw his name on a list yesterday and said you didn't recognize it, but have you given those names any more thought? Do you have any connection with this man?"

"Nope."

"So here's the thing—"

"It's a pretty fucking common name."

"Frank Hopkins?"

"Yeah, I mean . . ."

"So here's the thing. There was an envelope at the scene of the crime, addressed to Frank."

"He had the list?"

"Exact same list. The one with your name on it."

"Shit," Jessica said.

"Yep," Aaron said.

3

FRIDAY, SEPTEMBER 16, 1:33 P. M.

Ethan Dart was entering his own apartment when he heard the trill of the landline. He checked the digital readout on the handset, just to make sure it wasn't his mother, the only actual person, besides solicitors, who still called him at his home number. It was a number from Albany, New York, that he chose to ignore.

He went to make coffee, saw that there was a quarter pot left from yesterday (or was it the day before?), and poured it over ice, then got his guitar and returned to the living room. Sitting down in a shaft of pale sunlight coming in through the window, he watched dust motes rise up from the sofa he'd had for as long as he'd had this apartment. He was exhausted, and took a long, teeth-numbing swig of his iced coffee.

Settling the acoustic guitar on his knee, he strummed out a couple of chords, then tried to recall the words to the song he'd written the day before. They instantly came back to him. Reciting them now, he remembered deciding, the night before, that the song had been crap, but now he wasn't so sure. "Last on Your List." That name wasn't too bad. And maybe, just maybe, the song was actually about Hannah, whose apartment he had recently

departed. From what he knew about her, her list of con-
quests was pretty extensive. Not that his wasn't. Was he
falling in love? Would the song work better if the first line
was, "Woke in Hannah's dreams again last night"? Then
he could call the song "Hannah," a better title than "Last
on Your List." He tried it out, then fished around in the
glass ashtray for enough pot to fill a bowl. What he really
wanted was a goddamn cigarette.

Jittery, he stood up, did a few jumping jacks, then
checked the phone to see if Albany had left a message.
They had. He checked it, expecting some robocaller, but
got a real voice instead, a woman's voice, identifying
herself as Jessica Winslow and asking him to call her
back right away. He knew the name instantly; she'd
been on that strange list he'd received yesterday. In fact,
she'd been the name he was having trouble remembering the night before. Maybe that list really did have
something to do with one of the songwriters' agencies
he'd sent demos to. Albany, though? That didn't sound
right.

"Hi, Jessica?" he said. She'd answered her phone
before he even heard a ring.

"Is this Ethan Dart?"

"It is."

"My name's Jessica Winslow. I'm a special agent for
the Federal Bureau of Investigation, and I was hoping to
ask you some questions."

"Okay." Ethan sat back down on the sofa.

"Have you received a letter recently, one with a list of names?"

"I got it yesterday. Your name's on it, too."

A slight pause, then she said, "Yeah, it is. You remembered that?"

"Sure. I mean, I just got the list yesterday."

"Did it mean anything to you, the list? Do you know who it came from, or any of the other names?"

"No, it didn't mean anything. I thought it must be some kind of mistake."

"What about Frank Hopkins? Did that name mean anything to you?"

"No, none of them did." Ethan heard another voice—a male one—in the background say something.

"Has anything else unusual happened in your life recently?" she said. "Anyone threaten you? You make any enemies?"

"Uh, don't think so."

"Okay. Just checking. Do you still have the letter, or did you throw it out?"

"No, I still have it. Do you want me—"

"No, just leave it where it is, and don't touch it again. You're at home now, right?"

"Yeah."

"I'm going to send a local field agent over to your place to collect the letter. Can I confirm your address?"

"What's going on? Should I be worried?"

"We'll send an agent over, okay? Don't be worried,

at least not yet. We're still trying to figure out what's going on."

"That wasn't reassuring," Ethan said.

The agent laughed. "It wasn't, was it? Look, just don't touch the letter again before the agent arrives. Can you do that for me?"

"Sure," Ethan said.

After ending the call Ethan went and looked at the list, still sitting next to his laptop. He'd forgotten that he'd used the back of the letter to write down the lyrics for his new song, and now he was a little embarrassed that he'd be handing it over to federal agents. Not that they'd care. Who knew, maybe someone in the FBI would see those lyrics and realize what a genius he was and introduce him to his song-producer cousin. Ethan laughed in the empty apartment. Then, just for the sake of posterity, he took out his phone and photographed the back of the list.

4

The second person from the list that Jessica succeeded in finding was Arthur Kruse. She reached him on his cell phone while he was at work at the hospital, and when she asked about the list, it took him a moment to realize what it was she was talking about.

"Oh, right," he finally said.

"So you did receive a list yesterday in the mail?"

"Uh-huh."

She asked him the same questions she'd asked Ethan and got essentially the same responses. He didn't know anyone on the list. Nothing unusual had happened recently in his life. As far as he knew, he had no enemies.

"I'm also going to need access to that letter, and the envelope if you still have it," Jessica said. "Can you be at home in about half an hour?"

"I can't really," Arthur said. "I'm in the middle of my shift, and—"

"It's important."

"Sure," he said, knowing that between Gina and Maggie they'd be okay for the next hour or so. He didn't live far from the hospital, and he could be back in no time.

"And one more thing," Jessica said. "This is a long shot, I know, but do you know someone by the name of Gary Winslow?"

Arthur thought, then said, "It doesn't ring a bell."

"How old are you?"

"I'm forty-five."

"Your father's not named Arthur Kruse, or Art Kruse, as well, is he?"

"He was," said Arthur. "Art Kruse."

"Oh, I'm sorry. Is he dead?"

"Actually, no. I shouldn't have said 'was,' but I haven't seen him or spoken with him in over ten years."

"So his name is Art."

"It's Arthur but he goes by Art."

"So I don't suppose you remember if *he* knew anyone by the name of Gary Winslow?"

"I'm not sure I could name a single one of my father's friends. Didn't you say your name was Winslow?"

"Uh-huh. Gary's my father and I remember that he had a friend named Art Kruse, or I think I do, and somehow the name stuck with me. They were college friends, I think."

"My father went to Princeton."

"Okay. So they weren't college friends," Jessica said.

"Your father went to . . . ?"

"He went to UVM, but I know that he knew an Art Kruse. Does your father have a lake house?"

"No, but his parents did. I've seen pictures. Up at

Squam Lake in New Hampshire. I'm confused. What does your father and my father being friends have to do with the list?"

"I'm sorry. It is confusing. I'm an FBI agent but I also received a list in the mail, most likely the same list you received."

"Okay. That's why your name sounded a little bit familiar to me. So do *you* know what the list is about?"

"No idea. That's what we're trying to figure out. What we'd like to know is if there are any connections between the people who received a copy. Do you think there's any way you can call your father and find out if he had a friend named Gary Winslow, and where they met?"

"I don't even know how to reach him, honestly," Arthur said. "And if I did know how to reach him, I just don't think I'd be able to call."

"I understand. If there's a way for you to find out how I could get in touch with him, then maybe . . . ?"

"Sure."

Arthur drove back home in Richard's Subaru, past the barren fields and rotting farmhouses of the valley. One portion of the hazy sky had taken on a dark swollen look, and he wondered if a storm was coming through. Because his name had been brought up, Arthur thought a little bit about his father, wondering what his life was like now. He occasionally got a report from his sister, Samantha, who did talk to their father, but rarely saw him. Art Kruse lived in an over-fifty-five condominium complex in West

Palm Beach, Florida. Samantha said that he once claimed he had a girlfriend who lived in one of the other units, but she said it took him a little while to even come up with her name. With the possible exception of this girlfriend, it was clear to both Arthur and Samantha that their father was entirely alone. It bothered Samantha a little bit, but Arthur never thought about it.

Art had cut his son out of his life after finding out he was gay, but Arthur sometimes wondered if they would have had a relationship even if he'd never told him. His father was a hardcore Republican, a Fox News addict, priding himself on not being politically correct, which meant he got to say his racist, sexist, and homophobic remarks out loud and feel as though he was bucking a trend. When Arthur had come out to his father, two years after his parents' divorce, Art had given him a crooked smile, then said, "You'll probably tell me you're getting married next. Just don't expect me to come." In many ways, it had made things easier, his father's dismissal of him. When he and Richard actually did get married, Arthur mailed an invite to his father, fully expecting to hear back that he wasn't coming. Instead, he got no response, not even a refusal, and Arthur wrote him off for good. Richard once asked him if he thought about his father, and whether their relationship might one day be saved, and Arthur had answered truthfully that he rarely, if ever, thought about him.

Back at the house he only had to wait for less than five

minutes before a Lincoln Navigator pulled into his driveway, and two men, both dressed in gray suits, got out.

"Arthur Kruse?" one of the men asked, holding up a badge. He had a short white beard that extended only to his jawline. The pudgy skin under his jaw was pink and shaved.

Arthur showed them the letter and the envelope, both already deposited in his recycling bin. Wearing gloves, the second man, younger, clean-cut, very handsome, plucked both pieces of paper from among the catalogues and junk mail and frozen-food boxes.

"What's going on?" Arthur asked, wondering if these agents might divulge a little more information than Jessica Winslow had.

"Don't know exactly, bud," the man with the beard said, and Arthur recoiled a little at being called "bud."

The younger agent, the one who looked a little like Jimmy Smits back when he was on *NYPD Blue*, was sliding the two pieces of the letter into separate plastic bags. "That's all we needed from you, sir," he said, and Arthur walked them to the door, conscious, as he always was with new people, of his limp.

He watched them drive away through the frosted glass of the front-door window, then wandered back into the interior of the house. There was the sound of a very distant thunder crack, and he told himself he should get back to work. Instead, he sat down on one of the dining-room T-back chairs, and wondered what the list was all about, and why the FBI had become interested. Was Agent Winslow keeping something from him? It seemed probable.

He rubbed at the depleted muscles of his left thigh. He'd always felt that his leg was at its worst when the weather was bad. Or maybe he was just imagining it? The windows were suddenly dark, and he waited to hear the sound of rain on the roof. He should head back to work, but he kept thinking about how much he wanted to tell Richard about the recent details of his life—the list he'd gotten in the mail, the phone call from the FBI, and, now, the two agents who came to take possession of the letter. He allowed himself the rare luxury of imagining the conversation, Richard wanting to know details— *always* wanting to know details—like what did the agents look like. He'd tell him about Jimmy Smits, and the man with the beard that had been shaved along his jawline. *A George Lucas?* Richard would say, laughing. *Exactly*, Arthur would say back. *I hadn't thought of that.*

He allowed himself a few more minutes of this reverie, even letting Misty back into the picture, the way she'd lean up against one of their legs when they were talking, always looking for affection. He stopped thinking these thoughts when his throat began to ache. He needed to get back to work. It was raining now, but he didn't much care as he walked at his usual slow pace back to his car.

5

FRIDAY, SEPTEMBER 16, 6:00 P. M.

By six o'clock on that Friday night, Jessica had managed to positively identify a total of four people who had all received the list, not including herself or Frank Hopkins. Ethan Dart and Arthur Kruse, maybe because their names were the most unusual, had come relatively easily. Jessica had gotten in touch with several women named Caroline Geddes, all baffled by the question of whether they'd gotten a mysterious list in the mail, before she hit the jackpot with a University of Michigan professor. As she had done with Ethan and Arthur, Jessica called the nearest bureau and had them send someone out to retrieve the letter and envelope. She'd also gotten a positive hit with a Matthew Beaumont, despite the commonness of that name, after only about four or five dead ends. For some reason, as soon as she heard his voice when he answered the phone, she knew that the Matthew Beaumont who was the vice president of a financial company in Boston was the one. Why was that? She'd reached him at his office phone just before he was set to leave, and he agreed to meet with an agent. She asked the usual questions—he told her that none of the names had meant anything to him—then asked him his age, partly because he sounded young to be a vice president.

"I'm thirty-nine," he said.

"Oh, that's my age," Jessica said, before catching herself.

After hanging up she wondered what the ages of Ethan Dart and Caroline Geddes were. Arthur Kruse had told her he was forty-five. Ethan and Caroline sounded as though they were in their late thirties, early forties, as well. But what about Frank Hopkins? He'd been seventy-two.

She looked at the names for the hundredth time, trying to see if the ones she'd so far been unable to find gave her any other possible clues as to their age. Jay Coates could be any age, could easily be in his mid-thirties or in his seventies. Jay had been a popular name for a while. Jack Radebaugh sounded like the name of a slightly older man, but maybe she was just thinking that because the most famous Jack Radebaugh was a seventy-year-old business guru. But she'd talked with him already and he hadn't received the letter.

The last person she couldn't find was Alison Horne, and that was another name that could belong to someone of any age, but it was also such a common name that finding the right Alison Horne might prove to be very difficult.

Wanting to find out more about Frank Hopkins, she decided to call the Kennewick Police Department.

After identifying herself as an FBI agent, she asked to speak to whoever was in charge of the Frank Hopkins homicide.

"That's gone to state, honey," the receptionist said. "But Detective Hamilton's still here. He was at the scene of the crime if that's helpful to you."

"That'd be great."

After about thirty seconds, the detective came on the line and introduced himself.

"Detective, this is Agent Winslow of the Federal Bureau out of Albany. Do you have a minute?"

"Your first name isn't Jessica, is it?"

"It is. You've seen the list."

"Oh. To tell the truth I was kind of half joking. Was that actually your name on the list?"

"Yep. I received an identical letter to the one that was found near Frank Hopkins this morning. That's being kept under wraps for now, though."

"What is?"

"The existence of the letter, and the list."

"Oh, right, I heard that," the detective said. "So what's it all about? Do you know the other people on the list?"

"None of them. And we've tracked down a few of the others. No connection, at least not that we've figured."

"It's very strange, the whole thing," Detective Hamilton said.

"It's even stranger when your name is on it."

"I imagine it is."

"So what can you tell me about Frank Hopkins?"

"He'd lived up here in Kennewick his whole life. Married twice, no kids. He'd taken over a family-run resort that his parents had started called the Windward Resort."

"That's in Kennewick, too?" Jessica asked. Something about that name had seemed just a little bit familiar.

"On Kennewick Beach, yeah. It used to be kind of fancy way back when. The type of place that families would come to for a month at a time. All the meals included, organized shuffleboard, martinis on the veranda. But it's pretty down at the heels now. I think Frank kept it operating just so he'd have a bar to drink at while pretending he was running a business."

"He was an alcoholic?"

"I guess so. A functioning alcoholic like half the people I know. He never caused any trouble, though. Most people seemed to like him."

"Including you?"

"Sure, including me. I've been known to have an occasional Friday night drink at the Windward and Frank was always friendly."

"You were at the crime scene?"

"I was. I didn't get too close, but it was clear that it was a crime scene. Well, not clear, but for whatever reason I didn't think it was a natural death. It looked like someone had pushed his head pretty hard into the sand."

"I thought he was in a tide pool."

"It was a tide pool when he died, but the tide was going out."

"Right. And he had the envelope and list with him?"

"He was holding both of them, sort of crumpled up in his hand. The envelope didn't have a stamp on it."

"Okay, I hadn't heard that."

"You'll find out more if you talk with the State Police. The detective heading the investigation is named Mary Parkinson. She'll be helpful."

"I'll call her."

"So how many of the people on the list have you found?" the detective asked.

"Everyone but Jack Radebaugh, Alison Horne, and Jay Coates."

"Oh, really. That was fast. Anyone know anything?"

"Like I said, far as I know we're all strangers. Nothing in common except for the list."

"Well, you do have something in common then."

"Right. I suppose we do," Jessica said.

"There's a Jay Coates who's an actor in Hollywood. He has a website."

"Oh, you've been looking into it, too?"

"A little bit. I had some free time today, so I thought I'd google the names, see what came up."

"I did leave a message for Jay Coates the actor," Jessica said, "but haven't heard back. It's earlier in California so you never know. He might be at work."

"You think it's him?"

"Yeah, I do, but I don't know why. It's partly his age. So far everyone I've identified seems to be in their late thirties."

"Except for Frank Hopkins."

"Yes, except for Frank Hopkins."

Detective Hamilton said, "What about Jack Radebaugh. No luck on him yet?"

"No luck. Did you google him, as well?"

"I did. There weren't many. The big name was a kind of famous writer."

"I talked with him. He didn't get the letter in the mail, and he didn't know anyone else who was on the list."

"How old was he?"

"He's seventy."

There was a slight pause, and Jessica added, "If you think of anything else I should know about Hopkins, you'll call me?"

"Sure. Let me get your numbers."

After exchanging office and cell numbers they each hung up, Jessica sitting quietly for a moment, trying to dislodge whatever memory she had of the Windward Resort from her mind. It *had* rung a bell. A distant, distant bell.

She'd been to the southern coast of Maine at least twice in her life, but as far as she knew, she'd never been to Kennewick. She'd been to Camden for a very rainy Memorial Day weekend with Justin, her previous boy-friend. That was about three years ago. Prior to that she'd gone on a family vacation when she was thirteen years old—she remembered it because it was the first family summer vacation she'd gone on during which she wanted to be back home, hanging with friends. Her mom had rented a house in Kennebunkport that had been a disappointment. It was near a beach, but the beach was rocky, the water ice-cold even in August. She remembered their driving up and down the coast to visit shops and ice cream parlors in other small towns. And she remembered that her dad had been in a particularly mean-spirited mood while they'd been there. She only really remembered that because her mother had blown up one night at dinner and said that she was sick of living with two selfish teenagers. Had they visited Kennewick on that trip? She couldn't remember.

"Go home," Aaron said from the doorway.

Jessica turned in a daze to him. "I will. I want to make just one more call."

"Okay. Then I'm coming with you. I'm your escort."

"You're kidding me?"

"I'm not kidding. If you don't want it to be me, then I'll get someone else, but until I find out exactly what's going on, I don't want to take any chances."

"Okay, fine," Jessica said. "I'll come get you in five."

After Aaron left, she tried to call Jay Coates, the one in California, one more time. He didn't pick up, and she considered leaving a message, one a little more urgent than the one she'd left before, but decided against it. It probably wasn't him, anyway, and why scare him if it wasn't necessary.

6

Matthew Beaumont had forgotten that Nancy and he had dinner plans with the Robinsons, but walking into the kitchen and seeing his wife dressed in her favorite green dress made him remember.

"We're going out?" he said.

"You forgot."

"Only a little bit."

"I talked with Michelle and we agreed to meet at the restaurant. The reservation's for six-thirty, and Michaela's going to be here any moment, and that gives us just a few minutes to go over the kids' schedules with her, so please get dressed fast, and I don't think you have time for a shower."

In the bedroom Matthew found that Nancy had laid out an outfit for him, a pair of tan chinos and a button-down shirt that was supposed to be worn untucked. He stripped out of his suit, applied fresh deodorant, and got dressed, his mind going over the evening ahead, trying to figure out if he should tell the Robinsons about the letter he'd gotten the day before, and about the FBI agent who came and collected it from him at the office today. The agent had mentioned to him to keep the fact of the letter to himself, or more specifically, the other names on the letter, but had shrugged when Matthew told him that he'd already shown his wife. It was a good story, the letter, and if he was just having drinks with Pete Robinson, or with Michelle, for that matter, then he would definitely tell it. But he was mindful of Nancy's reaction to the list the evening before, and how suspicious she'd been, and didn't know how she'd be if he brought it up at dinner. And he definitely didn't know how she'd react when he told her that an agent had called him at his office, then sent another agent to take the letter away as some kind of evidence. Actually, he did know how she'd react. For one, she'd become convinced that it was some sort of sexual blackmail list. And she'd also freak out that Matthew had taken the list with him to work, instead of simply throwing it out at home. It would prove his guilt, somehow. But the only reason he'd taken the list with him into work was so that Nancy wouldn't happen upon it again and get upset.

When he came back downstairs, in his new outfit, he was assaulted by Alex racing through the foyer, wearing one sock and sliding on the floor, kicking off with his bare foot.

"Don't get a splinter," Matthew said, but Alex was already around the corner into the large living room.

He could hear Nancy speaking and entered the kitchen, where she was giving directions to Michaela, one of the teen girls from the neighborhood who'd been their primary babysitter for two years now. They loved Michaela because she could manage Alex, or at least she always reported at the end of the night that he'd been fine. His wife and the babysitter were on opposite sides of the granite island, and Matthew made sure to keep his gaze averted from any part of Michaela that wasn't her forehead. She'd recently transformed from a stick insect into a young woman with curves, and wore, like all the girls her age, yoga pants that still looked like nothing more than underwear to Matthew, and a striped shirt that didn't quite meet up with the top of the pants.

"Emma can do what she wants, of course. Don't worry about her. And if Alex can't settle down after dinner, then it's okay if he watches one of his shows but only from *his* Netflix account, don't let him log onto ours."

"He doesn't know the code," Matthew said.

"He probably does," Nancy said, while Michaela nodded, smiling. Didn't she used to have braces? Matthew couldn't remember, but if she did, she'd had them removed.

"Okay. He probably does."

"He's fine," Michaela said. "Last time he taught me a video game he likes to play. Okay if we do that again?"

"Sure," Matthew said, "but you might want to let him win if you don't want to see a temper tantrum."

"It's not a winning game, exactly," Michaela said. "More of a world-building game."

As they drove to the restaurant, Nancy was quiet for

thirty seconds, and Matthew was thinking of telling her about the FBI, when Nancy spoke first. "I don't think Michaela should keep babysitting if you're going to flirt with her the way you do. It's perverse."

Matthew sighed, as silently as he could, then said, calmly, "Nance, trust me, I was not flirting with Michaela. It's impossible because I have no interest in Michaela. She's a child."

"I'm just telling you—"

"I know what you're telling me, and I hear you, even though you're wrong. We can talk more about this, but not right now, okay? Let's try to have a decent night out with our friends."

Two hours later, as dessert arrived at their table, Matthew marveled that dinner with the Robinsons had actually been nice. Nancy, despite her earlier mood, seemed to relax as the evening went on. Glasshouses was a farm-to-table bistro that had recently expanded to include an outdoor patio with heat lamps, and that was where their table was, underneath the night sky. The cool air was filled with the smells from the wood-fired grill. Matthew's duck breast had been delicious, and he allowed himself one bite of the tarte tatin with salted caramel ice cream, telling himself he definitely would go on a run the next morning.

He was seated across from Michelle Robinson, and next to Pete, which allowed the men to talk Patriots while the women talked about their children. But after dessert they'd all agreed to one more drink each, and now Matthew was talking with Michelle and sipping port, while she told him about her trip down to New York to see *Hamilton*. No one would describe Michelle as beautiful. She had short legs and heavy hips, and her features were a little too large for her round face, but Matthew had always harbored a small crush on her. It had begun at a backyard barbecue the previous summer, one thrown by the Cartwrights, mutual friends of Matthew and his wife and the Robinsons. A late afternoon storm had marooned Matthew and Michelle inside the Cartwrights' pool house with a group of shivering children who had all fled from the pool. Matthew and Michelle had been looking at a shelf filled with children's toys, mostly neglected or broken or forgotten, and Michelle said, "I've entered the portion of my life where everything fills me with sadness."

"Have you?" said Matthew, shocked by the sudden confession.

She'd laughed. "Sorry, did I say that out loud? I'm being dramatic, or that's what Pete would say. I just feel like the exciting and mysterious parts of my life are over, and now everything fills me with nostalgia. Truthfully, I'm just being a baby about growing old."

"I think I know what you mean," Matthew said. "Being young was scary, but it was also interesting."

She laughed again, and because they were standing so close, Matthew could smell the wine on her breath. "I think that's what I miss," she said. "Life being interesting."

"Our kids are interesting."

"Your kids are a little younger than mine. Yes, they're interesting, but pretty soon they won't be interested in *you*. Again, I'm being a baby." She leaned in closer and squeezed Matthew's hand. "Please don't tell Nancy about this conversation. She wouldn't understand."

"I won't," he said. One of the kids, a scrawny girl wearing a swim vest, was tugging on Michelle's skirt.

"I'm cold," she said, and Michelle lifted her up and held her tight.

"Who are you again?" she asked the small child who had burrowed under her chin, shivering. Matthew rubbed the girl's back. The girl said her name, but her face was pressed against Michelle's sweater and neither of them heard it.

Matthew had thought about that moment a hundred times since then and the memory still had the power to make his chest hurt. It was ironic that he was now engaged in a conversation by candlelight with Michelle, and his wife would not be remotely jealous. Why was that? Was it because Michelle was a little overweight, a little older than them both? Maybe his wife had never noticed how beautiful Michelle's pale brown eyes were.

Five minutes after they'd gotten home, and after Nancy had paid Michaela and sent her on her way (Matthew deliberately never looking at her), he got a call from Pete Robinson.

"Michelle can't find her phone. You guys didn't pick it up off the table by any chance?"

It turned out that Michelle's phone, the same model as Nancy's, was in Nancy's purse, alongside her own. Pete said that he'd drive over to get it.

"I'm so embarrassed," Nancy said, and slurred the word. She was a little drunk, Matthew realized, a rare event.

"It's no big deal. It's not like you were trying to steal it. Were you trying to steal it?"

She smiled and asked if Matthew would wait outside for Pete. "I just want to go upstairs and get straight into bed."

Matthew put on his warmest sweater and went outside with the phone to wait. The Robinsons' Volvo pulled up, and he was surprised to see Michelle get out of the driver's side. He came down the flagstone path and met her with the phone.

"I thought you'd be Pete," he said.

"Disappointed?"

"No." He handed her the phone.

"Pete wanted to watch his highlights, and he probably shouldn't be driving anyway. I'm not sure I should be driving, but I guess I'm officially addicted to my phone."

"We all are."

They stood for a moment, the night silent around them, and Michelle suddenly said, "Matthew, how are you these days?"

Because the question surprised him, Matthew, without thinking, said, "I've been better. I worry about the kids, and Nancy, she's . . . I guess I worry about her, as well."

"It's not my place to say it, but I think she's hard on you."

Just hearing those words caused something to tighten in Matthew's chest. "She's upset at me all the time and I don't know why. And I don't know how to stop it."

"I'm not a marriage counselor," Michelle said, "but if I was, I'd say that it's not your fault. It's not up to you to stop it."

"I know that intellectually, but I don't always feel it."

"Understandable."

"How about you and Pete?" Matthew said.

She hesitated, then said, "He's been a good father, but he hasn't looked at me in years. All he's interested in is sports."

"Have you talked with him about it?"

"I have. He promises to do better, but nothing changes, and now I feel selfish for even wanting more. Do you talk with Nancy?"

"I don't think she sees herself the way that I see her, the way that other people see her. I don't know . . . I don't know what to do. But, no, I don't really talk with her."

The lamp above the front door, fitted with a motion sensor, went out, and Matthew and Michelle stood in the dark. He knew that if he took just a half-step forward they would be kissing, and that he'd never be able to take that back. But he also realized that Nancy already thought he was cheating with any number of women, so maybe he should just go ahead and do it.

He took a step forward just as Michelle did, and they began to kiss.

7

Ethan had ignored the text from Ashley, saying she was back from visiting her parents and did he want to grab a drink. Instead, he'd sent a text to Hannah, begging her to come over to his place. He hadn't heard back.

While he waited for the burrito to heat up in the microwave, he cracked open a Shiner Bock. As far as he knew, Ashley and Hannah, despite living together, weren't particularly good friends. That didn't mean that Ashley was going to be okay with the fact that he used to sleep with her and now he was exclusively sleeping with her housemate. But maybe she wouldn't mind too much. He thought of calling his oldest friend Marcus and asking him if he thought it was possible to pull off the roommate switch, but he could already hear Marcus's mocking laughter.

While waiting to hear from Hannah (God, he loved her aloofness), he did some deeper Google searches of the names that had been on the list he'd handed over to the FBI earlier in the day. One of the names had been Caroline Geddes, and he wondered if it was the same Caroline Geddes who was an assistant professor in the English Department at the University of Michigan. There was a picture of her, dark hair pulled back off a wide

forehead, and with a half-smile on her face that looked—
what was the word?—secretive, maybe. Ethan felt a click
of recognition looking at her. Not that he'd met her before
necessarily, but that he somehow knew her already.

Her faculty page included an email, and he sent her a
quick message:

Caroline, Did you get a strange list with your name on it?
If you didn't, please ignore this awkward email. If you did,
my name was on the list as well and I don't know why.
Email me. Ethan Dart

He closed his laptop, not expecting to get an email
back anytime soon, and went and crouched in front of
his record collection, looking for something to listen to.
What was he in the mood for? He picked Joni Mitchell,
playing side two of *The Hissing of Summer Lawns*, and
when he rechecked his emails he was surprised he already
had a response from Caroline.

Yes, that was me. An FBI agent nonchalantly took it away
and wouldn't answer any of my questions. What about you?

He wrote back:
Same. Something must be up. Should we be worried? I
feel more curious.

Caroline:
I'm curious, too. Also a little worried. Did you know any of
the other names on the list?

Ethan:

I didn't, no, and I looked them all up. Nothing rang a bell, but when I saw your faculty page . . . you seemed familiar to me. Don't know why.

Caroline:

Familiar meaning we might know each other? Your name doesn't ring a bell for me.

Ethan:

Really? I'm a famous musician.

Caroline:

Are you actually?

Ethan:

No, but I want to be, I guess. I'm aspiring. And now I'm embarrassed that I even made the stupid joke in the first place. Let's talk about something else? Where did you grow up?

They emailed back and forth for an hour, comparing biographies, trying to figure out if there was some connection between them. Except for their age—they were both in their middle thirties—they discovered that they had almost nothing in common. All they'd come up with was the fact that they both had had grandparents from the Boston area in Massachusetts.

Ethan wrote:

Maybe what connects us is that nothing connects us. It feels almost strange that we can't find anything.

She wrote:

You write songs. I like songs. I don't suppose that counts.

Ethan:

Well, you probably wouldn't like my songs. But you critique poetry, and I like poetry.

Caroline:

Liking poetry is far rarer than liking songs. What poets do you like?

Ethan thought for a moment, trying to construct a fast list that would impress her, then asked himself why he was trying to do that. Instead, he decided to just be honest.

Off the top of my head: John Berryman, Frank O'Hara, Weldon Kees, Robert Lowell. Also, a bunch of people you probably wouldn't consider poets: Joni Mitchell, Dylan, Leonard Cohen, James McMurtry, Willy Vlautin.

After sending that last email Ethan didn't hear back right away, and he wondered if his poetry selections had turned her off somehow. He went and flipped through his records, pulling out *Songs of Love and Hate*, and dropped the needle on its first track.

8

Caroline was in her bed, wide awake, emailing back and forth with a stranger. Her orange cat Estrella slept, as was her custom, on the edge of the lower right corner of the mattress, curled into a tight ball. Fable, her other cat, could be anywhere.

Ethan Dart, who'd emailed her out of the blue because of that strange letter, had just given her his list of favorite poets, and she was googling Weldon Kees, looking for a poem of his that she remembered liking. After a few minutes she found it and reread it to herself. An odd poem called "For My Daughter." It was the last line that had stuck with her: "I have no daughter. I desire none."

She was about to write back to Ethan when she got a second email from him.

I lost you when I called Dylan a poet, didn't I?

She smiled, and wrote:

No. You didn't lose me, but he's not a poet. He's a songwriter. No, I was looking up a poem by Weldon Kees I like called "For My Daughter." You don't hear very much about him these days.

Ethan wrote:

Phew, you're still there. I was missing you already. I love Kees, and sometimes I think I'm just romanticizing him because he went missing and no one ever saw him again. Do you know his poem "Crime Club"?

Caroline:

I don't, but I'll look it up.

Ethan:

Okay. I'll wait patiently while you read it. I'll try not to panic that you're leaving me.

Caroline and Ethan Dart emailed until just before dawn. She knew that it was that late not because of the soft gray glow that was filling her curtains but because Fable had come to wake her up, asking to be let out for his predawn reconnaissance.

It's nearly morning, she wrote and he wrote immediately back:

My least favorite time of day. Can we continue this conversation tomorrow night? Or maybe we shouldn't push our luck.

She wrote:

Sure, I could continue, but not until I get at least a little sleep.

84

She folded up her laptop, then brought it to her office to charge. The window curtains were now almost ablaze with morning light. Still, she crawled back under her covers, and thought about the very strange events of the last two days. First, the letter, and then the phone call from the FBI wanting to take possession of it, and now this long email exchange with a country singer from Austin, Texas, who loved Weldon Kees. She'd looked at the picture he had up on his website, and thought he looked a little like paintings she'd seen of Edmund Spenser. Same narrow, pointed nose, same dark brown eyes.

She pulled the covers over her head, creating a pocket of darkness, and lay for a time with her eyes still open.

9

Jessica Winslow lay awake in her bed, wondering if she'd even managed three solid hours of sleep. Aaron had escorted her home the night before, and she'd let him walk her into her house, even let him poke around for a while. She didn't offer him a drink, however, and he let her lead him to her front door.

"Come straight to work in the morning," he said. "Don't stop off anywhere public."

"Sure," she'd said, as she was bending down to pick up the single catalogue that had come through her mail slot.

"You taking this seriously?"

She looked up. Aaron seemed genuinely concerned, but she could also smell toothpaste on his breath, which meant that he'd brushed before leaving the office to escort her home. Which meant he was hoping to be asked to stay.

"I am," she said. "And I'll come straight to work in the morning if you promise to have a coffee and an elephant ear from Mia's waiting for me."

"That's the one on Clinton Ave?"

"That's the one."

"Okay. I'll see you then."

86

She'd spent the night compiling facts on the remaining names they had yet to identify, but didn't send any more emails, or make any more calls. Then she'd gotten into bed with the newest Lisa Gardner book, and read until she thought she might be able to fall asleep. She hadn't, not right away, her mind trying to connect the names on the list, trying to figure out what they might have in common. When she finally slept, she must have dreamed, because she remembered waking up at some point convinced that the dream she'd just had explained everything. She'd reached for the notebook she kept on her bedside table, but as soon as she'd opened it up to a blank sheet, her mind went blank as well. No vestige of the dream remained.

Even though Aaron was going to bring her coffee to the office, she made herself a cup at home. It was going to be one of those mornings. Dressed in her most comfortable suit, she stepped out into the misty day, scanning the blank windows of the surrounding townhouses. Like most residents of her development, she parked out front unless there was going to be a snowstorm and they'd need to plow. There was a parking lot available to all residents, but it was located on the far side of the swimming pool.

She tried listening to NPR on the way to work but her mind kept wandering, so she turned the radio off, and recited the names on the list to herself. Frank Hopkins. Jack Radebaugh. Arthur Kruse. Alison Horne. Jay Coates. Ethan Dart. Caroline Geddes. Matthew Beaumont. And that was eight. There was one more, right? For a total of nine. Then she remembered that she was the ninth name on the list. *Why nine?* she wondered. *Lists should be ten, shouldn't they?* She pulled into her parking spot at the field office. That was the first question she would ask Aaron: Why nine?

SATURDAY, SEPTEMBER 17, 8:00 A. M.

Matthew had reached the part of his run that took him through the town's conservation land, a pine forest that skirted the largest wetland in Dartford. He slowed down, trying to absorb the shushing sound of the gentle breeze going through the tops of the trees, trying to be in the moment.

He stopped and just stood there, listening, but mostly all he could hear was his own breath entering and leaving his lungs. He couldn't quite believe what had happened at the end of the previous night, standing in the dark with Michelle Robinson, making out like teenagers as curfew approached. He'd barely slept, going over and over in his mind what had happened, the solidity of her back against his hand, the softness of her mouth. How long had it lasted? Five minutes, maybe. Afterward, she had laughed, and said, "Well, that was interesting."

"We probably shouldn't be—"

"No, we definitely shouldn't be." Her hand was around his waist pressing their bodies together.

"And I should get back into the house, before Nancy . . ."

"Yes, you should. Definitely." She let go of him, and

leaned back against her car. "Maybe we should just chalk this up as a very nice interlude in our lives."

"That sounds about right. It was very nice."

They kissed once more, briefly but on the lips, and said goodnight.

Her words had been comforting, otherwise Matthew might be panicking right now that Michelle was telling Pete she was in love with someone else and wanted a divorce. No, that wasn't going to happen. It had just been a semi-drunken kiss between two married friends. Nothing more, and over time they'd forget all about it. What else could happen? Even the thought of starting an affair, of kissing in parked cars, and renting motel rooms, and lying to their spouses, made Matthew feel sweaty and nauseous. It would be a terrible idea, and people would get hurt.

He wondered what Michelle was thinking about right now. Should he send her a text message, ask her if there was a place they could meet and talk? But if he did that, then there'd be a text history on his phone. There'd be proof, even if he could somehow erase it. Also, it would be inviting more of what had happened the night before. No, the best thing to do was to pretend it had never happened.

One thing, though. Matthew might feel anxious, but he also felt happy. If nothing else, the memory of that kiss would carry him through a winter's worth of family troubles. The memory would always be there, ready for him to access. That would have to be enough. If Michelle and he had an affair, they would get found out. That's what always happened. And then he and Nancy would get divorced, and he'd probably never see the children again. She'd have custody, and she would hate him for what he had done, passing along all that hate to their children. Not only that, she'd probably pass along all of her neurotic tendencies too, his children becoming miniature versions of their mother. Or maybe not. Maybe they'd turn out okay. He had, after all. His own mother had been a mess all through his childhood. And now she hadn't left her house in over fifteen years, since he'd gone off to college. She lived on vegetable soup, and a steady diet of Hallmark movies, any movie really so long as it had a happy ending. Jesus, why was he thinking of his mother? He thought of Michelle again, and what it had been like to hold her in his arms.

Matthew had been slumped forward, his hands on his knees, even though he was no longer breathing deeply. He straightened up and did a couple of lunges, to stretch out some more. He'd already decided to do the big loop today and that meant two and a half more miles. More time to think of Michelle Robinson. But before he began to run again, he heard the snap of a twig behind him, then he was thrown forward onto the path by the enormous force of a .44-caliber bullet punching a hole dead-center between his shoulder blades, severing the spinal cord so that he was effectively brain-dead by the time he landed on the soft forest floor.

SEVEN

Matthew Beaumont

Jay Coates

Ethan Dart

Caroline Geddes

Frank Hopkins

Alison Horne

Arthur Kruse

Jack Radebaugh

Jessica Winslow

I

SATURDAY, SEPTEMBER 17, 8:04 A. M.

At the exact moment that a bullet ended the life of Matthew Beaumont, Alison Horne, who had gotten up very early on that Saturday in September, finished a glass of alkaline water and was laying out her yoga mat.

She was trying to relax, but her mind was racing. Had been racing since she'd woken up two hours earlier. This was a periodic problem, a sudden and overwhelming panic that the life she was leading was utterly without meaning or purpose. She'd felt that way before, on and off, all through her twenties and her thirties, but now time was a factor. She was going to be forty-one years old in December, and that thought filled her with a cold dread, a tightening in her stomach. She'd moved to New York nineteen years ago after graduating with a fine arts degree from Mather College in Connecticut, and had immediately gotten a string of jobs that seemed promising but led nowhere. She'd been a nanny for a wealthy couple who lived on the Upper East Side, a yoga instructor, and a portrait photographer specializing in actors' headshots. She'd also worked unpaid as an intern at a photography gallery in the Village, and she'd been taking her own photographs for as long as she could remember, shots of her friends mostly, and street shots of New York. Looking at some of those photographs now filled her with an almost sorrowful feeling of failure. They were like lesser copies of better photographs by better photographers. Some were okay, but none of them stood out. They were reminders that she wasn't special. And they were also reminders of her freewheeling twenties, and how they were never coming back. Most of the friends she'd photographed had left the city either to start families or to follow promising careers. And she was still here.

A year earlier, with the free time afforded her by her relationship with Jonathan Grant, Alison had taken up collage, utilizing some of her own pictures, combining them with printouts of text messages and emails, and rearranging them on canvases, painting over them with oil sticks.

Jonathan said he liked them, and even offered to try to get her a gallery show, but lately when she looked at the dozen pieces she'd produced, it was like looking at a foreign script. They were unreadable to her. She had no idea if they were any good, or if they were terrible. She'd put them at the back of her walk-in closet.

On good days she told herself that she was living a happy, comfortable life, that she was one of the lucky ones. She had a spacious one-bedroom in Manhattan with no financial worries. She had time to create art, read, work out, see friends. Her only responsibility was to Jonathan, who paid her bills in exchange for weekly sex (sometimes not even that) and an occasional dinner out at a top-end restaurant.

She'd been Jonathan's paid mistress for one year now. (Sometimes she told herself that she was his girlfriend, but she knew that wasn't really what she was.) He'd approached her when she'd been working as a hostess at a subterranean steak house in midtown Manhattan. It had been a particularly bad time for her, both financially and emotionally. She'd split with her boyfriend of five years, a mutual separation, but then he'd immediately taken up with a younger woman at his law firm, and within one year they'd married, bought a house in New Jersey, and were starting a family. She'd also just lost the best job she'd had in the city, as a photo editor for a start-up literary magazine that was being backed by a dot-com entrepreneur named Bruce Lamb. Apparently, the magazine had lost so much money in its first two years that it was no longer useful even as a tax write-off. Her friend Lucy had gotten her the job as a hostess at the Lodge. She wore tiny skirts and halter tops, but it was an easy job, and the tip sharing included the hostesses, which meant she was making far more per week than she had in the entire time she'd been in New York.

Jonathan Grant was a semi-regular at the Lodge, coming in by himself around nine and sitting at the bar. He wore nice suits, and reminded Alison of an actor her mother used to like called James Mason, with his deep voice and rigid posture. He always ordered the bar steak, a petit filet mignon with crabmeat and béarnaise sauce. On slow nights she'd chat with him, often about the wine he was drinking. One evening he stayed at the bar until late, then asked Alison if she wanted to go to a place he knew two blocks over, a Spanish tapas restaurant that had the best glasses of wine in the city. She must have hesitated when he'd asked her because he'd immediately put his hands up, and said, "Please say no, and don't feel bad about it. I just love talking wine with you and it would be nice to do it when you were actually tasting the wine yourself."

"I'll let you know how I feel at closing," she said, and went back to her station. She wanted to go with him. He might be as old as her father, but he also seemed harmless, and he was attractive. Still, as soon as he'd asked her the question a strange chill had rippled over her skin, almost like a premonition. She'd had those her whole life, little flickers of knowing. Like the time she'd been talking with her grandmother on the phone, and she'd gotten so cold that she had to run for a sweater after they'd hung up. The next time she laid eyes on her grandmother was when she was in an open casket, looking as though someone had replaced her body with a terrible non-breathing approximation. Her cold spells weren't always about death, though. When she'd first met Mrs. Talbot, their new neighbor in Greenwich when Alison was thirteen years old, she'd actually begun to shiver. Within a year, her father had left the family in order to move with Marianne Talbot to a brownstone in Philadelphia. He'd always been a distant, unhappy father, but after abandoning his family, he'd become almost a stranger. Alison hadn't spoken with him in a decade.

The way she thought about her premonitions was that they were mostly about change, but always change for the worse. And that's what death was, of course: just a change for the worse.

But she went out with Jonathan Grant, despite the coldness she'd felt when he asked her. And they had a good time. He talked about his children and his work, asked her questions about her own life. He didn't try to kiss her, even though she'd already decided that she'd probably let him. But on their third date, he offered her a proposition, starting off by saying, "I believe in straight talk. I think that's how I've made all of my money. So I'd like to put an offer before you."

She knew what the general idea of the proposition was going to be long before he got into the details, but it was the details that ultimately sold her. He owned an apartment near Gramercy Park and she could live there rent-free. In return he would like to see her once a week for a "physical engagement"—his unfortunate words—and he would also make sure that she received plenty of spending money and gifts.

"We haven't even slept together," Alison said. "How do you know you'd like it?"

"Because I like you. I'm not a fetishist, and don't care what your breasts look like or what acts you'd be willing to do. I don't care about any of that. I just want to be intimate with you, but I would entirely understand if you want to do that with me *first* before making a decision."

So, they did, that night, in a room at the Greenwich Hotel. True to his word, there was nothing strange or kinky about Jonathan's sexual behavior. He took a pill first, telling her it gave him his best chance of a successful erection, and then he took her to bed, gentle at first, a little boring, but before she knew it, he had taken control, changing their positions until he'd found the one that felt the best to both of them, and she had managed to easily have an orgasm. She lay on the comfortable bed, her body tired and relaxed, while he dialed down to room service for a cold bottle of white.

"So I'll be your whore?" she said.

"I believe the preferred nomenclature is 'mistress,' but you can call yourself anything you want. I'll understand if you don't want to do this."

"What if I meet someone else? What if I fall in love?"

"I'd be happy for you."

This was fourteen months ago. Despite the premonition that night at the Lodge, she felt as though the change that Jonathan had brought her had been mostly good. Her life was full of pleasure. She no longer worried about money. But she did worry about the purpose of her life, and she worried that she'd entered a kind of trap in this relationship with an older, married man. It wouldn't last forever, and what would she do after he was gone? How would she go back to a life without the steady income he provided?

The day loomed before her. She texted Doug to see if he was free for lunch, then remembered right after she texted that he had gone to upstate New York for the weekend with his boyfriend.

She paced her apartment, wondering why she was so shaky this morning, her limbs practically tingling. She'd felt strange for a couple of days now, and thinking back, she realized that it had started when she'd received that list in the mail with the names on it. It had been a while since one of her feelings had come over her, and that letter had done it. Which meant change was coming, and the bad kind.

She nearly fished through her kitchen garbage in order to look at the list again, but what would that accomplish? Instead, she called her favorite spa to see if she could get a pedicure appointment later in the morning.

2

SATURDAY, SEPTEMBER 17, 8:21 A. M.

He'd left his bedroom window open, and it was cold in the room when he woke up. Despite that, Arthur was under his heavy duvet and was perfectly warm. He lay for a moment, drifting up into consciousness, enjoying the feel of the cold air and his own body heat under the covers, and the way the curtain was flapping in the breeze. Light flickered across half of the high ceiling and he was transfixed by it. Then, as happened every morning, thoughts flooded in: Richard's death, a strange letter, the FBI agents. He was fully awake.

In the shower, he thought back on those few minutes of quiet bliss he'd had in bed that morning. It was happening more frequently these days, this lapse of time between waking up and then remembering that he'd lost Richard, and that he'd never be able to see him or talk to him again. He was conflicted. He loved these moments of time when he was able to just enjoy the fact that he was still alive, but he was also terrified that Richard was slipping away from him, becoming a half-remembered ghost of his past.

He forced himself to stop thinking about it and planned out his day instead. Saturdays were the hardest day of the week. He didn't have work, and he didn't have church, and the day stretched out before him like an endless, empty corridor. There was raking to do, and that would take up some of the day, and he'd been meaning to go see an exhibit at the Mead Art Museum, something called "A Collection of Medieval Devotional Objects," right up his alley. Between those two things, and eating, of course, plus maybe a movie after dinner, he'd manage to get through this Saturday.

3

SATURDAY, SEPTEMBER 17, 11:13 A. M.

Why nine?" Jessica said to Aaron as he sidled up to her cubicle.

"Huh?"

"Why nine people on the list, and why not ten? Isn't ten standard practice for these sorts of things? What's wrong?"

She noticed that Aaron was not so much listening to her as he was waiting to say something to her. She spun her chair the rest of the way around so that he was standing directly in front of her, both hands in his pants pockets.

"There's been another death."

"Who? Where?"

"Matthew Beaumont in Dartford, Massachusetts. He was shot while on his morning run."

"It's the same Matthew Beaumont—"

"Who got the letter? Yes. He works . . . worked in Boston. That was where his letter was collected from, yesterday."

"Jesus," Jessica said.

"You said it."

"How was he killed? You said shot? At what time?"

"I don't know what time he was shot, exactly, but I know that the body was discovered about ten in the morning. A local officer was able to identify him even though he wasn't carrying any identification, and since we'd flagged the name . . ."

"So whoever is doing this is a few hours from that location."

"Which could be almost anywhere," Aaron said.

"I know. It's just . . . that's two in two days."

"I think there was a part of me that still wondered whether there was just some massive cosmic coincidence at work. Nine random people wind up on a list, and one of those people is murdered. And then nothing more would happen. No more deaths, and we'd forget all about it."

"It's the second plane," Jessica said.

"What do you mean?"

"On 9/11, I remember watching the news after the first plane hit, and the world just thought it was a terrible accident. Then the second plane hit, and everything changed."

"Right, I remember that. This is the second plane, and now we need to get protection for everyone on that list. You included."

Jessica nodded. "I wish we could find everyone. I've been trying all morning. Do you know how many Alison Hornes there are in this country?"

"How do you know the Alison Horne you are looking for is even in this country?"

"I don't, obviously. But we need to find her. And we need to go to Dartford, Massachusetts."

Aaron took a hand out of his pocket and put it on the partition that separated the cubicles. "I'm assuming by 'we' you mean someone in the FBI. You know you can't be on this case."

Jessica knew that, and even though she was shaking her head, said, "I can at least keep looking for the people we haven't found, right?"

"Don't look at me. This is up to Ruth. That's really why I'm here. She's briefing us all in ten."

"Right," Jessica said. "Shit, she's going to put me on leave, isn't she?"

"She should. Send you on a secret vacation until we catch whoever's doing this. That's what you'd do if you were her, right?"

"I guess so," Jessica said, standing up, getting her phone from her desk. "Where was he shot?"

"Matthew Beaumont? In the back, apparently. He didn't see it coming."

"I just spoke with him yesterday. Jesus. I guess this is real."

Together they walked to Ruth Jackson's office.

4

Jay woke up in a filthy mood, the memories of his failed audition two days earlier fresh in his mind. He felt hungover, a dull headache behind his eyes, and he counted his drinks from the night before. A few light beers at his local bar, then two—or was it three?—hefty vodka rocks back in his apartment. He'd been on Craigslist, hunting through the personals for someone he could fuck, or, preferably, fuck up. He'd even messaged for a while with some straight-up prostitute, negotiating fees. She'd stopped writing him after he asked her what it would cost for him to fuck her from behind and then punch her in the kidneys. That had been the highlight of his evening, picturing her face when she received that message, but even then, he'd been thinking about the woman at the Brentwood Country Mart who he'd followed back to her apartment in Koreatown. Maybe he really should pay her a visit. He'd been thinking that last night, and he was thinking that again this morning. He found her on Instagram and scrolled through her pictures, thinking that they looked like every other Instagram feed from every other hot piece of ass. There she was curled up with a book to show everyone how smart she was. And there she was drinking prosecco with her girlfriends at brunch. And, of course, there were about three hundred pictures of her in a bikini because that's all she really wanted to show the world. Look at this body, and don't you wish you could fuck it. That's what it was all about, and he'd love to take her down a notch, or maybe two.

He put the phone down for a moment, and the dream he'd had the night before swam up briefly into his consciousness. It was a recurring dream, one he'd had for as long as he could remember. He'd killed someone and he needed to hide the body, and he was terrified of getting caught. Or else he'd already hidden the body but he knew it was going to be found. He tried hard to unpick the strands of last night's dream, wondering who he'd killed. Was it the blonde from Brentwood? He didn't think so. It had probably been Olivia Bauer, his high school girlfriend, the girl he'd lost his virginity to, and it wasn't the first dream in which he'd beaten her to death and hidden her in Eel Pond, that swampy, shallow pretend lake in the shitty town in New Hampshire he'd grown up in. No, he'd had that dream before, and it was always the same; he kept trying to weigh her down under the green surface of the pond by covering her body with rocks, but she kept bobbing back up to the surface.

He'd had that dream so many times he sometimes believed it was real.

Except for teaching a spin class at the gym from eleven to noon, Jay had a free day ahead of him. He did some push-ups, made himself a smoothie, then watched some porn without allowing himself to masturbate, not even touching himself. It was painful, but kind of invigorating at the same time. When he got bored with that, he checked his phone and saw that he had a voice mail message from a number he didn't recognize. It had been left the day before, and he assumed it was a sales call, but decided to listen to it just in case it had something to do with a job. Turned out to not be a sales call, but a Jessica Winslow from the Federal Bureau of Investigation, wanting him to call her back as soon as possible. His stomach twisted with a feeling of rage and fear. Jesus, was it that email he'd sent last night to that slut on Craigslist? That couldn't be it. She probably heard that stuff all the time, and besides, there was no way his account could be traced back to him. Also, he just realized, he'd gotten the phone call from the FBI yesterday afternoon and he'd sent the message on Craigslist last night. He relaxed a little. Still, that wasn't the first message of that kind he'd sent from his account. Maybe he should delete it, just in case, scrub his laptop.

He listened to the message again, trying to read her tone of voice. He couldn't tell a thing. It was probably nothing, hopefully nothing. Either way, he decided he didn't want to call her back. No matter what she had to say, it wasn't something he wanted to hear. He erased the message.

5

SATURDAY, SEPTEMBER 17, 2:05 P. M.

Caroline had risen late, then spent the morning grading papers, tweaking her lecture on George Eliot, and even spent half an hour memorizing a Weldon Kees poem. She made herself a grilled cheese sandwich for a late lunch, heating up some of the homemade tomato soup she'd put together at the beginning of the week. She brought the food out to her front porch, considered pouring herself a glass of wine, then decided not to.

It was warm, and slightly overcast, clouds stretched like gauze across the sky, or like a patient etherized upon the table. Estrella was on the porch with her, watching a cardinal through the screen. Fable was still outside; she'd seen him earlier stalking through the high grass of her neighbor's wild lawn.

She'd brought her phone with her outside and looked back over the email thread with that strange guy from Texas. It had been such an odd encounter that she couldn't shake it out of her mind. She supposed that for her students—for her contemporaries, probably, as well—having a long, flirty digital conversation was a regular occurrence, but it was new to her, and now she was consumed with thoughts of a man she'd never met.

No, that wasn't true. They *had* met, last night, even if it wasn't in person. In some ways it was the most significant conversation she'd had in years, so much more interesting than her occasional flirtations with self-satisfied academics at conferences. She flipped from her emails to her internet browser and looked at the few pictures of Ethan Dart that she'd found. On a whim, she searched for videos and found one on YouTube of him alone with a guitar on a stage, singing a song called "Just Because." It was from an event called Austin Showcase from a couple of years earlier. Ethan wore black jeans and a De La Soul T-shirt and he perched on a wooden stool while he played and sang. Caroline had limited knowledge of music, in general. She knew what she liked but didn't necessarily seek out new acts or go to shows. Most of what she listened to were CDs she'd owned since college—girl folksingers, and string quartets, and some Icelandic ambient stuff she'd inherited after her split with Alec. But she was relieved that she liked Ethan's song, the chorus repeating the line "Just because my boot was tapping didn't mean I liked the song," and she found herself unpacking that line for all its possible meanings.

As she was dipping the remainder of her sandwich into her soup, she noticed the police cruiser slowly turning into the driveway. A few random thoughts slipped through her mind: *Are my parents dead? Has my cat been found on the side of the road? Have they come to question me about Ethan Dart?* And that last thought made her realize they were probably there to follow up on the strange list. Two uniformed officers, one male, one female, one wide-hipped, one pigeon-toed, stepped from the cruiser and made their way to the porch.

6

SATURDAY, SEPTEMBER 17, 1:18 P. M.

An Austin patrol officer, just one, came to Ethan's apartment at roughly the same time as Caroline let the Ann Arbor police onto her porch. Officer Resendez knocked on Ethan's door while he was asleep. He'd already been up for a cup of coffee and three over-easy eggs, but he'd been so exhausted that he'd climbed back into bed and was still napping. The three sharp raps from Officer Resendez got incorporated into Ethan's dream, one in which he'd had to return to college in Lubbock to take one last exam in order to graduate. The raps, in his dream, were made by a large black vulture outside of one of the exam room's windows, pecking at a plane of glass. By the time Ethan had hoisted himself from the futon on his floor, and made his way to the door, peering through the eyehole to see a clean-shaven cop, the dream was gone.

"Hey," Ethan said to the policeman after opening the door about six inches.

"Are you Ethan Dart?"

"Uh-huh," he said, and coughed to clear his phlegmy throat. Was he about to get arrested?

"Do you mind coming with me to the station? You're being put under temporary protective custody. There's a federal agent on his or her way to the station who can explain it to you."

"Seriously? What's going on?"

"Honestly, I have no idea, man. But I'd find some comfortable clothes to put on. You don't know how long you'll be in them."

7

Jack Radebaugh heard the unusually loud thump of his mail being delivered through the slot in his front door and got up from the kitchen table to go take a look. There was a package from his wife in a manila envelope. She hadn't written a return address, but he knew her writing better than he knew his own.

He went back to the kitchen table with the thick package and slit it open using a steak knife. Inside was a stack of mail addressed to him at his old address. On the top letter was a sticky note, on which Harriet had written: *Change your address!*

He flipped through his mail, half of which could've been thrown out unopened. There were lapsed subscription notices, pleas for political donations, offers for credit cards. There was also his royalty check from his publishing house, a Christmas card from his old friend Earnest that was either very early or very, very late, and a thin white envelope, that, like the package it arrived in, had no return address. He opened it, and read a list of names, his included. He slid it on top of the pile of mail he intended on throwing out, then changed his mind, and moved it to the pile of keepers.

Three days earlier he'd received a call from a female FBI agent asking him if he'd received a list in the mail with his name on it. He'd told her that he hadn't, but now that he'd actually received such a list, he supposed that the thing to do would be to call her back. He wondered if he'd kept her number.

He got up and refilled his coffee mug, knowing he would take only a few sips, but liking the feel of the hot mug in his hands. Fall had arrived. Jack's favorite season anywhere, but especially in West Hartford, where he'd grown up, and where he was now living again, having bought his childhood house. It was a three-bedroom Tudor in a neighborhood of brick Tudors, each with its own fairytale profile—the steep roof, the narrow windows—and each with its own tidy front yard.

The square kitchen of his newly reacquired home was toward the back, and from its side window he could see into the backyard of his neighbor's property. That house had belonged to a family named Lambert when Jack was a boy. This was back in the early 1950s. There were three children in the Lambert family, all slightly older than Jack and his sister. There was a teenage girl, who still retained her English accent from the time before the Lamberts had emigrated to America. Two more girls, fraternal twins, liked to embroil Jack and his sister in strange games of imagination, usually involving the fairies that lived in their conjoined backyards. Jack remembered those games better than he remembered any of the Lamberts' faces.

He wondered what had happened to them. The parents would be dead now, of course, and those young girls would all be older than him. They'd most likely have children and grandchildren and successes and heartbreak. And the chances were that at least one of them was already dead.

Looking out at the Lamberts' old house now, he watched as a very thin woman with long brown hair stepped into the back sunroom, holding her own mug of coffee and staring into her backyard. The sunroom had not been part of his neighbor's house when he'd been a child. It was an addition, probably added in the 1970s or 1980s, a room almost entirely made of glass. He was calling it a sunroom even though he was pretty sure it went by another name that he couldn't quite remember. Words had been escaping him lately. They were like cigarette smoke. He'd open his mouth and the word would billow away on the wind. He could see its shape as it dissipated but the word was gone.

Jack, coming out of this reverie, refocused on his neighbor's house. The woman with the mug was now turned and looking directly at him, not with any animosity, but with curiosity, if anything. He raised a hand and she waved back, and then Jack stepped away from his kitchen window. There was a mirror in the front hall and Jack took a look at himself, making sure he had no food in his teeth, nothing crusty around his eyes, then he swept his fingers through his thick mane of gray hair, and made his way to his back porch. If the woman was still in her solarium—that was it, a goddamn solarium!—then he'd say hello.

It was colder outside than he thought it would be, and Jack buttoned up his cardigan as he wandered across toward his neighbor. The woman was still there, and she stepped outside as well, just as he reached the threshold of her property.

"Thought I'd introduce myself," Jack said.

"I'm Margaret," she said, putting out her hand, and taking three quick, awkward steps to shake his.

"I'm Jack. I'm—"

"I've been meaning to come over and introduce myself, and I even put together half of a welcome basket, but then ended up eating the muffins, and I don't even know why I'm telling you this. I'm sorry I haven't come over sooner."

"Nothing to be sorry about. I've only been here less than a month."

"I know. I just don't want you to think I'm not neighborly. I've got a pot of coffee on, if you want a cup."

"Sure," Jack said.

Once they were settled in the solarium/sunroom, Jack with another cup of coffee he didn't want, Margaret said, "I heard a rumor you used to live here."

"Oh, yeah? Who did you hear that from?"

"A fellow librarian, actually. At the branch just down the street where I work. She told me you used to live here, but before her time. She also said that you wrote a famous book."

"She's one for two. I did used to live here, but I hardly think my book was famous. Maybe it was for about a year and a half, right after it came out."

"What kind of book was it?"

"It was called *Say It Out Loud, Then Do It Out Loud*. It was—it is—a business book about always announcing your plans before you do them. I know what you're thinking— How do you write a whole book about that?—and I can barely remember how I did it. Wide margins, I guess. But it made me a lot of money once upon a time. And it turned me into a full-time consultant. I still occasionally do seminars all over the world."

"It rings a bell. My father probably bought it."

"Was your father a business man?"

"Yes. In the insurance business."

"Then he may well have bought my book."

Margaret had put out a platter with a few slices of coffee cake on it, and Jack took one and had a bite. It was very good. She looked expectantly at him, and he told her how much he liked it, and she confirmed his guess that it was homemade. While she talked with him about baking, and how it was her true love, he studied her. She had small features, a slightly pointed chin, and the skin on her cheeks was darker than the rest of her face, as though she'd had bad acne as a teenager. She was skinny, and sat slightly hunched forward, the same bad posture that Jack saw on so many young people. Her best feature was her long brown hair. It had that lustrous look that comes from a healthy diet, or maybe just plain genetics.

"So is it true you used to live here, in this neighborhood, I mean, when you were a kid?" she said, pushing her hair back off her forehead, and sitting up a little straighter.

"I grew up here. Right next door, same house I just bought. My father, like yours, worked in insurance."

"Wow. How long did you live here?"

"Until I went to college. Then my parents got divorced, and the house was sold. But except for vacation homes this was where I spent my childhood."

"You must have happy memories," she said.

"Why do you say that?"

"Because you've bought the house and moved back into it. Unless you plan on burning it down or something, I just figured . . ."

"No, you're right. It was mostly a happy childhood. And I love this neighborhood with all the brick houses."

"It must have changed."

"No, not at all. The city's changed, but this street is pretty much exactly how I remember it. It was where I started my life, so I suppose it's as good a place as any to finish it."

"Oh, don't say that," Margaret said, shifting forward, lowering her shoulders. "You don't even look like you're retired."

"I'm semi-retired, I guess. But I don't know . . . it feels, to me, that moving back here isn't temporary. It's final. I want to stop working completely, and my marriage is kaput. No, it's okay. One of those separations that is definitely best for everyone involved. And all this was happening, and then I went online and saw that this house was for sale. It was kismet. And now I'm ready for the next part of my life. How did you end up here?"

Margaret told him how she'd gone to college in Hartford, and gotten married right afterward, and even though they'd dreamed of moving to New York City, her husband Eric was offered a job at a local finance company, and she'd gotten a library degree, and was now working part-time at the nearest branch. They'd bought the house just a few months earlier.

"So, you're new here, too."

"Relatively. We'd been renting a place just a few blocks away. It was an in-law apartment at my husband's best friend's house, so we know the area. But, yes, we are new to this street, and you are pretty much the first neighbor I've had over for coffee."

"Well, I'm honored."

"And I'd love to have you over for dinner sometime. Maybe even grill out before the evenings get too cold."

"I'd like that," Jack said, assuming she was just being polite. He was also assuming that her mentioning a second social event meant this one was over. He stood up. "I have some work to do this morning," he said.

"Oh, okay." She stood, as well, and Jack saw an expression—anxiety, maybe, or possibly fear—cross her face. "I'm sorry. I didn't know I was keeping you . . ."

"Oh, no. Don't worry about it. It was lovely meeting you, but I do have a few things to do this morning, and if I stay here any longer, I'll eat all of that coffee cake."

Back in his own kitchen, Jack stood a little back from the window and watched as his nervous neighbor tidied up the room he'd just departed. He doubted she would make good on her offer of an invite for dinner, which was just as well. He had suspicions he wouldn't like her husband.

Jack turned back to the kitchen table and surveyed the two piles of mail he'd made. He remembered the FBI agent, and decided to go hunt down her phone number. He'd give her a call later that afternoon, or maybe he'd call her on Monday. Whatever it was, it could probably wait.

8

Detective Sam Hamilton had worked with Mary Parkinson, the state police detective, on two other occasions: one case, a foiled bank robbery, that had been cleared up within hours; and another, a hit-and-run, that remained unsolved. He'd gotten along with her just fine, although she was hard to read, one of those tight-lipped, weather-beaten New Englanders who looked like she'd been born with wrinkles on her face, and only spoke when it was absolutely necessary. Still, when she did speak, she was friendly enough, and she'd never shown any reticence about working with a local detective.

He'd been wanting to call her all day, to see if she'd provide an update on the Frank Hopkins homicide, but he'd forced himself to wait, not wanting to bother her so soon in the midst of an investigation. But after spending all day at home hunting the internet for possible connections between the nine names on the list, and finding very little, Sam decided to place the call.

"Detective Parkinson here."

"Mary, it's Sam. From Kennewick."

"Hi Sam. You must have something for me."

"I wish. I don't have anything. I was calling in the hopes that *you'd* update *me*."

"On Frank Hopkins?"

"Yeah."

"I'm off that case now, myself. Well, they told me I'm consulting, but it just went federal so there you have it."

"Seriously?"

"Seriously. Just happened about an hour ago."

"Why? Do you know?"

"There was another homicide. In Massachusetts."

"What do you mean?" Sam said.

"A Matthew Beaumont was killed this morning in Dartford, Massachusetts. Shot while he was out for his morning run. I'm sure you remember that he was one of the names on the list. Well, he'd gotten the same letter as Frank had, so now it's some kind of serial killer crossing state lines. Or that's what it looks like."

"Wow," Sam said. "I'm not surprised but I *am* surprised at the same time. If you know what I mean."

"I was surprised, too. I've been at this a long time, and when a homicide looks complicated, it mostly turns out that it's not."

"That's what I was thinking, as well."

"Well, it could still turn out that way," Detective Parkinson said. "Frank Hopkins was probably killed by some strung-out drug addict. You've still got those over in Kennewick, right?"

"Drug addicts?"

"Yes."

"A few," Sam said.

"Look, Sam, people keep walking by my desk looking to see if I'm off the phone yet. I'm sorry I don't have more information for you."

"You had plenty, Mary, thanks."

After ending the call Sam sat for a few minutes just staring out his second-floor window and thinking. Despite what Mary had said, that Frank's death could still just be the result of some desperate addict, Sam knew that the second death negated that possibility. Frank had died with a list in his hand. Nine names. And now another person named on that list had been killed as well. There was no scenario in which this was simply a coincidence.

Sam stood up and went to the built-in bookshelf on the opposite side of his office. It contained, among other books, his grandmother's entire collection of Agatha Christie novels. She hadn't explicitly left them to Sam in her will, but everyone in the family knew that she wanted him to have her books, and in particular the Christie collection, some of which were probably very valuable first editions.

For most of Sam's childhood he had spent summers at his grandmother's house in North Yorkshire. Patricia Barnard was his mother's mother, who had spent part of her adult life in Jamaica, arriving there from England in 1946 to take a post as a secretary at an export company. She'd fallen in love with Robert Hamilton, owner of a popular Kingston restaurant, and a Black Jamaican. She was married and pregnant within the year, giving birth to Rosemary, Sam's mother. Sam had asked his grandmother several times about what it had been like to be in an inter-racial marriage in the 1940s and 1950s. She'd always said that the worst of it was other people's bad manners—"just a funny look now and then, when we took the bus together."

Bob Hamilton, her husband, had died when their only daughter was just eighteen, and Patricia had moved back to England, settling into a family cottage in the Yorkshire Dales. And that stone cottage was where Sam had spent the best months of his childhood, given freedom to wander through the English countryside, and, more important, access to his grandmother's book collection. At the age of ten he'd read Agatha Christie's *Sleeping Murder* and fallen in love with it. After that, he was hooked on the genre. And he became a true Anglophile, obsessed with Cadbury chocolate, Arsenal football, and even the silly English sitcoms his grand-mother and he watched on her bulky television set in the sitting room. But it was the books that stuck with him most of all. He loved Agatha Christie and Dick Francis and Ruth Rendell, all his grandmother's favorites, and those books provided for him a worldview, one so different from that of his life growing up in Houma, his parents angry all the time and eventually divorcing during his senior year of high school.

Sam's friends and colleagues had been mostly surprised when he'd applied for the job in Kennewick, Maine, making jokes about how he was going to double the number of Jamaicans living in New England. But Jean Landry, the chief of police, during Sam's goodbye party, was the one who actually figured out Sam's real motivation. During her brief speech, she'd said, "I always knew that Sam, down deep, really wants to be Jessica Fletcher from Cabot Cove, Maine, and now he'll get his chance." And it was partly true. Although he returned to visit England often, even after his grandmother's death, he knew he couldn't work there. But he could work in New England, start a new life in a Maine village, and at least feel as though he was living the life he was born to live.

Staring at his grandmother's Agatha Christie books, arranged chronologically, he pulled out his hardcover edition of the book that would eventually come to be known as *And Then There Were None*, or *Ten Little Indians*. But the version that Sam Hamilton owned, in hardcover, bore the original title: *Ten Little Niggers*.

Sam remembered that after he'd finished *Sleeping Murder* he'd asked Nana Pat what he should read next.

"There's a book I think you'd really like," she said, "but I think I should buy a new copy for you."

"You don't have it?"

"I do, but it has a not-so-nice title. In fact, it was so not nice that they changed it. They've changed it a couple of times, actually."

She'd shown him the book and explained that it came from a nursery rhyme that had been popular many years ago. Sam had been fascinated, especially by the cover—a white, ghostly hand plucking at ten little African figures, some standing, some brandishing spears, some lying down. He'd read the book, of course, in one terrifying afternoon, not wanting to wait for Nana Pat to order a more appropriately titled version from the village bookstore.

Afterward, he'd followed her around the house while she'd tidied up, wanting to talk about what had happened in the novel, the scariest murders, the phonograph recording in which all of the victims had been accused of their crimes, how long the bodies were on the island after everyone was dead.

"Don't you want to know about the title?" she'd asked.

"I thought that it meant that everyone who got invited to the island was Black, but I don't think they were."

"No, they were all white. But don't go telling your parents that I let you read a book with that word in the title. Tell them it was called *And Then There Were None*."

"Dad uses that word all the time."

"What word?"

"Nigger."

"Does he?"

"Not all the time, but some of the time."

"It's okay for him, I guess, but it wasn't okay for Agatha Christie. Maybe it was at the time, but not now."

"How long does it take to die by hanging?" he'd asked.

Or something like that, probably. Sam brought the well-preserved hardcover with him to the leather club chair he liked to read in. On a whim he'd looked up what this particular copy was worth and discovered that it would go for about ten thousand dollars, despite the racist name, or maybe because of it. Not that he was planning on selling it, or any of his other beloved books. But he had decided to reread it, not for the first time. Whatever was happening with Frank Hopkins and the eight other unlucky souls on that list bore some resemblance to this particular novel. He opened it up to chapter one and read the first sentence: "In the corner of a first-class smoking carriage, Mr. Justice Wargrave, lately retired from the bench, puffed at a cigar and ran an interested eye through the political news in *The Times*."

9

SATURDAY, SEPTEMBER 17, 4:39 P. M.

Just as he'd expected on a beautiful Saturday afternoon, Arthur had been the only visitor at the Mead Art Museum to see the medieval devotional objects exhibit. There were about fifty pieces, all of which had been borrowed from a museum in Germany, and Arthur spent time looking at each one, reading each note. He was interested, but also strangely unmoved. There was a lovely bust of a female saint, carved in wood, several crucifixes, and multiple images of the Virgin Mary. He loved imagining these objects in their rightful time and rightful place, the mesmerizing effect they would have had on medieval parishioners, those poor people unlucky enough to be born in the Middle Ages. But the objects had no real emotional effect on him, except for maybe one piece. Two pieces really, a pair of beads that had been carved to be part of a rosary. Each bead had a face, one male, one female, healthy and full-cheeked on one side, but on the opposite side they were rendered as skulls and a few pieces of tattered flesh. On one of them it looked as though a lizard had burrowed into its chin. The note said they were memento mori beads, simple reminders that we are alive only a short time, and that we all have the same fate, to one day rot away.

Arthur was so taken with the beads that for about five minutes he seriously contemplated stealing one of them. He even ran his eyes along the ceiling to look for cameras, but then a museum guard, a tall, hunched-over woman with Coke bottle glasses, wandered by, and Arthur abandoned the plan.

But for the rest of the day he thought about the beads. The truth was, despite his church going, Arthur had struggled with his faith since Richard died. Actually, he'd struggled with his faith before then, since around the time he was rejected by his religious father for his sexual orientation. But after the accident—after coming to in the hospital to find out that Richard and their dog Misty were both gone in an instant, leaving him alone and crippled—all thoughts that he somehow lived in an ordered and benign universe were gone. He continued to attend church, and to periodically do the Sunday flowers, but only out of a sense of obligation and a way to fill some hours. And because he liked the kind of people who attended church, especially the older women. They seemed to have an appreciation for life, even for the small pleasures. And maybe he liked that they doted on him.

What was beautiful about the beads was that they were significant for anyone, for a person of faith or for an agnostic, which was what Arthur now considered himself to be. We all know that our time on earth is brief, the beads seemed to say. We know it, even if we don't always feel it. Our faces and bodies are only beautiful for a short time. Our bones outlast us. But instead of making him feel worse, the memento mori beads made him feel better. How lucky he was to have had Richard in his life for the years that he did. How lucky that he was still alive with the sun on his face, and the well-tended campus lawn under his feet. In the middle distance two college students threw a Frisbee back and forth, and it seemed indescribably beautiful. Life might be the blink of an eye, but he was somehow in it.

Back at his house he was surprised to find two strange cars in his driveway, one a police cruiser and one a black sedan that reminded him briefly of a hearse, but that was probably an aftereffect of the exhibit he'd gone to see.

He was told that he was under temporary police protection and was questioned by a federal agent at his kitchen table while a police officer briefly searched the house. It had to do with the letter he'd received, the one with nine names on it. The agent wouldn't tell him much, but it was clear that something bad must have happened to at least one of the other people who'd received the list. He was asked about all their names, and, as before, he said that none of them was familiar to him.

"How about any of the surnames?" the agent named Tom Urbino said. He was young, Arthur thought, maybe just thirty years old, with olive skin and deep-set eyes.

Arthur took another look at the photocopy of the list that was in front of him on the enamel-topped kitchen table. "No," he said, remembering his conversation on the phone with another FBI agent, Jessica Winslow. She had thought that his father and her father might be friends. Did his father have a friend named Winslow? If he had, Arthur had no memory of it.

He agreed to having a police officer parked outside his house for the duration of the night, and the agent left, while the officer, another young man, this one very blond and with a pimply chin, told Arthur he'd be doing the first shift from his police cruiser. "Lock your doors. Don't let anyone in. If you need anything you can call me."

"Can you tell me more about what's going on?" Arthur said, partly because he badly wanted to know, and partly because it eased his anxiety just to have someone to talk with.

"Honestly, I don't know much about it myself. I'm a low rung on a tall ladder, I guess."

"But does this sort of thing happen often? In your experience . . . ?"

"Well, no, I guess. But I'm new here."

Arthur, realizing he wasn't going to learn anything more, told the officer—he'd already forgotten his first name but his surname was Clift, like the actor—that if he wanted to stay in the house, it would be fine with him. But the officer said he was supposed to be outside in his vehicle.

Lying in bed that night, Arthur thought back over the surreal day: those carved faces reduced by death and time to grinning skulls; the two young men playing Frisbee in the quad; Arthur's thoughts on his walk, the way he'd suddenly felt at peace with the losses of his life. He'd always wondered what was worse: to feel emptiness and not know what would make it go away, or to feel emptiness and know exactly what was missing. Tonight, for whatever reason, he seemed to have the answer. He understood with evangelical clarity how fleeting our lives are, and how foolish it is to mourn those who've left too soon.

It was colder that night than it had been the night before and Arthur got up to close the window. After getting back into bed, he tucked the duvet tightly around him, placed his hands on his chest, and began the process of falling asleep. It wasn't such a problem these days, but Arthur had suffered on and off from insomnia for most of his adult life. He'd even been to a sleep specialist, and when he'd told her that he slept on his back with his hands folded across his chest, she'd told him he slept in the coffin position. And, now, every time he was falling asleep, he thought of that odd phrase.

Two hours later a stainless-steel canister that had been hidden in one of Arthur's empty suitcases on the floor of his closet began to silently release carbon monoxide into the room. It had been equipped with a specially modified valve that opened according to a timing system. Within an hour the carbon monoxide concentration in the bedroom was 3,200 parts per million and Arthur, still tucked under his covers, still in the coffin position, was gone from this world.

SIX

Matthew Beaumont

Jay Coates

Ethan Dart

Caroline Geddes

Frank Hopkins

Alison Horne

Arthur Kruse

Jack Radebaugh

Jessica Winslow

I

SUNDAY, SEPTEMBER 18, 2:01 P. M.

"Is there anywhere you can go? Anywhere you wanna go?"

"I've been thinking a little bit about that," Jessica said. She was in her most comfortable chair, the leather recliner, and Aaron Berlin was pacing back and forth across her living room, making her nervous. "Have a seat, why don't you? You want a beer?"

"I don't know why you're being casual about this. Three people on that list are dead, and one of them had police protection at the time."

"I'm not being casual about it, trust me. But wearing out my rug is not going to help."

"You have beer in the fridge?"

"Yep."

"Okay. You want one, too?"

"Sure. Why not?"

Aaron came back into the living room with two IPAs from Fort Orange Brewing. "Did I leave these here?" he said, as he handed her the tall can.

"Probably. I don't drink much beer."

Aaron sat, which was a start, although it was more like he was crouching on the final inch and a half of the seat of the chair by the entryway to the living room. The chair where Jessica usually dumped her mail.

"So, is there somewhere you can go, somewhere you have absolutely no connection to?"

"Was Arthur Kruse questioned yesterday afternoon?" Jessica said, ignoring his question. "You said he was, right? Do you know if he said anything about his father?"

"I don't, honestly. It's not my case, now, any more than it's yours."

"But you'll still get me his father's contact information if you can, right?"

He took a large swig of his beer, foam sticking to his unshaved upper lip area. Jessica took a sip of her own beer, and thought it was like sticking a pine cone in her mouth.

"I passed along what you'd said about your father and Arthur Kruse's father and their possible connection. I can get you his contact info, but you can't call him until after he's been questioned. You know that."

"I know that. I just can't help but think that there's something there. I mean, there has to be a connection between us."

"You keep saying that, and I agree. But don't you think it's a possibility that you were somehow just randomly selected?"

"I don't. Not really." Jessica sipped some more beer. It was growing on her. "I think if you randomly selected nine people in the United States, the results would be more diverse. Racially. Age-wise. Income bracket."

"There's some age diversity. People in their thirties and forties. Frank Hopkins was in his seventies. You're a woman of color. I don't know about income, exactly, but it doesn't seem like Ethan Dart is exactly rolling in the dough."

"Yes, but he's not poor, is he? He's not part of the under-class, even though his income is low. And I'm a woman of color but I'm adopted. It's significant. I know it is. There's no diversity among the parents of the nine people on the list."

"You don't know that."

"I don't know that, but I suspect that. And if it were a truly random list, then I still think why not have ten people on it instead of nine? Look, I know I'm just making assumptions, but it's not like I'm on this case so I'm going to go ahead and make them. And if I were on the case, what I would do is build up a profile of all of the parents and look for similarities there. That's where they're going to find them. And look for strange events in the parents' past, like unsolved cases, things like that."

Jessica was talking fast, and Aaron said, "Slow down a moment, will you?"

"Sorry. I'm speaking my thoughts out loud. It's just that I know that the nine people are not random, that there's a connection, and that whoever is doing this is not going to stop until we're all dead. God, I sound like I'm in a movie. I *feel* like I'm in a movie."

"It's going to get a lot harder for him or her as the days go on. There's going to be lots of police protection."

"Like for Arthur Kruse. No, I know. But there's not protection right now for Jay Coates, or for Alison Horne, or Jack Radebaugh."

"There will be. We'll find them." Aaron put his can of beer on the floor in front of him. It looked as though it was empty. "Look, I know you're avoiding this question, but I do think it would be better if you go someplace else while this case continues. Being here is not a good thing. Going to your local grocery store, going to the Club Room. Not a good idea. We can send you someplace, as you know, but if there's somewhere you want to visit . . ."

"I can think of a place. Maybe."

"Okay, good. Don't tell me about it. I'm going to get one more beer before I hit the road, and then you should make arrangements."

Aaron ducked into the bathroom first, before heading to the kitchen. Jessica thought of the place she had in mind. It was somewhere in mid-coast Maine, that was all she knew. Two years earlier she'd gone to her college friend Darlene's wedding, and ended up hanging out the entire time with a woman named Gwen Murphy. She'd known Gwen in college as well, but they hadn't been close. That weekend, however, they'd bonded, even fooling around a little after the reception, something Jessica hadn't done since college—fool around with a girl—back when she'd considered herself a true-blue bisexual. And one of the things she remembered from that wedding was Gwen telling her about a house she'd inherited from her grandmother, a cottage on a peninsula in Maine, and how Jessica should use it for her next vacation. She hadn't taken Gwen up on that offer, probably because she didn't know if it was an offer for her to have a vacation alone or a vacation with Gwen, but she thought she'd get in touch now. If the cottage was available, it might be perfect. And there was very little, almost nothing, to connect her with Gwen. They hadn't even texted or emailed since the wedding.

Aaron was pacing again, holding his second beer. He hadn't asked Jessica if she wanted one, which probably wasn't rudeness and had more to do with him knowing her well enough to know she wouldn't.

"You should go to work," she said.

"I should. Look, I have something for you." He pulled a flip phone out of his pocket. "It's a burner, in case you need to let me know where you are. I wouldn't trust your own cell phone, or your landline."

"I know." She took the phone from him.

At the door she kissed him on the lips, and when she sensed that he was about to ask her if she wanted him to stay, she pushed him back out onto the front step. Before closing the door, she spotted the unmarked police vehicle about fifty yards away.

Alone in her townhouse, she went to her desk and pulled out the overfilled, cluttered drawer where she put all the crap she didn't really need but didn't want to throw away either. She walked the drawer into her bedroom and dumped the contents out on her bed. There were programs from funerals she'd attended, takeout menus, old receipts, Christmas cards, an expired passport. There were also several business cards, and it took her a while, but she found Gwen Murphy's card. She was a real estate agent in Jamaica Plain, outside of Boston. Using the burner phone, she called the number listed.

"This is Gwen Murphy."

"Hi, Gwen, it's Jessica Winslow," she said. Then added, "From college," after noticing a slight pause.

"Yes, of course. Sorry, I'm driving."

"Are you alone?"

"Yeah. Go ahead, I've got you on speaker."

"I have a big favor to ask. Two big favors to ask. Do you remember at Darlene's wedding you mentioned that you owned a cottage in Maine?"

"Of course I do. I still have it."

"Is there someone there now?"

"No. It's empty. Why? Did you want to use it?"

"Actually, I *was* hoping I could use it. I know it's a lot to ask but I was thinking of heading up to Maine right away."

"That's fine with me," Gwen said. "Everything okay?"

"Without going too much into it, I need to get away, and I need to do it anonymously."

"Oh, okay," Gwen said, and Jessica could hear the change of tone in her voice. She knew her friend probably thought she was on the run from an abusive situation.

"So I need to ask you to not mention my going to your cottage to anyone. To keep this conversation a complete secret."

"Of course I can do that."

"I'm serious, Gwen, you have to promise to absolutely forget that I'll be there."

"I'm serious, Jessica, I will," Gwen said, her voice hushed, as though to prove how serious she was taking it. Then she provided Jessica with the address of the cottage on the St. George Peninsula, and where the extra key was kept. And she promised her that no one else would be showing up at the cottage.

After ending the call, Jessica thought for five minutes, convincing herself that hiding out in Maine was the best option, despite the fact that it felt like she was running away. She rinsed out her beer can and began to pack.

2

SUNDAY, SEPTEMBER 18, 4:07 P. M.

It was late afternoon and Alison hadn't left the apartment all weekend, not since she'd gotten back from her pedicure the morning before.

She'd told herself that it was a rare luxury, having a weekend all to herself, but now she was restless and bored. Ten years ago she could have called up any number of her friends who still lived in the city, but they had all left, except Doug, who was out of town, and Natalie, who, last time she checked, was still downtown, barely hanging on, a full-blown alcoholic living off a diminishing trust fund. When was the last time she and Natalie had hung out? Six months, at least, or maybe a year ago. She looked at her phone—she still had Natalie's number—and decided on a whim to give her a call. Maybe they could go to the Swan down in the East Village, drink Bloody Marys for dinner, then hang around all night, see who came in. It would be like stepping back in time.

She made the call, but an automated voice told her the number had been disconnected. She checked to see if she had Natalie's email address—she did—and wrote, "Hey Nat, Al here, wanted to see if you'd like to go on a Sunday evening bender for old times' sake. The Swan's still in business, isn't it?" Then, after sending the message, and feeling strange about it, she decided to look up Natalie, find out if she still even lived in New York. It took her a moment to come up with her last name—on her phone's contact list she was simply listed as Nat G—but it came to her. Gimbel, like the old department store. She punched in "Natalie Gimbel" and the first thing that came up was an obituary from two months ago. She clicked on it, and saw a picture of her old friend, smiling into the camera, sun-wrinkled and with streaks of gray in her hair. She'd actually left New York and had been living out in Sedona, Arizona. There was no cause of death, but the obituary stated that in lieu of flowers, please send donations to the Honeysuckle Treatment Center, and Alison connected the dots. How had she not heard? Had none of her old friends known, and if they had known, why hadn't they let her know?

Alison took a deep breath, but her windpipe felt constricted, as though she couldn't quite get enough oxygen. Her chest hurt, and her immaculate living room, and its objects, looked suddenly strange in her vision, unreal, as though she were seeing them for the first time. Her limbs felt hollow, and a voice in her head said, *You're dying, this is it*. But another voice said, *It's a panic attack. You had one before, in college. It felt just like this*. And the second voice won. She didn't call 911, but slowly waited for the feeling to pass, and eventually it did.

By dinnertime she felt almost human again, exhausted, and hungry enough to eat a yogurt. While she ate, she flipped through the channels on the television, but couldn't find anything to watch, so she logged onto Amazon Prime and binge-watched most of season two of *Fleabag*, a show she'd already watched a couple of times. In between the second and third episodes she opened a bottle of Vermentino and grabbed a single-serving packet of raw almonds. During the last episode she got a call from Jonathan, very surprising since it was late on Sunday evening. Pausing the television, she picked up and said, "Hi."

"Al," he said. He rarely called and when he did she always thought that his voice sounded so much older than he looked. A voice from an old movie, masculine and clipped.

She was about to make some quip about hearing from him on a Sunday, but said, instead, "Everything okay?"

"Yes and no," he said. "Jane's left me." Jane was his wife, and based on what he'd told Alison about her, she was supposed to be the type of wife who would never leave a marriage.

"What do you mean? For good?"

He cleared his throat. "It's a total shock, but she's actually met someone else, and she up and left yesterday afternoon. They have an apartment together already."

"Oh my God, Jonathan. How are you doing?"

"I'm dumbfounded, honestly, but I'm also . . . I'm also free now, I guess."

"Sounds like it."

"And the first person I thought of was you."

"Sweetheart," she said. It was her endearment for him, and she didn't use it very often.

"Want to go away for a few days? I was thinking I could bring you to my place in Bermuda. The weather will be—"

"Yes. Yes," she said, sitting up so fast that she kicked over the bottle of wine that was on the floor, spilling the small amount that was left.

"I have some things to do, but I thought that maybe we could leave toward the end of the week, be there by next weekend."

"I'd love that."

"Great. I'll get back to you with arrangements. I can book a private flight out of Teterboro, and I can get a car to bring you out. Are you sure you're up for spending all that time with an old man?"

"I'm thrilled. Really. I'm not just saying that, Jonathan."

After ending the call, Alison played her "going out" Spotify mix as loud as she thought she could without getting a noise complaint, looked up the weather in Bermuda, then started laying out clothing possibilities on her bed, even though it would be several days before she was going.

After making a list of items she'd need to buy that week, she listened to a very strange message from a man identifying himself as Agent Berlin of the Federal Bureau of Investigation, wondering if she'd received a piece of mail with a list on it that included her name. He left her his number to call, plus the local number of the FBI office in Manhattan, where she could ask for an Agent Garrett. She'd known that list was bad news, and she deleted the voice mail without taking down any of the numbers. She'd already decided she'd be better off not knowing. Besides, in a week's time she'd be in Bermuda.

3

SUNDAY, SEPTEMBER 18, 5:31 P. M.

Jack had spent too much of the day indoors, clicking through news stories on Google, making phone calls to various people in his employ, and decided that before it got too dark, he'd make himself a drink and sit outside and enjoy it.

There was a built-in cabinet in the dining room and that was where he'd set up his bar.

He cracked open a fresh bottle of Plymouth, thinking he'd make himself a martini, then remembered that he didn't have any olives. Never mind, he thought, and decided to make himself the drink he internally called "The Travis McGee," named for the favorite drink of the main character in a slew of thrillers he used to devour back in the day. They all had colors in the title, the books did, and he remembered one he thought was called *The Amber Place for Dying*, or something like that. He couldn't remember the author's name, it was something MacDonald, maybe John or Gregory, but the hero was Travis McGee, and for whatever reason, probably because it was a damn fine drink, he remembered how to make Travis McGee's favorite tipple.

After throwing a handful of ice into a tumbler, he

poured a little bit of dry sherry into the glass. Then he dumped out the sherry and filled it up with Plymouth Gin. He found a lemon in the refrigerator and added a few drops of lemon juice. He couldn't remember if you added some lemon peel but decided to do it anyway. It looked nice, and Jack had always considered drinking an aesthetic activity, above all else. He was going to bring his drink out to the back patio, but changed his mind, and went out the front door of the house, taking a seat on the bench that sat to the right of the front door. It wasn't comfortable, but it would be nice to watch the cars and the dogwalkers go by.

He balanced the drink on the metal seat of the bench and buttoned up his cardigan. Then he took a long sip of the delicious gin, and silently toasted whatever author it had been who had created Travis McGee.

Fewer cars were going by than he thought, then he realized it was a Sunday. But there were plenty of pedestrians, most of whom were walking with purpose, or at least seemed to be. There were several runners, mostly men. But even the walkers, especially the women, seemed to be walking with exaggerated strides, and they were all wearing exercise clothes, tight black leggings and brightly colored tops. And not only were they walking with grim determination, they were all talking at the same time, and it took Jack a moment to realize that they were on their phones, talking through the speakers that dangled from their headphones.

He finished his drink and was about to go inside for the evening when he spotted his neighbor—her name had already escaped him—walking along the sidewalk. Even if he hadn't known her, she would have stood out to him. First off, she wasn't wearing workout clothes. She was in jeans and a turtleneck sweater, and she was walking slowly, looking up at the leaves that still clung to the trees. She wasn't even wearing headphones.

"Hello," he said, and when she didn't seem to hear him, he said it again, louder.

She jumped a little, then turned her head. "You scared me. I was totally lost in my thoughts."

"Please go back to them. I'm sorry I interrupted."

"God, no. If you knew my thoughts, you wouldn't want to be lost in them. I didn't see you there. You blend into the side of your house."

Jack looked down at himself. He was wearing brown trousers, and a rust-red cardigan and he realized now that he probably was hidden against the brick exterior.

"I do," he said. "I was just about to go inside and get myself another drink. Will you join me on my bench?"

His neighbor, who had stepped up onto his lawn, shrugged and said that she would.

"What can I get you?" he asked, still trying to come up with her name.

"What were you having?"

"Gin on the rocks, which sounds like very serious drinking for a Sunday night, I now realize."

"It does. Although if you have some tonic, I'd drink a gin and tonic."

"I think I might."

When Jack had returned with two gin and tonics, she was sitting on the bench waiting for him. He handed her the glass, and she said, "I might have to suddenly leave you. My husband went into the office today, and he's due back soon, so I hope you don't mind . . ."

"I promise I won't be insulted when you leave me. This is a good spot. You'll be able to see him arrive from here."

"I will," she said, and took a sip of her drink.

"I'm embarrassed to admit this," Jack said, "but I've forgotten your name already. I blame old age."

"It's Margaret," she said. "And you hardly seem old at all."

"Margaret. That's right. And is that what people call you? Or do you have a nickname?"

"I think I'm the only Margaret left in the world. I'm not Maggie, or Megan, or Meg."

"Or Peg," Jack said.

"Right. Or Peg, although I don't think anyone these days is called Peg. No, I'm just Margaret. In college I had a boyfriend who called me Maggie and I loved it at the time, but then we broke up . . ."

"And no more Maggie."

"That's right."

They were quiet for a moment, both sipping at their

drinks. Jack said, "Does your husband always work on Sundays?"

"He's ambitious, and he says that if he goes in on Sundays, he can get more work done in eight hours than he gets done in the entire week. I don't mind. I spent the day reading, then decided I needed to get some exercise. You should meet him. I told him about you, and he looked up your book and said that he definitely remembers it. Why don't you come over for dinner?"

"Oh," Jack said, taken aback a little by how fast she'd spoken. "I'd be happy to have dinner with you and your husband."

"Okay. Let me think. What about this Thursday night? Do you think that would work?"

"I know that what I'm supposed to do right now is hem and haw and try to pretend that I'm mentally ticking through all of my upcoming social engagements, but I am pretty confident that I'm free on Thursday. I'd love to come."

"Great. Come at six. I know that's a little early, but we tend to eat early. And is there anything you don't eat?"

"I eat everything except octopus, but somehow I doubt you were thinking of cooking octopus."

"Why don't you eat octopus?"

"It does taste quite good, but I saw a documentary about them, and I kind of fell in love. They're very intelligent, and quite mysterious. I just can't bear it. I mean, I know that pigs are intelligent, and that chickens can bond with people, and all that, but somehow, it's different. Or I'm just a hypocrite."

"Fair enough. No octopus. And no need for you to bring anything besides yourself. And, right on cue, there he is."

She was looking down the street, where a black SUV was turning into her driveway. Out stepped a clean-cut man dressed in what looked like golf clothes to Jack. Slim-cut chinos and a tucked-in polo shirt. Margaret quickly finished her drink, handed the glass to Jack, and stood up. She took a couple of steps out onto Jack's front lawn, then waved her husband over. He walked to them, and Jack thought that Margaret seemed tense.

"Jack, this is Eric. Eric, this is the neighbor I was telling you about. Who wrote the book."

Jack stood up and shook Eric's hand. He'd been prepared for the forceful grip of a young finance guy but was still shocked by just how much it actually hurt.

"Yeah, she told me about your book," Eric said, "but couldn't tell me anything about it, of course. I looked you up. Six months on the *Times* bestseller list. Not too shabby."

"That was a long time ago," Jack said.

"Jack's going to come over to our house for dinner on Thursday night," Margaret said, looking up at Eric's profile. "It's all planned. There will be no octopus on the menu."

"Ri-ight," Eric said, furrowing his brow at Jack as

though *they* were the longtime friends, and Margaret was the stranger who said odd things.

"Margaret asked me what I ate, and I told her I ate anything but octopus."

"Oh, man. You been to that Spanish place downtown? Something something tapas bar. The octopus there is fucking delicious. You'd change your mind, I promise you."

Margaret threaded her arm through Eric's and said, "Let's leave Jack alone now. I need to start making dinner, anyway."

Her husband turned to her, and Jack found himself focusing on the tendons in Eric's neck. "You been drinking?" he said.

"I've had one drink, thanks to Jack's hospitality."

"You just kind of reek of gin. Whatcha making for dinner?"

"Come with me, and I'll tell you. Jack, thanks for the drink. Looking forward to Thursday."

They turned and made their way to their house, and Jack stood in place for a little while, feeling inordinately sad.

Back in the house he went from room to room, turning on lights. It was now fully dusk, his least favorite time of the day, and the only thing that kept the gloom from depressing him was a well-lit house. In the kitchen he opened up his refrigerator, wondering what he might have for dinner, even though he mostly felt like having another gin.

4

Jessica was looking at her travel bag, which was sitting on her coffee table. She was dressed in track pants and a hooded sweatshirt. It was going to be at least an eight-hour drive to get to Gwen's cottage in Maine, and she wanted to be comfortable.

She made a sudden decision, went into her study, opened the closet, and found a large cardboard box filled with old paperwork that she'd been meaning to shred for about six months now. She dumped the paperwork out onto the floor of the closet and brought the box back with her into the living room, then transferred all of her clothes and toiletries into the box. That was better.

She'd already turned her iPhone off and put it in her desk drawer. It was going to be strange to be without it, but her life was strange now, no matter what.

She picked up the cardboard box with both arms, and awkwardly swung open her door, stepped outside onto her front step, and closed the door behind her. She walked to her Camry, and stowed the cardboard box on the backseat, aware she was being watched from the blue sedan parked over by the communal swimming pool. She walked in the car's direction, waving at the occupant. The window rolled down as she got close enough to speak.

"Just letting you know I'm heading into the office to drop some things off. Then I'm coming straight back here."

The man in the driver's seat was familiar to her as a new agent at her office. He had the wide shoulders and distant eyes of a former member of the military. "That's good timing, actually. I'm at the end of my shift."

"You spot anything last night?"

"Just a late-night skinny dipper."

Jessica laughed. "You mean Bob. Every night at midnight until about October. Sorry you had to see that."

"Me too."

"Are you heading back to the office?"

"I'll follow you there, then return the car. You'll be checking in with Agent Berlin, right?"

"I will."

Jessica drove to the office, keeping an eye on the agent behind her. She pulled into the visitor's lot, and he veered away to park where the company cars were kept. She swept the car around in a U-turn and exited out of the lot, then headed north on 787. She planned on working her way across Vermont and then New Hampshire and then into Maine, staying away from toll roads. She'd brought her old road atlas with her and was actually looking forward to finding a place using a physical map instead of GPS.

She got mildly lost around Concord in New Hampshire and stopped for lunch at a diner. Sitting in a booth, waiting for her hamburger and drinking her Pepsi, she honestly had no idea what to do without her phone. Normally she'd be scrolling through the news or playing Threes or just checking out the weather. She felt unmoored, and focused instead on what was around her, the worn vinyl table, the waitress with a noticeable limp, the older couple each eating soup silently together. She wondered what it was going to be like in Maine at Gwen's cottage. She knew it had wireless, and she'd brought her personal laptop so she'd be able to follow any public information that was reported about the people on the list. The one concrete thing she planned on doing was calling Arthur Kruse's father, and finding out if he'd known her own dad. Other than that line of inquiry, she didn't know what her plans were, except to be invisible until the killer was apprehended. Hopefully, there were some good books at the cottage, since she'd neglected, stupidly, to pack any.

After eating her hamburger, Jessica went back outside to her car, and studied the map, figuring out the best route. It had begun to rain, a thin mist that swirled through the air, turning everything slightly out of focus. She found a college radio station that was playing a Valerie June song, put the wipers on the lowest setting, and set out for Maine.

She arrived at the cottage on the St. George Peninsula just after dusk. The thin rain had turned into driving sheets and high winds. She pulled the car as close as possible to the front door of the shingled cottage, but it took her five minutes to find the key that was hidden under the heart-shaped rock along the front garden. By the time she was inside with her box of clothes, she was soaked through and shivering. Before exploring the house, she stripped out of her clothes and took a long hot shower in the downstairs bathroom. Afterward she got into her flannel pajamas, unpacked her box, and went and looked through the kitchen for something to eat. The refrigerator was filled with mostly condiments, although there was one bottle of beer that turned out, after she'd taken a shockingly unpleasant sip, to be a hard cider. In one of the cabinets there was a can of Italian wedding soup, and she heated it up in a pan. That and the cider would have to be her dinner.

The two-bedroom cottage was small, with exposed ceiling beams that had been painted white, and lots of abstract paintings on the wall that on closer inspection all seemed to be seascapes. Jessica unpacked her things in the larger of the two bedrooms, then went and checked the bookshelf in the upstairs hall for something to read. She normally liked thrillers, but most of Gwen's books were contemporary literary fiction. She plucked out a book with an interesting title called *Started Early, Took My Dog* and decided to give it a shot. She read a quarter of the book tucked up in the unfamiliar bed, then turned out the bedside lamp, and listened to the wind for the hour it took her to fall into a shallow, nervous sleep.

5

MONDAY, SEPTEMBER 19, 3:33 P. M.

"Hey, detective," Clara said.

Sam Hamilton had been surprised to see her behind the front desk of the Windward Resort. Last time he'd run into Clara she'd been waitressing at the Kennewick Harbor Inn.

"You're back here now, Clara?" he said.

"I'm just filling in because Karen's on vacation. I'm still at the Inn as well."

"Busy over there?"

"At the inn? It's been crazy. Here, not so much."

Sam had noticed the slightly musty smell of the Windward as he'd walked across the worn linoleum to reach the front desk. He assumed that the only thing keeping the old hotel in business was the persistence of its owner. Now that he was gone, he doubted the Windward would stay open for a year.

Sam knew most of the year-round residents of Kennewick, at least by sight, if not by name, but he knew Clara particularly well because she'd shadowed him for a couple of days about eight years ago, back when she'd been a reporter on the Kennewick High School newspaper her senior year. He knew she'd gone to Boston University to study journalism, but a couple of years ago she'd returned to town and gotten work first at the Windward and then as a waitress at the Kennewick Harbor Inn. Rumor was that she'd come back to Kennewick because of Brad Romer, another local who was nowhere near good enough for her.

"Clara, do you think I could take a look at Frank's office? I'm sure the state police have been through it, but I thought I'd take a look-see myself."

She shrugged. "It's fine with me. You know where it is, right? I don't think it'll be locked."

"Yeah, I know."

Sam began to walk in the direction of the hallway that led to Frank's back office, but stopped, and said, "Any gossip around here? About Frank's death?"

Clara frowned while she thought about the question, and Frank thought how much she looked like her mother, June, one of the circle of Kennewick residents who took turns being the town's problematic drunk. "You mean, like who might have wanted to kill him?"

"That's a good place to start."

"No one, I think. Everyone liked Frank."

"Okay," Sam said.

Clara looked as though she were still thinking, so Sam said, "What about romances?"

"Frank?" she said and grimaced a little. "I don't think so. He had a crush on Shelly, but that was a one-way affair, for sure. No, sorry, Sam, I don't think I can help you."

"You'll let me know if you hear anything."

"I will, but the only rumors that go around aren't ones you'd be interested in."

"What do you mean?" Sam said.

"Oh, the big rumor is that the Windward is haunted. You didn't know that."

"No."

"Well, that's what the staff says. There's phantom smells up on the second floor of the annex, you know where I'm talking about, and apparently two of the cleaning ladies claim there's a ghost in the old ballroom."

"Hmm."

"Yeah, I didn't think you'd be too interested," Clara said. She was now leaning back in the high swivel chair behind the desk. Her face looked a little puffy, Sam thought.

"What do these ghost rumors have to do with Frank getting killed on the beach?"

"Do you know Milana? She's one of the cleaners. She said he was haunted by the ghosts and they made him go down there and drown himself." Clara did some approximation of an Eastern European accent.

"Not unless that ghost grabbed him from behind and pushed him into the water."

Clara grimaced again, and Sam apologized before making his way down to Frank's office.

It was a tiny space, made more cramped by the piled-up boxes against every wall. There was one desk, and one chair, the desk weighed down with paperwork. Not knowing where to start, Sam decided to sit down in the upholstered office chair, where Frank had sat all those years. Sam opened the middle drawer, crammed with old invoices and mini bottles of brandy, most empty, some still sealed. The other drawers were crammed with paperwork as well, all of it seemingly related to the running of the hotel. Sam, not even officially on this case, did not quite have the energy to go through all the piles. He did pull out one rubber-banded stack of thick creamy paper jammed down the side of the largest drawer; the rubber band, completely dried out, crumbled when he pulled at it, and he was looking at a bunch of yellowed menus from a Christmas Eve dinner in 1986. Shrimp cocktail, then beef Wellington. Sam was hit with a wave of sadness at the passage of time, wondering if anyone even remembered this particular dinner. Had anything significant happened? Love affairs? Breakups? How many of its guests were still alive?

He put the menus back where he'd found them and stared straight ahead. There was a bulletin board leaning on top of the desk and against the wall. Like everything else in this office it was crammed with hotel business: old receipts; Post-it Notes; job applications. Most were layered on top of one another, but there was one photograph pinned into the bulletin board, and although it was partially covered up along its edges, it was clear that Frank hadn't wanted to entirely cover it. Sam plucked it off the board. It was a family photograph, black and white and slightly faded. It showed a youngish couple, the man in a suit and a hat, the woman in a summer dress with polka dots. Between them were two children, a girl who was maybe twelve, and a younger boy, around eight. The boy was scowling slightly, as though he'd had to pose just a little too long for this particular photo. It was clearly Frank, his face hadn't changed much in all his years, and these were clearly his parents, the original owners of the hotel. They stood in front of the main entrance to the Windward, the carved wooden sign unchanged.

Sam sat still for some time, thinking, the photograph in his lap.

There is a method in all this, he thought. *The list is not accidental, not coincidental. And Frank was killed first.* In fact, the killer hand-delivered Frank's list directly to him, let him open it, then murdered him. Sam couldn't help but think that something Frank had done, or something that had been done to him, was crucial in figuring out what was going on.

And what the picture told Sam was that Frank's life, unlike most lives these days, had been spent entirely in one place. Here in Kennewick, Maine. At the Windward Resort. And that made Sam think that the answer to what was happening might be found here, at this decaying hotel, where Frank had spent his life. He thought of the ghosts that only the foreign cleaners could see, and he thought of all the people who had stayed here over the long years. It would be thousands for sure. Would it be hundreds of thousands?

Sam returned the photograph to the bulletin board, pushing the tack back through the already existing hole along its uppermost edge.

He wondered about Frank's older sister, and if she was still alive.

6

It had been several months since Tod Fischer had received a phone call from the woman he knew only as Linda. He imagined that Linda probably got a phone call from someone, maybe a Fred, only the first name and a voice over the phone. And Fred told Linda to call him. Information was passed along a chain of people who didn't know one another, all talking on unregistered cell phones.

The funny thing about Linda was that she always sounded so happy to hear his voice, as though they were old friends, or maybe just amiable coworkers, which he guessed they were in a way.

"Hi," she said. "It's Linda." She never used his name, maybe because she didn't know it. He was a phone number and a voice.

"It's been a while," Fischer said.

"I know, right?" said Linda. Fischer, who was watching his youngest boy play Pee Wee football on a misty field two towns from where they lived, said nothing, and eventually she added, "Do you have a pencil handy?"

She always asked that, and Fischer always said, "I do," even though what he had was a very good memory.

"Okay, then. Jessica Albers Winslow. I'll spell it out for you just in case." As she spelled out the name Fischer pictured the letters being written on a chalkboard. Once the name was there, he knew he'd never forget it. "Her date of birth is December 3, 1975, and her current address is 17 Tamarack Meadow Way, in Thornton, New York. Just outside of Albany."

"Okay. Got it," Fischer said. Because he was standing about fifteen yards back from the football field it had become impossible to tell which of the miniature black-and-red football players was Jerome, his son. He could tell, however, that his son's team, the Trojans, had just given up a touchdown.

"She's an FBI agent out of the Albany field office." There was a slight question mark in Linda's voice that Fischer ignored.

"Okay," he said.

"But the thing is, she's currently not in New York. The client believes that she is in Maine but does not know exactly where in Maine. She was tailed, but she was lost somewhere along Route 1 north of Thomaston and Rockland. She's driving a white Toyota Camry, the 2012 model, and her license number is—"

"Hold up, Linda, give me a moment," Fischer said. Yes, he had a very good memory, but wasn't sure he'd correctly memorize a license, along with all this other information. He trotted over to Suzie Maris, a mom who never missed one of her son's games, and a woman who carried a purse the size of a Thanksgiving turkey. He was pretty sure she'd have a pen and a piece of paper some-where in that purse.

She did, and he returned to where he'd been standing and took down the number.

"Ready for the good part?" Linda said.

"I'm always ready," he said.

"Fifteen thousand wired direct into your account upon acceptance of the job. Thirty-five thousand upon completion. Not too shabby."

"Not too shabby," he said. "Any special instructions?"

"Yes, actually. One word. Painless." She said it with a little lilt in her voice, as though she were telling him her cat's name.

"Okay, got it," he said. It wasn't a concern. "Painless" was his specialty.

"Do you accept, or do you want some time to think about it?"

"What's the timeline?"

"Oh, sorry. I forgot about that. ASAP is all it says. There's not a definitive timeline besides that."

"Okay."

"Okay, you accept?"

"Sure," Fischer said.

"Great," Linda said, genuine happiness in her voice, even though Fischer had never not accepted a job before. "You have all the details?" she said.

"I have them all, Linda, thanks."

That evening, after Valerie, his wife, had fallen asleep on the couch watching a home-decorating show, Fischer went down to his office in the finished basement. He booted up the computer he used for assignments and got a little bit of further information on Jessica Winslow, including a photograph of her on her LinkedIn page. He thought it was funny how quickly he came up with a picture of her, but he'd known many law enforcement officers and the one thing they all had in common was that they felt invincible. Looking at the photograph, he recognized, in a clinical way, that she was quite beautiful, not too physically dissimilar to his own wife. Same skin tone, high cheekbones, light brown eyes. It didn't particularly make him feel anything except for possibly a little bit of interest. He wondered if she'd served in the military as both he and his wife had. She had that look. And he wondered if she had a family, kids maybe. He wondered these things in the same way he'd wonder about someone whose obituary he was reading. He was looking at a dead woman. She was dead the moment he'd accepted the assignment, and because of that fact, the safety, economic and otherwise, of his own family was improved. That was how it worked, how it had always worked.

Fischer found another photograph of Jessica, this one from a small-town newspaper in which she was named high school athlete of the year as a soccer player. She stood alone on a playing field, wearing a maroon uniform, her foot on a soccer ball. Looking at the photograph, memorizing her features, he thought some more about that equation between her death and his family's safety, part of the ritual he went through every time he accepted an assignment. It wasn't hard to understand. Resources on this planet were limited, even if humans weren't always aware of that. And the world was a cruel and unforgiving place, another fact that Americans didn't always recognize. It was them or you, because there wasn't enough to go around, which meant, which had always meant, that your family needed protection. Money wasn't the only thing that served as protection in this world, but it was the most important thing. Fischer was sure of that.

He knew what he did wasn't moral, but what he'd been tasked to do in Afghanistan hadn't been moral either. It was simply the way the world worked.

He sent a text to Steve, letting him know that he wouldn't be around to help out at his garage for the next few days, and got an immediate text back, saying it wasn't a problem. Then Fischer retrieved the key hidden behind his fuse box and went to open up his gun locker.

7

After catching *Boyhood* with his friend Meghan, Ethan had gone to a bar that she liked in North Austin. They'd talked about the movie, which she'd loved and Ethan had tolerated. Well, more than tolerated, he guessed. It's just that the whole thing reminded him of his own childhood, and had left him feeling depressed and irritated. Meghan was drinking tequila, and he was drinking the three-dollar draft beer, and it was making him sleepy. When Meghan ran into a couple of friends she knew, he begged off and went home, even though it was early.

Caroline had texted him that afternoon that she was having dinner with colleagues, and he'd been strangely jealous. He'd told himself to not send her another text until the following day, but he couldn't help himself, and after getting into his bed with John Berryman's *The Dream Songs*, Ethan's heavily annotated version, he shot her a quick text, asking her if she was home yet. Five minutes later, she texted back. Just got here. You?

Same, he wrote. Then, before he lost his nerve, he quickly wrote, Can I call you? They had never talked on the phone.

After about thirty very long seconds, she wrote back, Are you sure we're ready for that step? Then sent an emoji, a laughing face, something she'd never done.

It's clearly thrown you because you've resorted to an emoji

Ha ha, she wrote back. Then, Sure, call me.

Ethan sat up in bed, propping pillows behind him, and made the call. "Hi there," she said, her voice a little deeper than he imagined it.

"Hey. Thanks for letting me call." He wondered what she thought of *his* voice, which presently sounded somewhat stupid in his own head.

"Are you about to tell me something serious? I'm suddenly worried."

"No, no. I just figured we'd been texting so much, and I wanted to hear your voice. Is that strange?"

"Everything is strange right now," Caroline said. "Don't you think?"

"You mean because of the police protection? I barely even notice it now. Sometimes I don't even see it."

"I see it, because I never go anywhere new. They park in the same place across the street from me."

"You went somewhere new tonight."

"That's true, I did. And I wanted to tell everyone about it at the dinner party, but I didn't. Do you tell people?"

"Nope. I mean, that's not entirely true. I told my friend

Hannah, but it was late at night and I'm not sure she even believed me. Charlie told me to keep it to myself, though."

"Who's Charlie?"

"Oh, sorry. The police officer in charge of my protection."

"You call him by his first name?"

"I do. He's become my bud. What do you call your police officer?"

"Officer Hanley. She's nice but she's very serious, and I can't imagine calling her by her first name."

"That's probably for the best. Someone named Officer Hanley sounds like someone who will keep you alive. Someone named Charlie is the guy bleeding out next to you after you've both been shot."

"But you'll be dying next to your new best bud," Caroline said. "It'll be romantic."

"Yes, you're right. If I've gotta go, I want Charlie by my side." Ethan had slid down along his bed and had relaxed. Talking to Caroline was going well.

"Are you scared?" she said.

"Of dying?"

"Well, not just dying, but dying soon. Dying because we're on the list."

"I am scared, I guess. I was very scared when they first told me they were going to put me under police protection, but now I've almost gotten used to it. Also, I google the names from the list every day looking for reports of death, and I haven't seen anyone's name come up since Matthew Beaumont."

"So you didn't see Arthur Kruse?"

"What?" Ethan pushed himself up a little onto his pile of pillows.

"I saw it today. There was a memorial held for an Arthur Kruse in Massachusetts. Nothing about how he died."

"How'd I miss that?"

"I think it's brand-new. I saw it this afternoon."

"So that's three."

"Yep, that's three," Caroline said. "Three that we know about, anyway. I thought that was why you wanted to call me."

"No, I just . . . I just wanted to actually talk to you for once, instead of texting."

"I'm glad you did. It's nice to hear your voice."

"Jesus. Did the article say when he died?"

"No. Nothing. It was just a short notice about his memorial service, and how he'd been an oncology nurse. You should ask Charlie about it. Maybe he has some information."

"Charlie and I don't talk about work together. We're more music buddies. And beer buddies. He talks a lot about craft breweries. I really am going to die with Charlie by my side, aren't I?"

"It sounds like it."

They both laughed a little, then were quiet for a moment.

"Awkward pause," Ethan said.

"It wasn't awkward. We were both thinking. Conversations should have more pauses, not fewer, I think."

"Very profound, professor."

"Thank you."

"So how about you, are you afraid of dying?" Ethan said.

"I'm nervous, for sure. But the thing is, I've always been nervous, about everything. I get nervous about every class I teach, and I get nervous when it's my turn to give my order at the coffee shop, and I get nervous for my weekly call to my mother, even though all we talk about is television and what she made for dinner the night before. But now I have something real to be nervous about. My name is on a list of people who seem to be dying, and it feels okay to be nervous. It's like my emotions match reality and suddenly I feel better. Does any of this make any sense?"

"I think so," Ethan said. "Why worry about your coffee order when you can worry about getting murdered?"

"I guess that's pretty much it."

"Sorry. I didn't mean to belittle the whole thing."

"No, you didn't," Caroline said, but Ethan could tell that his tone had lessened the conversation somehow. "Being slated for death puts things in perspective, I guess."

"Even though we're always slated for death."

"Exactly."

There was another slight pause, and Ethan forced himself to not comment on it. Instead, he said, "I know

I've asked you this already, but do you have any new theories about what our connection is? Why we're all on this list together?"

"Nothing new. I think it's random, that somehow we were randomly selected."

"My newest theory is that the list is a smokescreen," Ethan said. "Like maybe someone wanted to kill Frank Hopkins, the first one murdered. So they make a list of eight random people plus Frank, send the list out, then kill Frank, and the police are so worried about the list that they miss the obvious suspect sitting right in front of them."

"Except two more people have died," Caroline said.

"Maybe it's random. I mean, if you think about it, any list of nine people is a list of nine people who are going to die."

"But not a list of nine people who will be murdered."

"Right."

"That plot you described is the plot of an Agatha Christie novel, but I can't remember which one," Caroline said.

"It's from *The A. B. C. Murders*, one of the Poirot books."

"That's right. Are you a mystery fan?"

"When I was a kid, I was," Ethan said. "I read all the Agatha Christie books, and all the Fletch books, and Father Brown, and stuff like that. Then I discovered Charles Bukowski and Jack Kerouac and I stopped reading mysteries."

"I read all the Agatha Christies as a kid too. But then I discovered Jane Austen."

"Well, at least we have Agatha Christie in common."

"We have a lot of things in common. We both like poetry. We have a similar sense of humor. What else?"

"We're on a death list?"

"Yes, we're on a death list," Caroline said.

Another small silence, and Ethan forced himself to not fill it. Caroline said, "I should go to sleep, I think."

"Okay. I'm glad we talked on the phone. This was nice."

"It was. It was nice. Now we have something else in common."

"We both agree that talking on the phone is nice."

"It's very old-fashioned of us."

"Yeah, the kids today don't really talk on the phone."

"They don't."

"Can I call you again?" Ethan said.

"Anytime."

8

TUESDAY, SEPTEMBER 20, 1:03 P. M.

Fischer, driving north along Route 1, reached the outskirts of Rockland, Maine, and turned his Equinox around in the parking lot of a fish shack. He was about to start driving south when he decided that he should put some food into his stomach, even though he wasn't particularly hungry, and call Brandon back to see if he'd gotten any more information on where Jessica Winslow might be hiding out. Brandon was another one of Fischer's colleagues whom he knew only as a voice on the phone and an undoubtedly fake first name, but ever since he'd started working as a gun for hire, Brandon was the man to call for information about his quarry. Fischer thought of Brandon as the reference librarian of his particular profession.

He'd never been in Maine before, so Fischer, to mark the occasion, ordered a lobster roll, even though it was twenty dollars. He was asked if he wanted mayonnaise or butter, and because of his hesitation, the young pretty girl said, "How about both?" and he agreed.

It was cool outside, the sky threatening rain, but Fischer sat at one of the picnic tables. There was a single bar on his cell phone. He called Brandon.

"If she's on the run," Brandon said, "there's no one in that part of Maine that I can find who has any connection with her."

"What about Maine in general?"

"One of her friends lives in Portland, Maine."

"What kind of friend?"

"Don't know exactly. It's just someone she friended on her defunct Facebook account. A Jay Anderson. He's a barista. It's all I've got."

"Okay, thanks."

After eating his lobster roll—better with the melted butter was his amateur opinion—Fischer looked at his map app. It was clear that Jessica Winslow knew she was being targeted and had gone on the run. Whoever wanted her dead had someone tail her, and at some point, along Route 1, they lost her. It had probably been a single tail, so it wasn't surprising that they'd let her get ahead of them, especially being on a major road. But then they would have sped up, tried to catch up with her, and if they hadn't spotted her again, she had probably veered from Route 1. She could have gone inland, of course, but Fischer thought it made more sense that she would have turned onto the St. George Peninsula. It was where he would start to look. It wasn't exactly a small peninsula, comprised of three villages, but it had only one major road. Fischer decided to focus on the cottages and houses closest to the shore and look for her car. Jessica Winslow was upper-middle class. If she were looking for a place to hide out, she'd borrow one of her friend's summer places. It made the most sense.

Fischer drove onto the peninsula. There was farmland on either side, interspersed with wooded areas, some of the leaves already changing colors. The farther he went, the foggier it got. When he first saw the ocean, all he could see was the dark rocks and white foam of the shore. Fog shrouded everything else, although it was clearing in certain places and Fischer could see a dark tree-spiked island not far from the shore. He wondered for a moment if Jessica Winslow had gone to an island—he'd seen signs advertising ferry services—and thought that if she had, it was going to be very hard to find her. Putting it out of his mind, Fischer focused on scanning driveways for white cars, then trying to confirm if they were Camrys. In Tenant Harbor he saw a white Camry parked in front of the general store, and for a moment Fischer thought he'd hit the jackpot, but the license number was wrong.

He took a few side streets, most of which were dead ends, paying the most attention to the properties that looked like summer homes. Several had no cars parked in front of them—the season was definitely over—and several had long driveways or were surrounded by thickets of pine trees. He ignored these houses. If he had to, he'd check them out later, but for right now, he was just hoping to get lucky. He drove all the way to Port Clyde, the furthest village on the peninsula, and took a road out to a pretty lighthouse with a visitor's center. There was a white sedan in the parking lot that turned out to be a Corolla. Backtracking, he took another road that led him to the village center. A ferry was unloading passengers on a dock. He parked his car, put on his Toronto Raptors hat, and wandered through the town, looking at cars, but also looking at the harbor. The sky was still dark but there was a gap in the clouds where the late afternoon light was streaming through, illuminating a patch of the still water. Gulls wheeled overhead, and the air smelled sharply of the sea. Fischer had grown up on the Gulf Coast of Florida, in a family and a town that he'd been desperate to leave, entering the military the moment he'd been eligible. He never thought of himself as having particular feelings about the ocean one way or another, but the smell of it now, a different smell than the one in Florida despite its being the same ocean, somehow brought him back to his long, anxious childhood, his father sometimes employed but mostly not, his mother often absent, often drunk. Fischer had been the oldest of four kids and was more often than not the one who made dinner every night.

He hoped that he would find Jessica Winslow soon so that he could get back in his car and return home to Virginia and his own family.

He caught a young woman looking at him; she was coming off the ferry, wearing a backpack, and trailing a dog that was at least part pit bull on a leash. This woman had fair, freckled skin—not unlike Fischer's—and pale red hair. He raised his brow to acknowledge her and that made her look away. It didn't escape him that spotting

Jessica Winslow here in Maine might be easier than spotting her car. Everyone he'd seen so far had been white—a woman of color like Jessica would be fairly easy to spot. As a white man with a Black wife, and with three children, Fischer thought about race fairly often. People pretended that in America everyone was equal, but all that meant was that the ones in charge were happy to screw you over regardless of what color your skin was.

Back in his car Fischer drove out of the village and began to wend his way off the peninsula, taking side roads whenever possible, keeping his eyes on the parked cars in driveways. When he got back onto Route 1 he decided to go check out Rockland. According to his GPS it looked like a decent-size town. The tail that had lost Jessica just south of here would have sped right through to see if she were still heading north. So it was definitely possible that Rockland was her destination. Fischer drove into the town, parking his car on a main thoroughfare, either side lined with brick storefronts.

It was starting to get dark and Fischer knew that he wasn't going to find her today. Frankly, it would have been miraculous if he had. Still, he walked through the town, peering into storefronts, but really looking at the reflections of cars passing by, hunting for the color white. He passed a restaurant and read the outside menu, intrigued by the special of the night, which was sautéed cod cheeks. His wife was a great cook, but she wasn't inventive. She liked chicken and steak and hamburgers.

Not a big fan of fish, and definitely not a big fan of anything that reminded her too much of the animal she was eating. She loved pulled pork but wouldn't touch ribs, and it often freaked her out when she even saw her husband eating something with a bone in it, say. So whenever Fischer was out on an assignment he liked to take advantage of trying some adventurous foods. The menu he was looking at had oysters on it, and it had been a while since he'd had one of those. Definitely better to eat without Valerie staring at him from across the table with a look of horror on her face.

But first he needed a place to sleep. He'd passed several inns and motels on Route 1, but unless he absolutely had to, he preferred to not stay overnight at a place where he had to use a credit card. He was being overly cautious, he knew, but so far in his life being overly cautious had worked out for him. He got back in his car, and drove further north, hitting side roads until he found a trailhead with no cars parked in its lot. He walked about a hundred yards down a dark narrow trail hemmed in by thick stands of pine until he came to a clearing just big enough for his one-man tent. He set it up, then went back to his car.

His plan was to go back into town and eat at the fancy-looking restaurant that had the oysters and the cod cheeks. He'd see if he could get a window seat so he could watch cars and people go by. Then he'd drive back to the trailhead, park the car, and go sleep in the tent, making sure that he was up and back on the road by dawn. That gave him a whole day tomorrow to hunt for a white Camry and for Jessica Winslow. She was somewhere here and he'd find her.

9

For the first time since she'd arrived two days earlier, Jessica picked up the telephone that was secured to the kitchen wall of the cottage and checked for a dial tone. There was one, which surprised her, mostly because the phone itself was so old-fashioned. It was a pale green, the color of dated kitchens, and the handset was connected by a long, twisted cord.

The night before, she'd checked her messages; there was one from Aaron, congratulating her on giving her protective detail the slip, and also providing a phone number for Arthur Stearns Kruse, the father of Arthur Kruse. He'd told her to not call Kruse until the following day at the earliest, that he was set to be questioned by one of the agents in charge of the investigation.

Despite desperately wanting to speak with Art Kruse, to find out if he really did know her own father, she'd waited. Her first day in Maine had been spent almost entirely inside the cottage, although she'd taken an early morning walk, first down to a white lighthouse on the tip of a rocky peninsula. Because of a cold, impenetrable fog Jessica couldn't even see the ocean that no doubt stretched beyond the lighthouse, its lamp rotating, its horn blasting in periodic bursts. It was as though a gray curtain had descended along the shoreline. No, that wasn't quite it. It was like looking at nothing, as though the world simply ceased to exist beyond a certain point.

From the lighthouse she'd walked to the village of Port Clyde, a small cluster of docks and buildings along a busy harbor. There was one restaurant, one ice cream shop, one general store. Jessica went into the store and bought enough groceries and wine to last her a few days, then carried the heavy bags back up the hill to her cottage.

For the rest of the day, Jessica tried to acclimate to her new, temporary life. The book she'd started was good— all about life after a devastating plague—but in between bouts of reading she was nervous and restless, pacing through the house. At dinnertime she made herself pasta with clams and drank half a bottle of Chardonnay. Then she turned on the television, spent thirty minutes trying to figure out the three separate remotes, and finally settled in to watch *Rio Bravo* on TCM. She was familiar with the movie because it had been one of her father's favorites, although she didn't remember its being as funny as it was. It made her want to call him, even though that was impossible. He was in the memory wing of an assisted living facility, and, lately, he was having trouble recognizing family members when they stopped in to visit, let alone when they called.

I should call my mom, Jessica thought. At least to let her know that she was in the middle of a case and might be hard to reach for a while. She could also ask her mom about Art Kruse, although she doubted that her mother would know anything about him. Still, she supposed she could ask her mom to ask her dad about Art Kruse. Even though his condition was getting worse, he still had moments of lucidity, especially when it came to the distant past.

So the first call she made, the following morning at half past eleven, was to her mom's cell phone number, and received a chirpy "Hello."

"Mom, it's Jessica."

"Oh, my phone didn't recognize your number. I wonder why not?"

"I'm calling from a different number. That's why I'm calling you. I'm swamped with work and I'm off of my cell for a few days."

"What's going on? No, don't tell me. I'll only worry. Are you at home? Can I call you at your home number?"

"I haven't had a home number for three years, but if it's an emergency, send me an email okay?"

"Okay, honey. Guess where I am right now?"

"I don't know. Where?"

"I'm at Margie Lowry's house for lunch. You remember Margie?"

"Kind of, I think."

"You remember Danny Lowry?" A memory surfaced of a painfully shy boy with thick glasses and bright red hair. He'd been in Jessica's class from kindergarten all the way through senior year of high school, although she doubted they'd ever exchanged a single word.

"I remember Danny. You're at his mother's house?"

"She's having a little luncheon reunion for all the ex-troop leaders, the Brownie moms."

"Oh, fun. I won't keep you, but can I ask you to do one thing for me?"

"Of course," her mom said, and now Jessica could hear chatter in the background, the sound of elderly women gossiping.

"When are you next going to visit Dad?"

"I was thinking of going over this afternoon after lunch, because Margie now lives in Westford so I'm halfway there as it is."

"When you see him, can you ask him a question about one of his old friends? Someone named Art Kruse."

"Art Kruse? One of your father's old friends?"

"I'm pretty sure he was. The name doesn't mean anything to you?"

"Not really, honey, but maybe. You know your father—"

"I know. Just ask him. I'm not expecting much. Will you remember the name?"

"Can you text it to me?"

"I can't, actually."

"Right, right. No phone. You said it was Art Kruse. Can you spell it for me?"

Jessica spelled out the name, and her mother promised

to ask her father about him. She doubted it would lead to anything, but it couldn't hurt.

After finishing the call with her mother, she punched in the number that Aaron had given her for Art Kruse in Florida. After several rings, a man's voice, hoarse-sounding, said, "Hello?"

"Is this Art Kruse?" Jessica said.

"Depends on who's calling."

"Mr. Kruse, this is Agent Winslow calling from the Federal Bureau of Investigation. I'm pretty sure that you've talked, already, with my colleague . . ."

"Yes, yesterday. He gave me a list of about a hundred people, none of whom I'd heard of, but wouldn't tell me what it was all about. Something to do with my son's death, I guess."

"I'm very sorry about that, by the way, Mr. Kruse," Jessica said.

"Oh, well. We weren't close, but he was my son, I guess."

"I'm not going to ask you a lot of questions, but I did want to follow up on just one of the names, and make sure that he's not someone whom you know. Is that okay?"

"Sure. I doubt I can give you any more information today than I could give you yesterday, but go ahead anyway."

"It's Gary Winslow. He'd be about the same age as you are now. Take a moment and think about it." She wondered if he'd remember that she introduced herself as Agent Winslow and make a connection, but somehow doubted it.

He cleared his throat. "I knew a couple of Garys in my lifetime, and it's possible that one of them was named Winslow, but I'm not so sure."

"How did you know this person?"

"Well, let me think a moment. It was a long time ago now, but I think there was a Gary who came to visit at the lake house in New Hampshire. I would've been in college then."

"Whose lake house?"

"My parents bought a lake house up on Squam after I graduated from high school. It's not there anymore, or it's there but no one in the Kruse family owns it. I remember there was this kid, Gary, with long hippie hair and a beard. His parents were friends with my parents. And I think those parents were called Winslow. I'm not really sure about any of this, but it sort of rings a bell."

"Do you remember anything else about Gary, other than the hair?"

There was a long pause, and Jessica wished very badly that she could see Art Kruse's face at this particular moment. Even listening to him on the phone she felt certain he was holding something back. "Nope," he finally said. "Bit of a druggie, I remember thinking."

"What about Gary's parents. What do you remember about them?"

"I'm not too sure I could pick them out of a lineup.

They looked like my own parents, and they all played cards together. And I remember my mother complaining that they'd overstayed their welcome."

"How long did they stay?"

"I have no idea. A couple of weeks, probably, and Gary stayed the whole summer."

"Gary stayed the whole summer?"

"Yeah, he got a job up there at the gas station on the lake, and he stayed with us."

"So you must have known him pretty well."

"Like I said, not really."

Jessica asked him a few more questions, hoping to shake something loose, but he either couldn't remember much about her father or he wasn't saying. Before ending the call, she told him again how sorry she was about his son.

"Right," he said.

"I spoke with him, on the phone, less than a week ago. He seemed very nice."

"Yeah, well, I guess he made his choices." Jessica imagined she heard a little crack in his voice, some vestige of emotion, but maybe it was just the hoarseness of his voice. Like her own father, he'd probably been a heavy smoker.

IO

WEDNESDAY, SEPTEMBER 21, 3:03 P. M.

Fischer had been in his car for the majority of the day, systematically working his way south from Rockland, checking every small coastal village, every side road, every dead end, for any sign of Jessica Winslow or her car.

He was beginning to worry that whoever had tailed her as she fled to Maine, then lost her south of Rockland, might have truly lost her. If she'd continued to head north, and the tail had missed her on Route 1, then she could be anywhere. She could be in Canada for all he knew. And if that was the case, then Fischer was going to need either a miracle or some outside help to locate her.

But for now, he was operating on the assumption that she had turned off Route 1 somewhere between Damariscotta and Rockland. He was in Damariscotta now, sitting in his parked car, studying a map he'd bought at a general store called Renys, when his cell phone rang. It was Brandon.

"Hey," Fischer said.

"Hey. Any luck?"

"No, nothing."

"It's possible I have something," Brandon said.

"Please tell me."

"It might be nothing, but I've compiled a list of all of Jessica Winslow's contacts from her defunct Facebook page, plus also her LinkedIn page that she doesn't use anymore, and I even managed to scrape a few names from her old Friendster account. I've been going through the social media accounts of everyone on that list, and one of her contacts, a Gwen Murphy, who was in her graduating class at college, has an Instagram account. Murphy lives in Boston now but there are a lot of pictures of Maine on her feed. Looks as though she has a house there. The majority of the pictures are from Port Clyde, which is a village—"

"On St. George Peninsula."

"That's right. You've been there already, I take it," Brandon said.

"I have but I'll go back and give it a second look."

"It's not much but I thought I'd report it."

Fischer started his car, very happy to have a lead, even if it turned out to amount to nothing. All along he had thought that Jessica Winslow might have borrowed a summer place that belonged to one of her friends. It made sense. And maybe Gwen Murphy was that friend. He turned off the main road back onto the peninsula, passing through the now-familiar landscape of rolling meadows and early fall color and low afternoon light. It was nice here, in Maine, and he'd already been starting to think about taking the family on a vacation, maybe next summer. They usually rented a house in the Smoky

Mountains, but Maine would be a nice change of pace. Being close to the ocean did remind him of his shitty childhood in Florida, but he could get over it. Besides, his youngest daughter, like him, loved any kind of seafood.

When he reached the outskirts of Port Clyde, Fischer slowed down so that he could look at all the cars in the driveways. He drove toward the lighthouse again, wanting to get a look at it when the fog wasn't so thick. He parked and got out of the car. He was amazed how many islands were visible, some not too far from the shore. The water was speckled with lobster buoys, catching the remaining light in the day. He wanted to stay for a while, just take it all in, but got back in his car and drove into the center of the village, looking for any side streets he hadn't tried yet. The first left heading northwest from the general store was Horse Point Road, and he turned down it. The road rose slightly to provide expansive views of the harbor, and several of the quaint shingled cottages had signs out front, advertising themselves as rental properties.

About three-quarters of a mile down the road Fischer spotted a white Camry parked in front of a two-story gray house with blue trim. He slowed, just long enough to confirm that the license plate was correct, that it was Jessica Winslow's car.

He'd found her.

A small surge of excitement coursed through him, prickling the back of his neck. But as he scanned the house before turning back to the road, he caught a glimpse of a figure in a first-floor window, looking out toward him.

He'd been spotted, as well.

Horse Point Road was a dead end, and he turned around slowly. He considered for a brief moment pulling into the driveway of the house that Jessica Winslow was hiding in, busting down the front door, and taking her in the house, but it would be foolish on so many levels. She was an FBI agent and would almost certainly have a gun. And even if he got the drop on her there would be no way he could make her death painless, and that was one of the instructions from his client.

He drove back down the road, not turning his head to look at either the car or the cottage. Maybe there was a chance that she simply thought he'd come down a dead-end road by accident.

WEDNESDAY, SEPTEMBER 21, 4:22 P. M.

Jessica Winslow was on the phone with her father when she spotted the gray Chevy Equinox slow down in front of her house. Inside the car, the man—although she supposed it could have been a woman—turned his head to look at her car. He wore a baseball cap but that was all that she could see.

Her road was a dead end so she told her dad she'd call him right back, and raced upstairs to the guest bedroom, grabbing the pair of fancy binoculars that she'd spotted on the top of a bookshelf earlier. She went to the master bedroom, put a desk chair in front of one of the two front-facing windows, and adjusted the focus on the binoculars. She only had to wait about thirty seconds before the car, not slowing down this time, cruised past the house. She got a good look at the license plate, but it was smeared with mud, and all she could make out was the number 3 and maybe an *L*.

The fact that the plate number was obscured, intentionally, meant that she'd been found. A combination of fear and triumph surged through her. He was so close. And how had he managed it? She assumed that she'd been followed from Albany, or possibly her phone conversation with Gwen had been tapped, although how that was possible she had no idea. And if she had been followed here, then it must have been a multi-car job. She hadn't spotted anything.

She did wonder if the person in the car was the architect behind the list, or merely some employee. Maybe someone sent to kill her, or maybe someone just sent to find her. Her whole body hummed with what felt like electricity, and she went and got her handgun—the Glock 27—just to have it near her.

She was trying to decide what to do next when she remembered that she needed to call her father back, if only because she had told him that she would. When she'd asked him about Arthur Kruse there'd been a long silence, followed by his asking if Arthur was someone he should know.

"No, Dad," Jessica had said. "I was just curious *if* you knew him. He's someone you would have known many years ago."

Another pause. Then, he said, "I keep wondering where I left my car."

That had been the last thing he'd said before Jessica quickly told him she'd call him back. She didn't really need to; he wouldn't remember the phone conversation. But because she'd said she would, she called him anyway.

"Hi, Dad, it's Jessica calling you back. Your daughter."

"I know you're my daughter."

"I just thought I'd say a proper goodbye since we got cut off abruptly before."

"That's a good thing," he said, and he sounded as though he had a little cold.

"What's a good thing?"

"A proper goodbye! No one really says them anymore."

She laughed. "No, they don't, do they? Okay, Dad, I'm off. I love you."

"Were you the one asking me about little Artie Kruse?"

Jessica, who'd still been sitting on the chair in her bedroom, stood up. "Yeah, that was me."

"He was a little fascist, that much I know."

"When did you know him, Dad?"

"Well, I don't know how well I really knew him ever, but I stayed at his parents' house up at Squam Lake one summer."

"Oh, yeah, I heard that."

"And I wanted him to talk about it, to talk about what we'd done. But he wouldn't. He pretended it had never happened."

"He pretended what never happened?"

"What we'd done. When we were kids."

"Oh, yeah," Jessica said, keeping her voice gentle. Her father was starting to sound agitated, the way he got when some memory was just out of reach. "Why do you think he didn't want to talk about it?"

"Because he didn't want to think about it, that's why? That's why people don't want to talk about things, usually."

"I agree. But you didn't want to forget, Dad. You must have wanted to remember because you wanted to talk about it with him."

"What are we talking about again, Rose?"

Rose was Jessica's mother's name, but she ignored the slipup. She knew her dad was about to lose the thread, so she said, "We're talking about Art Kruse, little Artie Kruse you called him, and what he didn't want to talk about."

There was a long silence, and Jessica knew that she'd lost him. When he spoke again, he said, "Am I supposed to know him?"

"No, I don't suppose so, Dad," she said. "It must be close to your dinnertime there."

"Probably macaroni and cheese again."

"Is that a bad thing?"

"No, I guess not."

"All right, Dad, I love you, and I'm going to hang up now."

"I love you, too, Rosie."

Jessica began to pace, her handgun in her holster toward the back of her hip. There was so much to think about, and she was trying to organize her thoughts. First of all, there was a connection, a definite connection, between her father and Arthur Kruse's father, and something—something bad—that they had done. Whatever that bad thing was, it was the key to what was going on. She was sure of it. But the more pressing matter was the gray Equinox that had slowed down in front of her house. She'd been marked, but she'd also marked him. She wondered if he would try to get to her tonight, and she somehow doubted it. She was in a locked house with a gun. She felt relatively safe. A part of her was actually hoping he'd make an attempt.

She did wonder if he'd seen her in the window as he first drove past, if he knew that she'd spotted him. If that was the case, he might just take off, assuming that she'd call in reinforcements. But she wasn't going to do that, at least not yet. She thought she could get to this guy. She knew what his car looked like, and she knew he was in the area. It was getting dark now, and she would batten down the hatches. Tomorrow she would hunt him down.

12

WEDNESDAY, SEPTEMBER 21, 11:41 P. M.

Fischer had lost the last game, so he put eight quarters into the coin slots to release the pool balls, then racked them, while Donald Bennett looked on with the forced concentration of the very drunk, leaning a little on his pool stick.

"Rack 'em right this time," he said.

"Sure thing, boss," Fischer said. "But it won't make a difference. You still break like a pussy."

Donald made a sound that began as a word but ended in a raspberry, and smiling broadly, stumbled toward Fischer, taking playful swings at him. The fingers of his right hand grazed Fischer's wig, the dark one with the slight mullet cut that made him look like the type of idiot who just might lose a game of pool to the drunkest guy in the bar.

He'd spotted Donald two hours earlier, saying something to the tired bartender that made her roll her eyes as soon as she turned her back to him to fetch his Miller Lite from the cooler. The bar was called the Lobster Pot, a single-story concrete structure that was just off the main road, halfway back up the peninsula from Port Clyde. Fischer, since arriving at eight, had slowly nursed three beers, and eaten one dry hamburger, while looking for someone who might be of some use to him. But there were surprisingly few solo drinkers—or not surprisingly, considering it was a Wednesday in September. One woman came in alone, teetering on stiletto heels, but she'd been there to gossip to the bartender, drink one amaretto sour, and leave. And there'd been a lone male drinker, a guy in his sixties who drank his draft beer almost as slowly as Fischer was drinking his. And despite his greasy hair and threadbare coat the guy looked intelligent and, more important, wary.

Fischer had been about to give up when Donald Bennett arrived, unsteady already. As he'd settled onto the vinyl-covered stool, the bartender held her hand out to him, palm up, fingers cupped. He'd slapped her hand, saying, "What's up?" in a loud, braying voice, then he'd laughed and dug into his jean pockets to hand over his keys. Then he'd said something else to her that Fischer couldn't make out.

"The same, Donald," she responded, after dropping his keys into an empty goldfish bowl at the back of the bar.

While getting his beer Fischer clocked the eye-roll. The dough-faced man in the jean jacket and the Steelers cap was a regular, and an unliked one.

All Fischer had to do was buy a roll of quarters from the bartender, then go over to the pool table. After shooting a little by himself, the man came over, introduced himself as Donald Bennett, made a few suggestions on how Fischer should hold his stick, then asked to play a game. By the time they'd played seven times, and Fischer had bought Donald three beers and two shots, they were best friends. Fischer had told Donald that he was from New Hampshire, that he'd just driven down to check out some property for sale, that he was thinking about opening up a paint gun place. Donald didn't know much about that—he repaired the netting on lobster traps for a living—but he did know that if Fischer was looking for some poontang he'd come to the wrong goddamn bar. Then he'd laughed like a hyena, revealing a row of teeth that looked like rotten stumps. If he was in a movie, Fischer thought, he'd be a cliché that would make his wife groan and talk back at the screen.

"You live around here, huh?" Fischer said.

Donald told him that even though he lived less than a mile away, Teri, the bartender, always took his keys when he came in.

"Like you couldn't drive one fucking mile after a few beers," Fischer said, incredulously.

"*Right*. That fucking bitch." He looked toward the bar to make sure she hadn't heard him.

Fischer drove Donald back to his place that night, a small farmhouse he'd inherited from his parents after they were both dead. Inside, there was wallpaper peeling off the walls, and it smelled like cigarette smoke and rotting flesh. They drank fireballs, and Fischer said, "I lied to you, good buddy, about why I'm here in Maine."

"Oh, yeah?" Donald lit a cigarette, then flicked the spent match onto the floor. The chair that Fischer sat in was covered in some kind of plaid synthetic material, and there were several darkened, rippled patches in the upholstery where a match had been left to smolder. He was amazed that Donald Bennet had somehow gone this long without burning himself to death in his own house.

"Look, I'm only telling you because you're a good guy, and maybe you can help," Fischer said. "I can even pay you, man, I'm flush right now. My girlfriend's living down here in Port Clyde. She dumped me about three months ago and took about fifty thousand of my money with her."

"What the fuck, man," Donald said, waving the tip of his cigarette.

"Yeah, no shit. Thing is, she might have spotted me, and she knows my car, and now I'm wondering—"

"You want some help getting that money back from her because I'll help you do that."

Fischer, who'd really just wanted a place to sleep for the night, and maybe a different car to drive tomorrow, thought about what Donald had said. Maybe this waste of a human being could be more helpful than he'd originally thought.

"Why'd she take your money, man?" Donald said, his voice high, and genuinely curious, as though he couldn't quite fathom how anyone would want to hurt his new best friend.

Fischer was thinking and didn't immediately answer. And when he moved his eyes from the Styrofoam drop ceiling back down to Donald Bennett, he wasn't surprised that his new friend had passed out, still sitting up, cigarette smoldering between his fingers. Fischer put out the man's cigarette, then draped an old granny square afghan around his sleeping form and went to check out the rest of the house.

As he poked around, careful not to leave his fingerprints on any hard surfaces, he thought some more about possibilities for the following day, and the ways in which Donald Bennett might be helpful. The house had three small bedrooms on the second floor. One had clearly been the master bedroom, where Donald's parents had slept, and it looked unchanged, the windows covered by heavy brown drapes, the bed covered in a chenille bedspread, and another homemade afghan comforter. A thin layer of dust had attached itself to everything in the room.

Donald was clearly sleeping in his own childhood room, unchanged, apparently, as well. There was a Nickelback poster on the wall, and a futon mattress without a sheet on it. Next to the mattress was an overflowing ashtray and several wadded-up tissues. The third upstairs room was the source of the house's bad smell. It was entirely filled with bags of garbage, some of them split open and leaking. Fischer stepped inside enough to quickly flip the light switch and heard the scurry of some kind of rodent finding a place to hide. Who had started to bring the trash upstairs? He assumed it had been whichever parent had survived the other. Donald seemed just bright enough to know where trash went, but he'd yet to clear out this room.

After texting his wife to say goodnight and let her know the power tool conference in Ohio was going well, he settled down, fully dressed, on top of the made bed in the Bennetts' master bedroom and managed to get six solid hours of sleep.

13

THURSDAY, SEPTEMBER 22, 10:43 A. M.

She didn't know much about the person who'd written the list, the person who'd so far killed at least three people, but she did know that he wasn't randomly shooting his victims in the street. At least not yet. So far, he had drowned Frank Hopkins in shallow water on a public beach, shot Matthew Beaumont from behind in an isolated location, and poisoned Arthur Kruse with an elaborate contraption. In all three cases there had been no witnesses. Because of that, Jessica felt relatively safe drinking her morning coffee on a bench outside of the Port Clyde General Store.

It was a cold, sunny morning, and she gripped the to-go cup with both hands to keep them warm. Her body was shivering but she was worried less about that than she was about her numb hands. Her Glock was in her side holster, and she might need quick hands to get to it.

There was a constant but slow-moving stream of cars coming and going through Port Clyde. Passengers were gathering on the dock to take the ferry to Monhegan Island, and small boats were coming over from nearby islands, some people just to get coffee or breakfast and head back. The sun came out from behind a three-story bed-and-breakfast, and Jessica moved along the bench to sit in its ineffective light. It was then that she saw the car she'd been waiting for, the dark gray Chevy, pulling into the ferry parking lot, then pulling out again to head back up the incline that led out of the village.

Leaving her coffee cup behind, Jessica raced to her own car, starting it up and speeding away from the curb, scattering gravel. She told herself to slow down, that they were on a peninsula, and there were limited places to go. After cresting a small hill she spotted the car up ahead, heading northeast. Between them was a FedEx truck. She would have liked to keep the truck right where it was, but it was trundling along under the speed limit, and she lost sight of the Chevy, so she accelerated around it on a corner, and kept up her speed until she could see the car again. She followed at what felt like a reasonable distance; in some ways she didn't particularly mind if she was spotted. She had a gun with her, and if he figured out she was trailing him, then let him try to get the drop on her.

They passed through the village of Tenants Harbor, dipped down a hill to cross an inlet at low tide, then back up an incline to where the Chevy turned right down a side road. Jessica followed, slowing down now, figuring that in the unlikely event she hadn't been spotted, then why risk it now, and she drove a mile to the end of the road without spotting the Chevy again. She turned around and went slowly back down the dark, wooded street, checking driveways, then spotting a dirt road she'd missed. She took it, the road bending sharply, passing an abandoned granite works building, then dead-ending. Either the Chevy had pulled into the closed garage of the weathered ranch house that was the final building on this road, or it had cut down the narrow, weed-choked driveway that went past a faded sign advertising the Long Cove Quarry.

Jessica thought: *This is a trap.*

But she also had a gun, now resting on her passenger seat, the safety off. And trap or not, this was an opportunity. Her body flush with adrenaline, she drove her car down the single track, through dense pockets of trees on either side, and emerged into an open space scattered here and there with piles of discarded granite and rusted machinery. There were cliffs on all sides, and a swimming hole shimmered in the sun, reflecting the colored leaves of the trees that lined the top of the cliffs.

The Equinox was parked twenty yards away. Jessica stopped her own car, killed the engine, and took hold of her gun. A man stepped out of the car, looking directly at her. He wore a baseball cap, as he'd done when she'd spotted him the day before. It was a Steelers hat, which seemed wrong somehow. He looked toward her, raised his arms slowly to show that his hands were empty.

She stepped out of the car, the gun down by her side, her finger resting along the short barrel. She took a few steps toward him, and yelled out, "Get down on the ground," raising her gun slightly, but not so that it pointed at him.

Jessica didn't hear anything, and she didn't feel anything, but for a discernible moment, she knew she'd been foolish, that she'd lost this particular game. The man in front of her was bait, and she was now on the hook.

The bullet, moving faster than the sound it had made coming from the Remington M24, struck Jessica Winslow in the back of her skull, sending her pitching forward onto a slab of speckled granite.

Donald Bennett stood frozen for a moment, confused even though he had heard the gunshot, and watched the woman in the fleece jacket lift in the air slightly before hitting the ground like a head-shot doe. He'd been giddy with excitement all morning at the thought of getting revenge on his new buddy's girlfriend, but now he wasn't sure what was happening. He just knew it was something bad.

He didn't hear the next shot, the one that hit him in the dead center of his chest.

When Fischer got to his Equinox, stowing his rifle in his trunk, he detected the faint sound of a distant siren, probably nothing to do with him. But, still, he felt suddenly exposed out in the daylight, in a quarry with two dead bodies and only one exit. He made the quick decision to leave the bodies where they had fallen and drove out of the quarry as fast as he could. When he'd first started in this business, he'd been meticulous about covering up his crimes, but over the years, he worried less and less about it. In real life, the police just weren't as good as TV shows and movies made them out to be.

As he was leaving the peninsula, a police car went past him going the other way. Maybe the gunshots had been reported, but he was already turning south on Route 1. He looked at his watch, realized that if he pushed through without stopping, he could be back in bed with his wife by midnight.

FIVE

Matthew Beaumont

Jay Coates

Ethan Dart

Caroline Geddes

Frank Hopkins

Alison Horne

Arthur Kruse

Jack Radebaugh

Jessica Winslow

I

THURSDAY, SEPTEMBER 22, 6:00 P. M.

It was drizzling rain, but the walk from his house to his neighbor's was less than fifty yards, so Jack Radebaugh wasn't wearing any kind of jacket when he pushed the doorbell, cradling two bottles of wine in his free arm.

Margaret answered the door, and for a moment he thought he might have the wrong night because a look of surprise, or maybe fright, crossed her face. But then she said, "Oh, I told you to bring nothing, and you bring two bottles of wine." She held out her hands and he handed her the wine.

"I didn't know what we'd be having so I brought a bottle of red and a bottle of white."

"Come in. Eric just called and he's leaving the office now, so he'll be here any minute."

"It smells delicious in here," Jack said.

"Braised beef ribs. I hope that's okay."

"It sounds perfect."

Margaret led him to a high-ceilinged living room and indicated an expensive-looking white couch for him to sit on. On the coffee table in front of the couch was a platter of appetizers. Rounds of bread topped with a little bit of smoked salmon, a dollop of what looked like sour cream, and a sprinkling of chives.

"What can I get you to drink?" Margaret said. She was wiping her hands along her corduroy skirt, and Jack thought she seemed nervous, or if not nervous, then harried. There was a sheen of sweat along her forehead.

"Well, what do you have?"

"I can make you whatever you'd like. Be creative."

Jack asked for a gin martini, and Margaret disappeared into the kitchen to make him one. He looked around the room, which was immaculate but a little sparse. There was no clutter, and nothing particularly personal about it. There were also no bookshelves or books, which struck Jack as odd since Margaret was a librarian.

She returned with his drink just as the front door opened, and Eric shouted out, "Sorry, sorry," very loudly into the house. Margaret spilled a little of the gin as she handed him the large martini glass. He took an immediate sip and set it down on the coffee table, standing up just as Eric walked into the living room, shedding a raincoat.

"Yep, I'm an asshole," Eric said. "The guest is already here, and I'm just coming in." He was talking theatrically, as though he were trying to project out to some nonexistent back row.

"I just got here," Jack said, reaching a hand over the couch to shake Eric's hand, bracing himself for the tight squeeze.

"Hey, I know that *you* don't think I'm an asshole, but this one does." He grinned at Margaret, who seemed embarrassed.

"As far as I know, I've never in my life called you an asshole, and you are right on time, Eric, so no worries."

"So she says. Look, do I have time to grab a beer and a shower and get back down here in time for dinner or would that fuck everything up?"

"It's fine with me," Jack said, at the same time as Margaret said, "Not a problem."

After Eric had grabbed a can of beer, then gone upstairs for his shower, Jack told Margaret how much he liked the martini.

"Oh," she said. "Thank you. It's funny. I used to make them for my dad, when I was a little kid. Doesn't sound appropriate now, I guess."

"No, it sounds sweet."

"I'm going to go get my wine and join you, since we won't be eating for a little while."

After she'd settled down on an uncomfortable-looking modern chair, she said, "Eric can be a little much for people, sometimes. He's really a good guy, at heart, but I'm worried he's going to try to impress you and end up looking like a jerk."

"I've met every type of person in my life, and I already like Eric because you like Eric, so don't worry about it."

"Okay. Thanks. At least the food will be good, I think."

"How'd you two meet?"

While she recounted a more detailed version of how she and Eric had met in college, Jack wondered again why good women wound up with bad men. It wasn't life's greatest mystery, but it certainly was one of them. Eric, of course, would be exactly what he seemed on first impression. An insecure bully who lorded it over those he felt superior to, and groveled to those he believed had more power than him. And he would beat down this poor woman until she either left him or she had a nervous breakdown. Jack knew that he was making a lot of assumptions about a man he'd spent less than ten minutes with, but he was sure that he was right.

The rest of the evening unfolded along the lines he thought it would. After Eric returned from his shower, dressed in jeans and a green Oxford shirt, he was initially okay, as though the beer had calmed him down enough so that he actually made decent small talk with Jack. But as the evening went on, as everyone drank a little too much, Eric began to criticize his wife. It started with the food. He asked for salt and pepper to be brought to the table, even though he was sitting closest to the kitchen. After Margaret got them for him, he sprinkled heavy amounts of both on his braised ribs, then passed the shakers to Jack. "Don't be polite, Jack," he said, "Margaret doesn't understand how to season food."

"I think it tastes perfect," Jack said, even though, he had to admit, it was a little underseasoned.

"He's just being polite, honey. No offense, but it needed salt."

"I guess we have different taste buds," Margaret said.

Eric, in a voice that sounded as though he were containing his rage, said, "Actually, that's scientifically not even true, but we don't have to get into it right now."

After this exchange, there was a brief pause in the conversation, everyone tucking into their food. Jack broke it by telling them the story of the list he'd gotten in the mail. He hadn't planned on telling anyone about it, but it seemed like neutral territory with which to get the evening back on track.

"So, they are taking it pretty seriously," Margaret said, after Jack told them about the offer of police protection.

"I guess so. They certainly spent more time asking questions than answering them, so I have no idea what it's about."

"You're a big-deal author," Eric said. "I'm sure you have some enemies out there."

"Maybe. I don't know. But I didn't recognize any of the other names."

"So, is there a policeman sitting outside on the street right now?" Margaret said, pouring herself some more of the red wine that Jack had brought.

"No, I turned the police protection down. They tried pretty hard to convince me, but it seemed like a waste of time. Besides, I'm traveling tomorrow. I'm just not worried about it."

"Other people on that list have died?" she said.

"Again, they didn't tell me much, but I looked up some of the names and there are some recent suspicious deaths, so who knows. Maybe I just don't care that much. I know that sounds awful, but I'm an old man, and I've lived most of my life. If someone wants to take a shot at me, what do I care?"

Dessert was butterscotch pudding, something Jack's mother used to make, in the days of the dinosaur. The first taste brought him back in time with such a ferocity that it was almost too much to bear.

"I haven't had butterscotch pudding since I was a kid," Jack said, then wondered if that sounded like an insult.

"It's very sweet," Eric said, pursing his lips.

"It's delicious," Jack said.

"Thanks," Margaret said. Jack thought she looked tired, as though the night had worn her down. He decided that as soon as he finished his dessert, he'd say that it was time for him to leave. Unfortunately, just as he was getting ready to make his announcement, Eric asked him about his book, almost as though he'd been waiting until after the meal.

"I ordered it on Amazon, so I haven't read it yet, but I read the comments. You're a guru, man."

Jack had long ago lost any interest in the world of business, or in his book, but he sat politely with Eric and gave him the big picture philosophy to his approach, going into his consultant mode. He even broke out a couple of amusing stories from the six-month book tour he'd taken after the book had landed on the *New York Times* best-seller list. Margaret cleared the table, and Eric drank a beer while Jack had a cup of tea. In a more perfect world, Jack imagined Eric clearing the table while Margaret and he talked about anything but business. After finishing his tea, Jack stood up and declared that it was past his bedtime. At the door, Margaret, her face shiny from doing the dishes, thanked him for coming, and Jack told her it was the best meal he'd had in years.

Eric, standing two feet behind Margaret, said, "Then you've got to go to Quarto, downtown, man, if you haven't been. It's the best restaurant in Hartford. Trust me, a whole lot better than what we ate tonight." He was swaying slightly, his big fist around the bottle of beer, and Jack imagined for a moment the sheer pleasure he'd get from punching this man in the nose.

It was cold outside, but it had stopped raining, and Jack stood for a moment in front of his own door, taking deep breaths of the fresh air. A car went slowly past, disturbing the puddles on the street. He didn't feel fearful, even though he did wonder what it would be like to be afraid of dying. He tried to imagine it, but then he was wondering what the conversation was like at his neighbors' house at this particular moment. Eric would be making her feel bad about something she'd said or done or cooked that evening. Maybe one day she'd leave him, Jack thought, even though he doubted it. He opened the door to his childhood house and stepped into the hallway, confused for a moment, smelling butterscotch pudding in the house, even though that was impossible.

2

FRIDAY, SEPTEMBER 23, 10:09 A. M.

He doesn't want to hurt them," Aaron Levin said. He was in Ruth Jackson's office, the door closed. He'd been offered a chair but was still standing.

"He hurt Frank Hopkins, didn't he?"

"Frank is an outlier. Jessica thought so, as well. He was drowned, so he knew he was going to die. He had the letter, but it wasn't stamped so someone had delivered it directly to him. He was in his seventies."

"Jack Radebaugh is seventy."

"So both of them are outliers."

"How many outliers are you allowed to have in a list of nine names?" Ruth said. She hadn't changed her position, leaning back in her ergonomic chair, since Aaron had entered the office.

"How the fuck do I know, Ruth. Jesus."

She frowned. "I know you're emotional because of what happened with Jessica, but don't take it out on me, okay?"

"Sorry. You're right. I don't even remember what I came in here to tell you."

"That he doesn't want to hurt them."

"Right. Except for Frank Hopkins, Matthew Beaumont was shot in the back, Arthur Kruse was gassed while he was sleeping, and Jess got shot from behind as well. Like he doesn't want them to know it's coming."

Ruth said, "Donald Bennett knew it was coming, or might have known."

It took Aaron a moment to recognize the name. Donald Bennett had been the other dead person on the scene, a local man who had probably been brought there by whoever shot Jess. At least it was clear that he hadn't ridden in Jess's car. Teri Michaud, bartender at the Lobster Pot, said that Donald Bennett, a regular, had left the bar with a strange man who'd paid in cash, a greasy-looking guy with a mullet. The current theory was that Donald Bennett had been recruited by whoever had shot Jess.

"I've thought about him, too," Aaron said. "If Bennett had agreed to help the shooter out, to somehow get Jess to this isolated place, then Bennett is guilty too. So it doesn't matter how he dies." Aaron flicked a piece of lint from his suit pants. "If you're innocent, he makes sure you die without knowing it's happening."

"It's a theory," Ruth said.

"Which means that Frank Hopkins was guilty of something. But he died first so we can't exactly interview him about it."

"Look," said Ruth. "Can we table this for now? I have some calls to make."

"Oh, right. I'm sorry. I really just came in here to find out if there was anything new."

"It's been an hour."

"So."

"Actually, there *is* something new," Ruth said. She smiled, and Aaron, who liked Ruth, suddenly wanted to slap that smile off her face. "They found Jay Coates."

"What? Dead or alive?"

"Alive. He's down in Decatur, Georgia. He got the letter but threw it out. That's all I know about it."

"How old is he?"

"Like I said, that's all I know about it. He's a tech guy or something, so he's probably not that old. Not retired, anyway."

"Okay. So that's everyone now except for Alison Horne."

"That sounds right to me."

"Are they going to question Jay Coates about his parents?" Aaron said, looking out of Ruth's window at the car park below.

"I'm sure they are, Aaron. I'm sure they're going to question him about everything."

"That was one of the things that Jessica said to me, the last time we talked face-to-face. She said that if she were in charge, she'd build up a profile of the parents, and look for similarities there, that the answer was there."

"I think she was right about that," Ruth said, and moved fractionally, tipping her chair forward.

"Did you hear something?"

"I'm not going to tell you everything I hear because, right now, Aaron, I'm a little concerned about you."

"Oh, there *is* a connection between the parents?"

Ruth moved her chair another inch and settled her feet solidly on the floor. "I don't know that there is. I do know that, geographically, if you look at the parents, they are clustered generally in the New England area."

"That's interesting."

"So now that I've given you the one piece of information that I have to give, I need to send you on your way. I'm putting you on the Brundy case to pick up where Jessica had left off."

"I thought Ellen was going to be doing that."

"She was and now she's not, and now you are, which means that you need to be prepared to testify, even though the chances of this going to trial are less than zero."

Back at his desk, Aaron looked at the Brundy files but he couldn't concentrate. At the back of his file drawer was a pint of Dewar's and two short glasses. He'd always imagined that some late night working at the office he'd pull out the bottle and the glasses and have a drink with a colleague. He'd seen it done enough in stupid cop shows. But somehow it had never happened. He slid the bottle into the inside pocket of his suit jacket and went upstairs to the quiet bathroom on the fifth floor. There he locked himself in a cubicle, sat on the lid of the toilet seat, and drank some whiskey. Then he put his face in both of his hands and cried as quietly as he could for about two minutes.

3

WEDNESDAY, SEPTEMBER 28, 5:45 P.M.

Jay Coates, a forty-one-year-old cloud security specialist living in Decatur, Georgia, had finally decided that he'd made a huge mistake when he'd told the pretty-sounding police officer on the phone that, yes, he *had* received a mysterious list in the mail about a month ago. He should have owned up to his lie as soon as the two federal agents showed up at his apartment building and asked if he'd come back with them to their office to answer questions. But the two men, both in gray suits, both with gray hair, although one of the officers was white and the other was Black, were so serious-looking, and had such deep voices, that Jay couldn't bring himself to admit he'd never received a list.

"Will I be questioned by the woman who called me? She said her name was Officer Chen." Jay said, and the men looked briefly confused.

The older of the two, the Black man, shook his head slowly, and said, "We'll be questioning you."

He was brought to an interrogation room with recording equipment, and soundproofing on the walls, and then he knew that he couldn't tell the truth. Fortunately, it wasn't too hard to lie. When he'd spoken to the nice police officer on the phone, she had given him enough details about the list so that he could plausibly talk about it.

"I did get a list like that. I think I did, anyways," he'd said to her.

"Can you describe it?"

"Uh, it was a while ago. Like you said, about a month maybe."

"Was it nine names listed on a blank piece of paper, including your own?"

"Yeah, that sounds familiar."

"Did you recognize any of the other names?"

"I don't think so."

"Do you remember any of the names now?"

"No. I just remember that my name was on the list. Sorry."

"Don't be sorry. That's totally fine. I mean, why you would think it would mean anything at all . . ."

"Right. I know, right."

So he simply told the agents what he'd told Officer Chen on the phone. He didn't remember the exact date, or any of the other names, but his was on it. Jay Coates. After the termination of the interview, he'd decided that it was going to be okay, that no one would ever find out he'd lied, just as no one had ever found out about that time in high school when he'd told his two best friends that he'd lost his virginity at fencing camp.

But now it was almost a week later, and when he left his forty-four-unit apartment building he was always aware of the nondescript Chevrolet that tailed him to the office park where he worked. And when he returned at night and walked in the early dusk from the parking lot to his building's entrance, he felt eyes on him. He'd been told to live his life as normally as possible, but to always alert the agent in charge—another man in a gray suit, but without any hair to turn gray—if he planned on doing anything, going anywhere, outside of his normal schedule. But he didn't. He just went back and forth to work, and he ordered takeout every night. Tonight, he was ordering pizza again, even though he knew he shouldn't, and he even found himself adding extra cheese to his large pepperoni, and then ordering the two-liter bottle of Dr Pepper. He played Dark Souls II while waiting for his pizza, and then watched a documentary about sharks while he ate.

Going to sleep that night, on several pillows because his acid reflux was back, he thought about a fantasy he used to have, one in which he was the unwitting subject of an experiment. Without his knowing it, scientists had implanted recording devices in his eyes and his ears so that a team could observe an average life—his average life—twenty-four hours a day. They would see the world as he saw it. In this fantasy, he'd imagine the group of observers watching his every move, seeing the way he made his scrambled eggs in the morning, and the way he cleaned his dishes, and the people he put up with at work without ever complaining or acting out. The scientists would take notes, and try to be impartial, but they wouldn't be able to observe him without coming to admire his simple life, his intelligence and goodness, and they would also recognize how no one around him seemed to care. They'd recognize that he never got credit for anything. People just took him for granted, or were rude, or dismissive. Sometimes, he would let the fantasy keep running so that he would imagine one of the scientists quitting her job, quitting her profession, so that she could come and be with him. It would make a cool book, he used to think, and maybe even a better movie, and he thought about writing it himself, but knew that he probably never would.

But now that he actually was being watched by anonymous police officers in gray cars, he wasn't sure how much he liked it. He wondered if they were looking at his browsing history as well, and for that reason, ever since telling the woman on the phone that he was on a list, he'd stopped going to certain websites. And he missed them. Lying in bed now, with his eyes closed, he conjured up the image of Evie Aurora, a cam girl who had always been happy to see him, back in the good old days before he ever got that phone call from the FBI.

4

SATURDAY, OCTOBER 1, 10:30 A. M.

Jay Coates, the Jay Coates that lived in Los Angeles, California, was preparing for his weekly talk with his mother by doing a couple of tai chi moves while staring out of his apartment window at the smoggy sky.

His phone rang right on cue. 10:30 his time, 12:30 hers.

"Hi, Mom," he said.

"Hi, darling. I haven't caught you at a bad time, have I?"

"Nope. I was expecting your call."

"Oh, good. I just finished my lunch."

"What did you have?" Jay said, and then finished his moves with the phone in his hand as he heard her say something about a tomato salad.

"Are you there, darling? I think you're breaking up."

"I'm here."

"Oh, good. Tell me about you. Did you get that commercial you were going for?"

"They wanted me for it, but I turned it down. I mean, it would have been okay money, but that's not what I came out here to do, you know?" He went on to tell her about a fantastic play he was going to be in, and when she asked if she could come out and see it, he told her it was only being performed for industry insiders. He wasn't sure she bought it, but she moved on. It was hard to lie about having acting success, since acting was a public performance. Sometimes he told her that he wrote screenplays as well, and that he'd sold a few, although who knew when they'd go into production. She always wanted to know if he'd written a part for himself, like Matt and Ben did in *Good Will Hunting*, and he'd told her that he wasn't that egotistical. His mother had grown up in Cambridge, Massachusetts, and she acted as though she were somehow related to Matt Damon and Ben Affleck, talking about them constantly.

"Did you hear what I just said, Jay?"

"What? Sorry, you dropped out there, for a moment."

"I have some news about your father."

She often had news about his father, despite the fact that he'd left her over twenty years ago. "Oh, what's that?" Jay said.

"You know I don't follow him on Facebook, but my friend Stella still does, and she told me that he's trying to sell vitamin supplements or something like that. She said it looked like a total scam, and it made me think he must be desperate for money."

"He's a loser, Mom, you know that."

"As you know I don't have very warm feelings toward your father, Jay, but I don't like to hear you say that."

"Then stop bringing him up."

"Well, I hear you loud and clear, my dear. I won't speak another word about it. What movies have you seen lately? I just saw something with Bradley Cooper that was very good."

Twenty minutes later, after several failed attempts, Jay managed to end the call with his mother. To calm himself down, he decided to go on a run. As he was lacing up his running shoes, his mind went to Jeremy Evans, his best friend from grade school, and the time that Jeremy had gotten a pair of Air Jordans for his twelfth birthday. Jay had been so jealous of the fancy sneakers that he'd broken into Jeremy's ground-floor bedroom through an open window during church hours, stolen the Air Jordans, and tossed them into a dumpster behind a convenience store. He hadn't thought about that for years; it was probably the combination of hearing his mother's voice on the phone, then lacing up his own sneakers that brought it bubbling up. He found himself luxuriating in the memory. Jeremy's grief at losing those sneakers had been a momentous experience for Jay. He'd done something in secret that made someone else feel bad and made him feel good. It had been a transformative moment.

After cuing up his running mix, he left his condo, thinking he'd do three miles at least.

5

WEDNESDAY, OCTOBER 5, 8:49 P. M.

Ethan and Caroline still emailed, but they'd spent more time on the phone lately, and they'd even taken up skyping. Ethan sometimes believed skyping was the safest mode of conversation. He assumed that the police or the FBI or some lunatic killer was constantly listening in on any conversation that went between their cell phones. Skype felt private, somehow, even if it wasn't. It also meant that he could look at Caroline instead of looking only at the words she typed or listening to her voice on the cell. He'd become enamored by her face. His mother used to collect small ceramic animals that were dressed like tiny humans. They had a name, although Ethan couldn't remember exactly what it was—woodland creatures, or something like that—and whenever she'd gotten a new piece for her collection, she'd stare at all their little faces and say again and again how cute they were.

Caroline's face reminded Ethan of a woodland creature, not something he'd ever tell her. She had a small mouth and a small nose, but large eyes and a large forehead, made larger by the brown hair that she always pulled back into a loose bun. Her skin was so pale that it almost seemed reflective, as did her pale brown eyes. Ethan thought she alternated between looking like a young girl and looking like an old lady. Again, these were things he hadn't told her.

But he had told her almost everything else. About how he subsisted on the meager royalties from the one song he'd sold over five years ago, a song that had been retrofitted into a national commercial for jeans. About all his relationships with women, about his fear that he had no talent, that he was wasting his life on the pursuit of an unattainable dream. He told her about his year-long relationship with Phoebe Faunce, another singer-songwriter, and how she'd died from an Oxycontin overdose while he'd slept beside her. And he even told her about what his parents' friend Bob O'Neal had done to him in the dunes near a Cape Cod rental they had all shared one summer week when Ethan was twelve. In return, Caroline had spoken at length about her family dynamics and the particular insidious cruelty of her own father, and how, when she'd finally confronted her mother about him after he died a few years earlier, her mother had said that she married her father *because* he'd been cruel, not in spite of it.

And they talked about the list, and the police presence that had become part of their lives, and, once, they had talked late into the night about their own impending deaths, and whether they thought the police would catch whoever had killed Frank Hopkins, Matthew Beaumont, and Arthur Kruse.

"I think they'll get him or her," Ethan said. He had

propped several pillows under his head, and was lying on his side, looking at Caroline doing the same thing from her house in Michigan.

"Really?"

"I don't know. He's stopped now, for a while, anyway."

"That's because we're all being watched," Caroline said. "But they can't watch us forever. I think he's just biding his time."

"You're probably right. He killed as many of us as he could kill before the police presence got out of hand, and now he's just waiting. There's no real rush, unless they figure out who he is."

"I hope so," Caroline said.

"I read somewhere that human beings can't actually conceive of their own deaths, that if we could we'd all be paralyzed by fear."

"I study poetry for a living and, trust me, poets must be the exception to that particular rule. Lots of conception of mortality."

"What about your students?" Ethan said.

Caroline frowned, then laughed. "I think you're onto something there. My students definitely have no conception they will one day die, which is probably why they seem so unmoved by poetry."

Ethan didn't immediately respond; his mind was trying to unearth a thought. These silences—comfortable silences, for the most part—had become part of their routine, especially when they talked on Skype. "They might catch him," he said, at last. "They clearly have a lead."

"Oh, we're back to that. Do you mean our parents are the lead?"

"Uh-huh."

A few days earlier both Ethan and Caroline had been contacted by different federal agents, and asked questions about their parents. Shortly after that, their parents had been questioned as well. Ethan had talked with his mom immediately after she'd been interviewed, and she told him that they had a long list of names, people they wondered if she knew.

"Caroline Geddes? Jay Coates? Jessica Winslow?" Ethan had asked.

"I don't think so. The last names sound familiar. They asked me about a Wayne Coates, and I told them I knew a Wayne Chalfant, you remember him, don't you, that nice retarded man who worked at the grocery store?"

"So you didn't know any of the actual people they mentioned?"

"No, I didn't, honey, but maybe I'm getting old and forgetful. I mean, that's what your father tells me, anyway."

"I don't think you're getting forgetful, Mom," he lied. "And, really, the agents are just fishing. What about Mary Louise Gauthier? Or Meg Gauthier?"

She had paused, then said, "Yes, I think they did ask me about her. Why? Do you know all these people? I wish you'd tell me more, Ethan, I don't like what's happening to my baby boy."

Gauthier was the maiden name of Caroline's mother, and Ethan had confirmed that the agents had asked her about his mother as well. This was why it was obvious that there was a lead that the FBI were following. It might be a false lead— probably *was* a false lead—but they thought they'd found some connection that had to do with the parents of the people on the list.

"Mom," Ethan had said during his last conversation with his mother. "This is a strange question, but could anyone want to get revenge on you? Did you ever have anything to do with hurting a child maybe? I mean, just accidentally."

There was the slightest pause, maybe only noticeable to Ethan because he was so familiar with the rhythms of his mom's speech, but then she said, "Of course not. I would never hurt anyone."

"No, I know, Mom. But what if it were an accident or something?"

Again, a slight pause, and for a moment he thought she was going to tell him something significant, but, instead, she said, "I don't know why you're asking me these questions."

Caroline was falling asleep—he could tell by the way she had just folded her pillow in half, and let her head fall onto it—and Ethan said, "I'll let you go. Do you want to skype tomorrow?"

She yawned, but propped herself up on her elbow. "I read a poem the other day and thought of us."

"Oh, yeah?"

"It's a recently published Philip Larkin poem called 'We Met at the End of the Party.'"

"How is it a recently published Philip Larkin poem?"

"Posthumously published, I should've said."

"You want to read it to me?"

"No, not right now. You're right, I'm tired. It just made me think of us, like we've met but maybe it's too late."

"That's grim."

Caroline smiled. She had a small mouth but a large smile. He could see a sliver of her pink gumline. "It is, I know, but I can't help how it made me feel. Look it up and read it."

"Okay, I will."

After ending the call, Ethan got up to use the bathroom, brushing his teeth and getting a glass of water from the kitchen. As he passed the sliding glass doors that led to the small backyard, he thought he heard something outside. Pulling the curtain aside he saw the feral cat he'd named Townes chowing down on the cat food he'd left out on the brick patio. It was a full moon, and there was a yellow sheen across the scrubby yard with its two lawn chairs, its rusty Weber grill.

Back in bed, he found the Larkin poem online; it had been published in *The New Yorker* a few years earlier. It was clearly about being old, about meeting someone and falling in love when there's not much time left, and it bothered him that Caroline had thought of them when she read it. He almost called her back but decided to let her sleep, instead. He'd text her first thing in the morning.

6

Jonathan's house in Bermuda was not what she had expected. Alison had imagined a swank newly built mansion in a gated community, but she'd been brought to a ramshackle nineteenth-century colonial on a narrow twisty street in St. George's. There was an overgrown garden, and the rooms were filled with musty furniture and threadbare oriental rugs. Alison loved it there. Every morning she would ride a scooter down to Tobacco Bay and swim until she was exhausted, then bake herself in the sun. In the afternoons she'd retreat to the coolness of the house with its high-ceilinged rooms. There was wireless, of course, but except for that, there was nothing modern in the house at all. The kitchen was probably the most recently updated room, and that might have happened sometime in the 1950s.

Being with Jonathan all day was not what she had expected either. He spent a lot of time in his office on his laptop, or taking phone calls in the garden, but he'd take a walk with her every evening around six when the day had cooled. They'd circle a quiet park that smelled of flowers, her arm linked through his. Since his wife's departure something had changed in him; he was colder, quieter, but prone to asking sudden strange questions. Did Alison think anyone in the world was truly happy? Did she believe in an interventionist God? It was possible that this was Jonathan's true personality, and she'd just never seen it emerge during their weekly get-togethers. He'd even stopped wanting to have sex with her, although he seemed happy to have her with him in the king-size four-poster bed. He'd fall asleep with a hand on her thigh and a paperback novel perched on his chest. Some nights he'd have bad dreams that would cause him to say indecipherable words. Once, when he moaned, she woke him up, and he looked at her like he had no idea who she was.

The house had belonged to his parents, and he'd been coming there since he was a young boy. There were framed family photographs hung along the upstairs hall, and there were oil paintings in the large sitting room, one of his parents, and one each of Jonathan and his sister, when they were both little kids, probably eight and ten. She asked him about his family, and he wouldn't say much, just that they were all gone now, and he should probably sell the house sooner rather than later. A local woman came every other afternoon to clean, and Jonathan always made it a point to chat with her; they'd known each other for fifty years, he said, longer than he'd known anybody. She did very little cleaning, just some dusting and vacuuming, so Alison had begun several house projects on her own, mostly working her way through closets and storage spaces, looking for silver to polish, or new artwork to display. One day she found a set of etched cocktail glasses from the 1960s, cleaned them up and served rum swizzles to Jonathan for cocktail hour. But her best find had been an old Instamatic Kodak camera, probably also from the 1960s, plus a whole box of film. She started taking photographs of the house, and of the village, not knowing whether the film was still good. After she'd finished a roll, she'd brought it to a small processing shop in Hamilton and had it developed. The pictures were beautiful, she thought. And now she was working her way through the rest of the rolls, feeling as though the old camera, maybe in combination with the old house, and this new part of the world, had reignited her passion for photography.

They'd been there a week and a half when Jonathan told her he needed to go on a business trip to the West Coast. Before he'd even finished the words a feeling of dread descended on her. She didn't want to go back to New York. She didn't want to leave this house. He must have seen it on her face because he quickly said, "Stay here if you want. I'll only be gone a week or so and then I'll come back here to be with you."

She'd been relieved, but the day he'd left to go to the airport there'd been driving rain all afternoon, and the cold, creeping sensation that something was wrong in her life had returned to her. It wasn't quite a premonition, but she felt a negative energy in her bones. Lying that night in the enormous bed and staring at the network of cracks along the yellowed ceiling, she tried to quell the feeling by picturing herself swimming in the warm Atlantic Ocean, but the image of Tobacco Bay kept turning into something else. Cold, gray water, pocked with steady rain. A slack tide. Wheeling gulls. Dark, seaweed-fringed rocks.

She got out of bed, and wandered the top floor of the house, eventually slipping underneath the slightly musty-smelling sheets of a single bed in a corner bedroom. The wallpaper was patterned with small blue flowers.

7

It was fully autumn now, Caroline's favorite season, and the drive from her cottage to her mother's house on the other side of Ann Arbor was so peaceful she was tempted to skip lunch with her mom and just keep driving.

She was listening to a Lucinda Williams album recommended by Ethan, and the majority of the trees were at peak color, oranges and yellows and reds. The sky was a cold blue, and steady wind was whipping dead leaves through the air. She felt as though she could have stayed in this particular moment forever, but her mother was waiting for her, and a police officer was watching her every move. She parked behind her mother's Taurus and walked across the leaf-strewn lawn to the open door of the ranch her mother had bought two years earlier in order to be closer to her daughter.

Lunch was an elaborate chicken casserole and a spinach salad with nuts and pomegranate seeds. This was a sign that her mother was feeling well. When she was depressed, *bluesy* was her word for it, one of the first things she stopped doing was cooking nice meals.

They ate in the dining room, Meg's elderly labradoodle sleeping underneath the table.

"I've met someone," Caroline said, surprising herself.

"Oh," Meg said, her eyes lighting up. "Who is it?"

"I should back up. I *have* met someone nice, but I haven't actually met him yet, not face-to-face. We talk on the phone. He's a singer-songwriter in Texas."

"Interesting. How did you meet him in the first place?"

She considered lying, but her mother had always had a good nose for lies. "He's actually on that stupid list, same as me. That's how we started talking to each other."

Her mother took a sip of Riesling. "Haven't they caught someone yet? Do they tell you anything?"

"If they've caught someone, they haven't told me about it, and I'm still getting followed around by policemen, so it seems unlikely. And I don't know anything more about it than you do."

Meg rubbed the side of her face, then looked down at her food. "I know they're watching you, but I still hope you're being extra careful. I get so worried . . ."

"I don't know what else I could do to be extra careful. I'm just waiting until they catch who even is doing this. They haven't called you back, have they?"

"Who hasn't called me back?"

"The FBI. The ones who questioned you. They haven't called back, have they?"

"Are they going to? I told them all I knew, and it wasn't much, I think."

Caroline had already quizzed her mother about the questions she'd been asked by the FBI, and her mother had sworn that she'd answered truthfully. Despite believing her, Caroline also suspected that her mother might be suppressing important memories. It wouldn't be the first time.

"Mom, remember when you and Dad broke up the first time, right after Julius left for college?"

"I remember when Julius left for college because he was so happy to get out of the house, we thought we'd never see him again."

"But do you remember kicking Dad out of the house?"

"He left around then, didn't he? He told me he was going to stay in a hotel and it turned out he was staying with that grad student who was his girlfriend at the time."

"You kicked him out, Mom. You changed the locks and threw all his books out the window of his den. Then a few years later I asked you about it, and you said you didn't remember."

Meg took a deep breath and focused her eyes on the wide window that looked out at the sugar maple that dominated her backyard.

"I had a doctor a while ago, I think it was Doctor Penny, and she told me that one of the advantages of depression was that for lots of people who suffer from it, we don't always remember it. There are parts of my life I just don't seem to remember, and it turns out that those parts aren't worth remembering."

Despite her mother's ups and downs, Caroline had probably only ever seen her cry on one or two occasions.

But Meg seemed almost close to tears now, her voice throaty, and one of her eyes glistening.

"I'm sorry to be bringing this up," Caroline said. "It's just that . . . it's obvious, to me at least, that the agents who are investigating this list think that the connection might be between the parents of the people on the list. That's why they called you, right? They asked you about a series of names?"

"I told them I didn't know any of those names. Caroline, trust me, if I did, I'd have told them."

"I know, Mom. I'm not accusing you of holding anything back, but I wonder if there was something from way back when, maybe even when you were a child, that might have some importance. You probably don't remember this either, but when you've been very depressed sometimes you've told me that you deserve it, and once you told me that you were a bad child, and that you were paying a price."

"Well, I'm not sure that I was a very nice child, really. At least according to your grandmother." Meg moved a piece of chicken onto her fork and put it in her mouth.

"But you can't remember anything specific?"

"We had a neighbor, I think their last names were Landry, and the little boy was probably about three years younger than me, and he'd come over every day to see if I wanted to play with him. Which I didn't, of course. At first, I would tell my mother to say I wasn't there, but then I started going to the door myself when he'd ring the bell, and telling him to meet me down at the park in five minutes. And I just wouldn't go. The sad thing was, he kept coming back."

Caroline had heard this story before as an example of her mother's childhood cruelty. "The FBI didn't ask you about anyone named Landry, did they?"

"Oh, no. The only name that was vaguely familiar to me was Jack Radebaugh but then I realized that he's an author of some book I think your father bought. No, Holly, no chicken for you. Maybe after we clean up." The dog had woken up.

They would normally have taken a walk after lunch, especially with the weather so nice, but it seemed unnecessarily risky, so they made coffee and sat outside on the stone patio. They talked about *Grey's Anatomy*, Meg's favorite show, and they talked about Julius, of course, who had been in a motorcycle accident in Mongolia of all places, and was staying there, recuperating, for now. Dark clouds had moved into the sky, and Caroline's fingertips had turned white, but her mother didn't seem to notice. There was a pause in conversation, and Caroline was about to stand up and move them both inside, when her mother said, "I did have a terrible dream when I was a kid, and it's something I've never really stopped thinking about it."

"Oh, what's that?" Caroline said.

"It'll sound silly, I know, but it was so vivid, and I can still see it. I think sometimes I still dream about it, like the way I still keep dreaming that I've forgotten my locker combination at school."

"What was the dream?"

"I am probably around ten or eleven years old, and I've run away from home with a bunch of other kids. My friends, I guess, although I can't really remember who they were. But we've all run away, and, somehow, we've managed to steal a great big boat and we're sailing across the ocean. It has two masts and a sail, and it's a wooden boat, like an old pirate ship, I guess you'd say. And there's a plank, of course. And what I remember most from the dream is that we all decide that one of us—one of the kids—has to walk the plank. I'm worried it's going to be me, but we choose another little girl, and we tie her up, and tell her that she has to walk off the end of the plank or we'll all die."

A gust of wind whipped her mother's scarf up across her mouth for a moment, and she pulled it away to keep talking.

"That's it. That's the dream."

"So the girl walked off the plank?"

"Yes. We tied her up and she was crying but she went into the ocean and didn't come back up. It was awful. It makes me sick just to think of it now."

"You don't remember names?"

"From the dream?" Meg said. "No. They were just other kids, like me."

"I wonder what it means."

Meg stood, and so did Caroline. Together they walked through the sliding doors into the warm house. "Does it always have to mean something?" Meg said. "It was just a scary dream. Kids have scary dreams."

8

Jack got back to his house in West Hartford at dusk, and went from room to room turning lamps on. He'd driven up from Summit, New Jersey, where he'd had lunch with his attorney, then visited his wife very briefly, standing in their front yard, where she handed him the papers he'd asked for.

"You look thin," she'd said. He'd thanked her and she told him it wasn't a compliment.

Later, driving on the parkway under a densely clouded sky, he wished he'd said, "This is me in the winter of my life." That phrase—*the winter of my life*—had been rattling around in his mind for a while. It was still in his mind now that he was back in his childhood home in Hartford, turning on lamps and pulling curtains. He was only going to be here for one night, so he went to the refrigerator to see if there was the possibility of scrounging something for dinner or if he should go out. But looking at the withered vegetables, some ancient cheese, and half a dozen eggs that might be past their sell-by date, he realized he wasn't hungry, just jumpy. He pulled on his jacket and went outside to take a walk.

He didn't go far, just doing a loop of the nearby

residential streets. It was an interesting time to take a walk, not fully dark out yet, but with lights on in the houses, and people going about their business, curtains still open. He saw a woman pouring herself a glass of wine in her kitchen, a man on a fancy stationary bike that came with its own television screen, kids watching cartoons, and even saw a young couple in a long embrace in front of a wall-sized television showing the news. Back in his own neighborhood he glanced toward his neighbors' house, wondering if Margaret and her awful husband—Eric was his name—were in. Without thinking about it, he found himself skirting along his own driveway, immediately next to their house, then standing in the black shadow of a high hedge with a view into the well-lighted solarium at the back of their house.

It was empty, but there was a glass of water on the coffee table in front of the sofa, along with a hardcover book that was splayed open facedown. Jack waited, and Margaret appeared, carrying a glass of red wine, and sitting back down on the sofa. She pushed her long hair back off her forehead, and swung one leg underneath her, leaning back against an armrest. He thought she'd pick up her book again, but she just sat there, holding her wine, not sipping at it, and staring out into the darkness. For a terrible moment he thought she was looking at him, but her eyes were off to the side a little, and besides, it was far too dark outside to see anything.

The awful thing about loneliness, Jack thought, not for the first time, is that it isn't always cured by other people. That was his experience, anyway. Spending time in the company of other people, even people he loved, made him feel lonelier than he did when he was by himself. He'd felt this way almost his entire life, since his sister had died, really, all those years ago, and since his parents had never recovered from that loss.

He heard the sound of a car, then flinched as headlights briefly illuminated him. Eric was home, turning into the drive, then quickly dousing his lights. Jack wondered if he had been spotted. He didn't think so, but stood as still as possible in the dark shadow of the hedge, trying to figure out what he would say if he was caught.

Margaret must have heard the car as well, turning her head in that direction. She had a long, elegant neck and something about the way she was posed, head turned, glass of wine in hand, made her seem like a classical painting. She put the wine down, and took a deep breath, and Jack saw everything in her face. Sadness, wariness, and maybe a touch of genuine love. She got up and went to meet her husband, and Jack took the opportunity to walk to his own side door.

Before reentering his house, he heard Eric's loud voice, as he was met at the door.

"Looks like your boyfriend's back in town," he said, and it took Jack a moment to realize he was talking about him.

9

The message was from Madison. Two breathless sentences. "Call me right away. You're not going to believe my news." And there was a text, as well. CALL ME and some kind of emoji face that Jay didn't really get, a flushed face with tiny hands in front of it, some kind of celebration thing. For a brief moment, Jay actually thought that he might be sick. Madison had clearly gotten a job, and as far as he knew—and she told him everything—it was either the local commercial (not worthy of the breathless message) or the three-episode arc on that crap FX sitcom that had just gotten renewed for a second season. It had to be the sitcom, and he honestly didn't know if he could handle talking with Madison right now, acting excited for her, telling her how she deserved it. Jesus. He really was going to be sick.

He'd met Madison at an acting class in the valley two years earlier. He'd taken her out for drinks after the final class, then fucked her at his friend Michael's bungalow that he'd been taking care of while Michael was in London. Madison shared a one-bedroom with another actress, who was home that night, and there was no way that Jay was going to bring her to his house and let her know where he lived, so they'd ended up at the bungalow.

He thought he'd never see her again, but then he'd run into her six weeks later at a bar in Hollywood, and they'd had a few drinks together. She told him, with an exaggerated sad face, that she'd started dating someone new, a fellow barista at the Starbucks where she worked. He was relieved, having zero intention of another mediocre sexual encounter. But they'd had fun having drinks. She was stupid, which Jay liked because it meant he could explain things to her. And she was a terrible actress, which Jay doubly liked, because it meant there was no way she would get a job before he did.

And now here he was, and he was about to have to congratulate her on landing a goddamn sitcom. It was unbearable. Instead of delaying it, he decided to pull the Band-Aid off and call her right back.

"You got the sitcom?" he said.

"Uh-huh," she said, casually, and then let out a squeal that caused Jay to move the phone away from his ear.

He let her talk for about two minutes, which was all he could take, then said, "I wasn't going to tell you right away, because I want you to have your moment, and I'm so excited for you, Mads, but I just talked with my mom and she had some bad news."

"Oh, no."

"She has like stage-five lung cancer."

"Oh, no!"

"Yeah. So I've got to deal with this, you know, figure out what do next. So if I'm not able—"

"Of course not. I get it. Go take care of your mom, Jay. Let me know if you need anything."

"I will. I promise."

After the phone call Jay wondered if he could get away with never talking with Madison again. Probably. He imagined she was pretty used to guys simply ghosting her. Still, she had once called him her "new best friend" . . .

He could kill her.

And even just having that thought put him in a much better mood.

She'd definitely hit a few bars tonight to celebrate, and if he timed it right he could be waiting for her outside of her complex . . . no, it wouldn't work. He knew her, after all. There'd be phone records, if nothing else. And even though she was going to become completely unbearable the more acting jobs she got, she wasn't worth the effort of bashing her head in. It would be like stomping on a baby bird. So easy and so meaningless.

He put his phone down on the arm of his couch. His fingers were white from gripping it so hard. He went to the kitchen and took a long swallow from the bottle of Ketel One he kept in the freezer, then did some tai chi in his bedroom to try to calm down. Afterward he allowed himself some fantasies, then made himself stop. He needed to actually do something, and not just think about it—it was the only way to make himself feel better.

That night he found a speakeasy bar in downtown LA, a place he knew there'd be no chance of running into either Madison or any of her friends. He got a corner booth, drank vodka and soda water with two limes, and watched the girls come and go, talking of Leonardo DiCaprio. The worst were the really young ones in mini-dresses and heels, laughing like hyenas at whatever some much older guy was saying. They were so pleased with themselves, thinking that they were somehow hot enough to actually make it in Hollywood, listening to wannabe dudes tell them about their screenplays. It took him a while, but he finally spotted the right girl. She had pale red hair and was wearing jeans and a slutty top. She'd come in with her friend, but now her friend was talking to some guy, and he knew the redhead was getting fed up. She kept checking her phone, taking tiny sips at her own vodka and soda, and wishing her stupid friend with her loud cackling laugh would shut the fuck up. Jay knew he could peel this one from the herd and get her alone at some point. But then the front door swung inward, and the redhead turned and spotted some guy who'd come to meet her, and suddenly she was all smiles, flipping her hair, sliding down the bar to let this douchebag with an ironic moustache sit down.

Jay finished his drink and left the bar. He wandered through downtown for a while, found a place with patio seating that would allow him to watch the street, and got one more drink. Two girls came in, bought Corona

Lights, and sat at the next table from his. They were already drunk, talking loudly with midwestern accents, and glancing in his direction trying to decide if he was a movie star or not. Jay kept his eyes on his phone, even fake texting to make it look as though he was waiting for someone. He wondered what it would be like picking up these two ugly girls from Wisconsin or Minnesota or wherever, and telling them that he'd just booked a major television role. One or both of them would probably want to fuck him, something he had zero interest in. However, if he could get one of them alone . . .

"Excuse me, are you an actor?" It was the older of the two, with big thighs and dyed-blond hair.

"Nope," he said. "What about you two, you actresses?"

They both laughed uncontrollably at this, and told him they were just visiting Los Angeles for the first time, and that morning they'd seen Josh Lucas crossing the street and getting into an SUV.

"I don't know who that is."

"He was in *Sweet Home Alabama*," they both said at almost the same time.

"I don't watch movies," he said. "Probably because I work on them, and know that they're total bullshit."

"What do you do?"

"I'm a fight coordinator on film sets. I could tell you stories about all your favorite movie stars, but you wouldn't like them much."

They practically squealed, then invited him to join

them. He told them he was in the middle of an important text conversation, and maybe he'd join them in a bit. Sipping his drink, he continued to stare at his phone, considering what to do next. A wave of disgust was beginning to sweep through him. Disgust at the two stupid girls at the next table, disgust at some casting director actually having given Madison a professional acting job, disgust at the idiot city he lived in, crawling with human insects. Jay finished his drink, got up, and went through the bar area and out the other side. He had decided to give up, and go home, spend some time on the internet. He'd been hoping for more but tonight was not the night.

An Uber pulled up across the street and let out a blonde in a tiny skirt and some kind of halter top. She swayed for a moment on the sidewalk, looking at her phone, then studied the street. He thought she might walk toward the bar, but turned instead in the opposite direction, staggering along the sidewalk.

Could this actually be it?

She turned onto a cross street and he followed her, keeping his head down in case there were any traffic cameras around. They were in a residential area, old Spanish-style apartment buildings that had once been chic, now filled with new Hollywood arrivals and drug addicts. She was about twenty yards in front of him, but she kept stopping to stare at her phone, the light illuminating a messy head of blond hair, and an overly made-up face. His heart raced. In his leather jacket pocket was the heft of a hunting knife he'd bought over a year ago at a vintage market. He put his hand around it and an almost sexual thrill surged through his body, a rolling sensation, like great drugs. Now he was only about ten yards behind her, between streetlamps, and in the shadow of a row of desiccated palm trees. He quickened his pace.

The first strike from the stainless-steel baton hit him across his right ear, breaking his temporal bone, knocking him to the ground. A ringing sensation howled through his brain, and his first thought was that the police had caught him, even though he hadn't done anything yet, then he felt a rush of warm blood sheet down his neck and under his shirt, and he felt scared.

The second blow from the baton hit him about two inches above his ear and with much more force. His body slumped, his face hitting the pavement. That second hit was enough to kill him—he was dying already—but a few more rained down upon his head before the perpetrator walked briskly away, passing a drunk girl on her phone, saying, "I'm right out front, what do you mean it's too late?"

FOUR

Matthew Beaumont

Jay Coates

Ethan Dart

Caroline Geddes

Frank Hopkins

Alison Horne

Arthur Kruse

Jack Radebaugh

Jessica Winslow

MONDAY, OCTOBER 17, 4:40 P. M.

Jay Coates of Decatur, Georgia, had been sitting in the interrogation room at the police station for over an hour. No one had checked in on him, or offered him water, or even told him why he was there. Earlier, he'd been at work, and two uniformed police officers had showed up to escort him to the station. Jay could only imagine what his coworkers were thinking now. He didn't know whether to be upset or kind of thrilled. But either way, he was not happy to be here now, waiting, studying the room, trying not to look directly at the observation mirror across from him and wondering who was on the other side.

To calm himself, he tried to estimate the dimension of the room, deciding it was eight by ten, exactly. That had been too easy, and he decided to do another mental exercise, seeing how far he could count using the Fibonacci sequence. It was something he used to do years ago, in college, when he was particularly nervous, or bored, in a class. He was at 317,811 when the door banged open and two plainclothes officers came in, a man in a tan suit with long arms and a heavy brow and a younger woman with a buzz cut who sat down off to the side. The man in the suit kept standing, pacing a little back and forth behind the chair that was opposite Jay, until he finally said, "I'm going to give you one chance, Coates, and only one. If I find out you are lying to me, I'm going to throw the book at you for obstruction of justice. Do you understand?"

Jay opened his mouth to say something, but the policeman kept talking. "I will personally ensure you do time for this. Real time, understand? And if you so much as try to tell me another lie in this room today, help me, Jesus, it's not going to be pretty. And if you so much as pretend you don't understand what's going on here . . ."

He shook his head slowly back and forth. Jay looked at the female police officer, who sat impassively in her chair, looking back at him.

"Do all of us a favor, Coates," the man in the suit said, his voice softer now. "I'm going to ask you a question and I want you to tell me the truth."

Jay, whose whole body felt as though it were pooling under him, looked at the police officer, and felt himself nodding.

"Okay, Coates. Here we go. One simple question: Did you receive a letter on Thursday, September 15? Did that letter contain a list of nine names, including yours? Think before you answer, because I'm not going to ask you twice."

Jay looked at the woman, but she was idly looking at the back of her hand now, as though this whole process was boring her.

"Why are you looking at her?" the man said.

Jay looked at him, and said, "No. No. I never received a letter." And both officers looked at each other, almost without interest, as he broke down and cried.

2

WEDNESDAY, OCTOBER 19, 1:15 P. M.

As the plane touched down in Sarasota, Sam Hamilton, seated in the second-to-last row, turned the page of his book. He was in no rush to stand hunched under the baggage compartments waiting for everyone to dis-embark ahead of him. He was rereading *And Then There Were None* for the second time since the murder of Frank Hopkins. After he'd booked this trip to Florida in order to visit Frank's surviving sister, he'd dropped by Kennewick's only bookstore, a ramshackle barn filled with used books that went by the somewhat pretentious name of Ragged Claws Books. Sam had known what poem that name came from at one point, but he'd long since forgotten. After saying hello to Charles Montgomery, the owner, and the only person ever working at the store, Sam had gone to the mystery section, where he'd found an old Pocket Books paperback copy of *And Then There Were None*. He knew he wanted to bring the book with him to Florida and he also knew that he didn't want to bring his own copy.

He wasn't sure rereading the book was helpful, but it felt like something proactive to do. And it kept his mind on the case. The question he kept asking himself, the question that everyone tasked with this case was probably asking themselves, was what was the connection between the nine people on the list? In a way that was also one of the questions from *And Then There Were None*. Ten strangers are brought to an island, and systematically murdered. They don't know one another, have never met, yet they are forced into a deadly situation together. Sam thought their connection was obvious, that it was forged the very moment they all arrived on the island. And it was the same with the list of nine people who received letters, all now targeted for murder.

Sam wondered why he was so fixated on the book. For all he knew, the killer had never read it, never even heard of it. It wasn't as though the nine names were incorporated into some sort of nursery rhyme. And there was a major difference between what happened in the book and what was happening now. The difference was that early in the novel the characters realize that because there is no one on the island but them, the killer must be among them. That wasn't the case with the list of nine names, but even so, Sam did wonder if the killer had put him-or-herself on the list. According to Mary Parkinson from the state police, no one had successfully located Alison Horne yet. Was that important? Sam, just going from his gut, didn't think so.

The person Sam was interested in was Jack Radebaugh, only because of his age. Six of the people on the list were in their thirties or early forties, while two were in their

seventies. Sam didn't think this was particularly important except for the fact that Frank Hopkins had been killed
in such a different way than the other four victims. He'd
been murdered in a manner that ensured he knew it was
happening. He'd felt pain, and probably panic. Everyone
else had either been shot or attacked from behind or
asphyxiated in their sleep. But not Frank.

"Excuse me, sir."

Sam looked up at the stewardess who had spoken
to him and realized that the plane was almost entirely
empty. He apologized and made his way down the aisle.

After picking up his rental car and driving to the
motel he'd booked on Siesta Key, Sam checked in, then
changed into a pair of lightweight chinos and a light blue
short-sleeved polo. It felt good to be temporarily back in
tropical weather, the warm air heavy with an impending
afternoon storm. He had talked with Cynthia Hopkins,
Frank's older sister, on the phone twice, once to ask her
questions, and once to arrange this visit. She had told him
during both phone calls that she had hearing issues and
wasn't good on the phone, and that was the reason for
Sam making the trip. He knew it was probably a waste of
time, but he'd taken the two days off anyway, booking a
round-trip flight from Portland to Sarasota that included
a stayover. Cynthia was expecting him at four in the
afternoon. It was two o'clock now, and the motel he'd
booked was within walking distance of Cynthia's house.
He decided to go for a walk down toward the beach.

At exactly four o'clock Sam rang the doorbell of Frank Hopkins's sister's house. It was a bungalow with pink stucco siding; the shabby front yard was packed dirt decorated with a few patches of yellow grass. The door opened six inches and Cynthia Hopkins peered out. Her round face was a mass of wrinkles, the skin patchy with sun damage.

Sam, unsure of whether she was going to remember this planned visit, said, "Mrs. Hopkins, I'm Detective Sam Hamilton. We spoke on the phone."

"I remember," she said, swinging the door all the way open and inviting him in. "I don't hear as well as I used to but I'm not forgetful. Not yet, anyway."

She led him through the overly warm house and to a screened-in patio where she indicated a wicker chair for Sam to sit on. "What can I get you?" she asked.

"Nothing, unless you're having something yourself."

"I should have had you come at five because that's when I like to have a gin and tonic."

"Don't let me stop you. We can pretend it's five o'clock."

"No. I'll wait. When you get to be my age it's important to have set rituals." She sat down across from him on an identical chair and crossed one leg over another. She was wearing white pants and a flowery blouse under a pink cardigan. She didn't look much like Frank, Sam thought; for one thing, she was taller than he was, more weather-beaten, her face almost simian with all her wrinkles.

"I'm sorry about your brother," Sam said.

"Thank you," she said, her voice gravelly, and Sam imagined that the deep lines on her face had been caused not just by Florida sun but by a lifetime of cocktail hours and cigarettes.

"Were you close?"

"No, we were never very close, but we never fought, or anything like that. I was the quiet, studious child, and he was gregarious, like both our parents. They all loved the hotel business, and I couldn't think of anything worse. Imagine living somewhere where there are constant houseguests. As soon as I could I moved to Boston and got a job at Houghton Mifflin—it's a publishing company—and that is where I met my husband. Like me, he was content with a less sociable life. We never had children, but we sure read a lot of books."

"Your husband is . . ."

"He died in 2003, just a few years after we'd moved ourselves permanently down here to Siesta Key. Frank made his only visit to see me right after Patrick died. He promised to come for another trip but never had the time, I suppose. That's what happens when you run a hotel. Have you discovered who killed him, my brother?"

Sam, surprised by the sudden question, said, "No. But whoever did kill your brother is killing other people as well. Their names were all on a list together."

"That makes some sense, because I struggled through

a very hard-to-follow phone conversation with another policeman who asked me a list of names, none of which were remotely familiar to me."

"Do you mind if I ask you again?" Sam said.

"What? The names? I don't mind but I doubt any of my answers have changed."

Sam recited the names—he had them memorized—and she appeared to think about each one, eventually telling him that the names meant nothing to her.

"I hope that's not all you came down here to do," she said.

"No, actually. I wanted to ask you about the history of the Windward, to ask you if you remember any scandals happening in its past, anything out of the ordinary."

"When you say past . . ."

"It could be something that happened when you and Frank were kids, or something more recent, I suppose."

"Let me think about that for a moment. You know, maybe I will have that gin and tonic a little earlier, just for today."

"If you tell me how you like it, and where everything is, I'd be happy to make it for you while you think."

"So long as you make one for yourself."

"I'd be happy to," Sam said, and she directed him to the kitchen. He crossed the terrazzo floor of the living room and entered the bright alcove. On top of a spotless countertop was a bottle of Gordon's gin and a bottle of Publix brand tonic water. He found some nice highball glasses and made two drinks, bringing them back with him to the patio.

"This is a treat," she said. "Being served my evening cocktail by a man."

Sam settled back into his chair and took a sip of the drink. He was worried he'd made it too strong, but Cynthia took a sip as well, and declared it very good.

"Any thoughts?" Sam said.

"About the hotel's history? Two, I suppose. They both happened while I was still living at the Windward so we're talking ancient history at this point."

"It doesn't matter. I'm interested."

"Well, then, the biggest scandal happened when I was eighteen, right before I left for college. This would be the summer of 1961. There were two guests staying with us, a man and a woman, and after what happened I remember everyone talking about how they had never believed they were husband and wife in the first place, even though they'd apparently presented themselves that way. I don't remember anything about them even though I was occasionally working the front desk back then." She paused to sip at her drink, taking her time as though she were trying hard to remember. "They were a middle-aged couple, but on the day they were supposed to check out they never came out of their rooms. A cleaning woman let herself in and found them both dead. From what people said at the time it looked as though he'd killed her with a straight razor, then got into the bathtub and slit his own wrists. I remember the police coming and a bunch of journalists. And I remember that everyone had a different opinion about what had happened. It wasn't clear whether he'd murdered her, then committed suicide, or if it was some kind of suicide pact. I do remember it turned out that they were both married to other people."

"Do you remember their names?"

"I knew you were going to ask me that, and I'm afraid that I don't. All I remember is that they checked in under very obvious fake names. Something like John and Jane Smith. But, no, I don't remember their real names, but I do remember the room number. Twenty-two. It was one of the rooms in the old motel unit that was torn down in the 1970s. And I don't think that room was ever rented again."

"And you're sure it was 1961."

"Yes, that part I'm sure about because it was the year I left for college."

"You said there was another incident."

"This one's not quite so lurid, and I think I only remember it because I was a kid when it happened." She took another sip of her drink, her eyes looking upward as though she were gathering her thoughts. "And I'm sorry to say that I don't remember the name for this one, either, but when I was about twelve or thirteen a girl who was staying at the Windward crawled into one of the crevices along the base of the seawall and drowned when the tide rose."

"Did you know her?"

"I didn't. It was Frank who used to get to know all of the kids who came and stayed for the summer. I spent my time reading in my room. Oh, how funny, I was just going to say that you should ask Frank about the little girl, but of course you can't do that."

"No," Sam said, and paused as Cynthia shifted in her chair. After a moment, Sam said, "When you say the seawall . . ."

"The jetty on Kennewick Beach."

"Where Frank died . . ."

"Yes, of course. I hadn't made that connection, but, yes. He must have died right near where that girl died all those years ago. It was terrible, of course. Much worse, somehow, than the couple dying in the room. Because it was a young girl, and an accident. Nowadays, if it happened, they'd probably put a chain-link fence all around the jetty, and warnings everywhere. But back then . . . I suppose that life just went on."

Sam stayed for the length of the drink, the two of them chatting some more about what her childhood had been like at the Windward. She had a good memory, and he liked listening to her talk. But he was hungry, and he also wanted to get back to his laptop in his motel room and search for both of the incidents she'd told him about, so he left as soon as he could. He stopped at a seafood restaurant in a strip mall and had another gin and tonic while waiting for them to prepare some grouper tacos to go, then went back to the motel with the food, turned the air conditioning to high, and began to hunt the internet to find out how good Cynthia Hopkins's memory really was.

3

Caroline had texted to say that she had too much work to do and maybe they should take a night off from talking with each other, and Ethan felt as though she'd slid a long knife into his gut. He wrote back: sure thing, work hard. Then he dug out his denim jacket and walked to Casino el Camino. It had been a long while since he'd been there, which was exactly what Lauren, the bartender, said to him as he ordered a mule.

He'd been asked by Officer Resendez to limit the time he spent in public places, but he hadn't been explicitly told to stay home. And he didn't care tonight, even though a day earlier he had googled the name Jay Coates, as he did every day, and found out that a Jay Coates had been murdered in the city of Los Angeles the previous weekend. The list was getting shorter.

On his third mule, Ethan spotted a pair of women in a back booth who looked familiar. It took a moment, but he figured out they were both servers at a club he used to play at when he'd been in a short-lived band called the Buckets. He wandered over and they invited him to join them; he bought a pitcher of Lone Star and slid into the booth. An hour after he'd sat down it occurred to him that he'd hooked up with the prettier, chunkier girl at the table, about two years ago after one of his shows. Her name was Alicia, but she pronounced it with four syllables instead of three, and it seemed like she remembered their night together because she kept pressing her knee up against his under the table.

They all left together at closing time. Jennifer had already ordered a Lyft, jumping into it as soon as they were out on the street, leaving Alicia and him together. They walked to his place, Ethan telling her about a new song he'd written for a female vocalist, and maybe she'd sing a little of it for him if he played it on his guitar for her. He'd used that line before, and for a brief, panicky moment he thought he might have used it on Alicia before, back when they'd first hooked up, but if he did, she didn't show it.

Back at his place Alicia rolled a joint while he tuned his guitar and printed out the lyrics he'd written. She actually had a pretty voice, and the song was better than he remembered. They went through it a couple of times, then made out on the couch, Alicia asking him if he remembered doing this before. "Why do you think I came over to say hi to you?" he said.

After they'd moved to the futon and turned out the lights, Ethan thought of Caroline for the first time since getting back to the apartment. He had a sudden longing to be alone, to open his laptop and see if she'd join him on Skype. He looked at Alicia, visible enough in the moonlight coming through his window for him to see that her eyes were barely open. Her breath was sharp with alcohol.

"Hey, Alicia," he said. "I'm going to go put on a record. Close your eyes but don't fall asleep on me, okay?"

"Of course not," she said.

He got up, put on a Rachael Yamagata record, then sat for two songs on the sofa. When he crept back into the bedroom, he was happy to find Alicia on her stomach, one leg kicked out from under the covers, and gently snoring.

He went back to the couch, opened up his laptop, and looked for a halfway point between Austin, Texas, and Ann Arbor, Michigan. There were some nice cabins near the Shawnee National Forest that seemed as good a spot as any. He texted Caroline:

I missed you tonight. Want to meet at Rolling Brook Cabins in Makanda, Illinois?

4

FRIDAY, OCTOBER 21, 11:15 P. M.

Caroline looked at the text from Ethan and wrote back: Yes. When?

You pick a date, he wrote. I'm always free.

Caroline opened up her calendar, although she pretty much knew her schedule. She'd be free the following weekend, and even though she had a ton of grading to do, she'd gotten a lot done tonight, and she could do extra all week. The thought of seeing Ethan face-to-face was tying her stomach into knots, but not necessarily in a bad way. She told herself that if it was awkward, that if they had no physical connection, or something, then at least they could stay friends. That much had been established.

Meet on Friday? she wrote.

I can do that, Ethan wrote back.

Caroline: It's Halloween Weekend

Ethan: Is that a big weekend for you? Should we cancel?

Caroline: It's a very big weekend for my students. Lots of sexy outfits.

Ethan: You invited to a party?

Caroline: Always. One of my colleagues always has something on the Saturday night around Halloween.

Ethan: Should we make it another weekend?

Caroline: God, no. Seeing you will mean I don't have to think about a costume.

Ethan: Slutty Sylvia Plath

Caroline: I did that two years ago. People would remember. What about you? Party?

Ethan: There's a party I could go to but I'd much rather go to Illinois

Caroline: I'm glad. What was going to be your costume?

Ethan: Down-and-out rock star. Same costume every year

They texted back and forth for another hour and by the end of it, Ethan had booked two nights at the cabin for the following Friday and Saturday nights.

Caroline got into bed and tried not to worry about seeing Ethan, and what he'd expect, and what it might feel like to be with him. Instead she worried about who she'd get to watch Estrella and Fable, and she worried about the dangers of traveling to a place that would put her and Ethan together, considering they were both on someone's kill list. Maybe it was stupid to even attempt to get together. But part of her didn't care, or at least didn't care enough. The feeling she had when she was talking with Ethan, or even emailing or texting him, was so intense, so freeing, that she needed to see if that feeling would persist when they were face-to-face. She sometimes wondered if she'd ever truly been in love before. Her only serious boyfriend had been Alec Gresham, whom she'd met at Oxford, when she was there for her Fulbright. He'd moved to America for two years to be with her as she completed a PhD in Ithaca, and by the end of his stay, they had felt more like best friends than lovers. No, that wasn't true. She loved him then, and she still loved him, in a way. But she had never felt about him the way she suddenly now felt about Ethan. A quote from *Sense and Sensibility* kept running through her head: "It is not time or opportunity that is to determine intimacy—it is disposition alone. Seven years would be insufficient to make some people acquainted with each other, and seven days are more than enough for others." Was that what Ethan and she had—a disposition? Or maybe it was only their circumstance, but she needed to find out one way or another.

The next morning she talked to Maeve, an adjunct and fellow feline lover she'd gotten to know, and Maeve agreed to take care of her cats over the weekend ("I might just steal them from you") and then she talked with Officer Hanley, who was in charge of her police protection detail. Officer Hanley told her that she'd arrange to have police officers posted outside of the Rolling Brook Cabins in Illinois, that she'd get back to her with details. At the end of the phone conversation, Liz said, "That's a long way to go for a booty call," and punctuated the sentence, as she often did, with a loud laugh.

"Yeah, it is," Caroline said, resisting the urge to tell her it wasn't exactly a booty call, even though she kind of knew it was.

5

Jack Radebaugh made the phone call from the comfortable bed in his high-end hotel room. There were two rings, and then an answer. "Ellen Mercer here."

"Agent Mercer, hi. This is Jack Radebaugh. I spoke with you after—"

"Hi Jack, I know who you are. How are you?"

"I'm fine. Everything is fine. But I remembered you telling me that if I thought of anything, of any possible connection . . ."

"Right."

"Well, the other names on the list are still not familiar to me, but I did do some googling, actually, and I read that Frank Hopkins owned the Windward Resort. Is that true?"

"It is."

"Well, unless I'm mistaken, I'm pretty sure that I stayed at the Windward Resort. It was in Kennewick, Maine, right?"

"Yes, that's right."

"This was about a thousand years ago, when I was eleven. I was there with my family for most of that summer."

"So do you remember Frank Hopkins?" the agent said.

284

"No. I mean, I hardly think he'd have been running the resort in 1956."

"Actually, he *was* there in 1956. His parents ran the resort before he did, and he lived there his whole life, as far as we know."

"Oh."

"So it's very possible that you did meet him when you were there. You would have been roughly the same age."

Jack took a drink from the complimentary bottle of mineral water on his bedside table. "I might have known him— there were a ton of kids my age there, and I don't really remember their names."

"Of course, I understand."

"Look, I'm sure it's purely coincidental, but you did tell me—"

"No. No, of course, I'm so glad you called. Anything you think of, even if it's a coincidence, could be helpful. How about any of the other names?"

"No, I'm afraid not."

"Well, if you think of anything . . ."

"I will let you know, I promise."

"And one more thing, Jack, I've been meaning to ask whether you'd reconsider having some police protection. Even if it's just an occasional unmarked vehicle outside of your house at certain hours."

"I'm traveling right now, so they'd be guarding an empty house. But, really, the answer is that I'm fine without it. Thanks, but no thanks."

He could hear her sigh across the line. "All right, then. Thank you for letting us know about the Windward Resort. And don't hesitate if you remember something else. *Anything else*."

After ending the call, Jack wondered for a moment if contacting the FBI had been the right thing to do, and whether he should have told her what happened to his sister at the Windward Resort.

There was a knock on the door. Just before calling Agent Mercer, Jack had called down for room service, but he thought it was too soon for them to be at his door. He slid gingerly off the bed—he always felt particularly old when he traveled for business—and walked to his door, opening it just enough to see a short Latino man holding a tray with his Cobb salad on it, plus his half-bottle of wine. Jack brought the tray to the table in front of the room's only windows, three adjacent panes that provided a panorama of flat farmland for as far as he could see. There was low sunlight striking his window but somewhere in the middle distance he could see a dark cloud, striations underneath it, a rainstorm hitting some distant point. For a brief, scary moment, Jack completely forgot where he was, then remembered that he was on the outskirts of Indianapolis.

He sat, and peeled the Saran Wrap off of his salad. The whole thing, including the grilled chicken and the bacon, was ice cold. No wonder it came right away, since it had clearly been premade and sitting in the refrigerator. He twisted the cap off his wine and poured himself a glass.

6

The Rolling Brook Cabins didn't look like much from the outside but inside they were borderline luxurious. It looked like something you'd see in an LL Bean catalog, dark wood furnishings, fishing prints on the wall, and the bed was covered by a white blanket with red, green, and yellow stripes. There was a working fireplace, and two upholstered lodge chairs, and the bathroom had a deep tub in it.

Ethan had gotten there first, then texted Caroline to say that he'd checked in, and she should come straight to the cabin. She'd texted back to say that she was half an hour away. Nervous, he paced the cabin, wondering if he had time to take a quick shower, then decided that he didn't. He kept wandering over to the window and pulling the curtain back to see if Caroline had arrived. He was hardly aware of the police cruiser, even though the officer had identified himself to Ethan after he'd checked in.

He went and looked in the refrigerator. There was a complimentary bottle of white wine and a fruit plate, covered with plastic wrap. He left them both there. In his backpack he had his one hitter, packed with some pretty

287

potent indica, but he wanted to be straight when he first saw Caroline. It seemed important, somehow.

There was a knock on the door, and his heart hammered in his chest. He went and swung it open, and there was Caroline, taller than he thought she'd be, her cheeks flushed, a smile on her face.

"I'm nervous," she said.

"I'm nervous, too. Why?"

"Right."

She came inside the cabin, put down her overnight bag, and they embraced. It felt good, but also surreal, like the world had suddenly added a dimension and Ethan was rushing to catch up with the feeling.

"What should we do now?" she said.

"What do you want to do?"

"I asked you first."

"I think we should get into bed with each other," Ethan said. "I don't care whether we have sex or anything, but I want to lie by your side and be able to touch you and kiss you."

"That's what I want to do too."

Two hours later they were drinking the wine and eating the fruit in bed, both enormously relieved that they felt as close to each other now as they'd felt for the past few weeks. Periodically, one of them, or both of them, would suddenly laugh.

"If anyone saw us . . ." Caroline said.

"I don't care. I'm so happy to be here with you."

"I am, too."

An hour later they both lay facing each other, sheet and blankets pulled up tight around their naked bodies. They were both exhausted. "'We met at the end of the party,'" Ethan said.

Caroline looked confused for a moment, then laughed. "You're quoting poetry at me."

"It was the poem you found."

"Yes," she said. "'We met at the end of the party, when all the drinks were dead.'"

"Do you know the rest?"

"Some of it. Not all of it. I'm done quoting poetry."

"I'm glad we did this," Ethan said.

"Think how strange it is, the way we met."

"I think about it all the time."

"Do you believe it was somehow fated?" Caroline said.

After a pause, Ethan said, "No, I don't. I don't believe in soul mates or that there's only one perfect match for all of us out there. I think there are many perfect matches, and sometimes people never find theirs, or they find two or more. It's random."

"I agree with you. I don't believe in soul mates, but I do believe in disposition."

"Oh, yeah?" Ethan said.

"In some ways we're not alike, but we have similar dispositions. It's everything, I think, and I'm very glad we did this."

"Me, too. If nothing else, this is the most comfortable bed I've ever slept in."

"Ha. It is, isn't it?" Caroline said.

They fell deeply asleep, aided by the liquid benzodiazepine that had been injected into the wine through the cork. Neither was awakened by the injections they then received, first of much higher doses of the same benzodiazepine, followed by injections of fatal doses of morphine. Caroline, nearly forty pounds lighter than the man in whose arms she was sleeping, convulsed slightly, her brain starved of oxygen, then died.

THREE

Matthew Beaumont

Jay Coates

Ethan Dart

Caroline Geddes

Frank Hopkins

Alison Horne

Arthur Kruse

Jack Radebaugh

Jessica Winslow

I

SATURDAY, OCTOBER 29, 2:22 A. M.

Twenty minutes later, Ethan Dart died in the same manner as Caroline Geddes had.

TWO

Matthew Beaumont

Jay Coates

Ethan Dart

Caroline Geddes

Frank Hopkins

Alison Horne

Arthur Kruse

Jack Radebaugh

Jessica Winslow

I

SUNDAY, OCTOBER 30, 4:39 P. M.

The Saints game had just started, and Sam Hamilton cracked open a beer, even though he had no intention of sitting down in front of the television. He was in his study, the volume of the TV turned up loud enough so that he could hear if anything momentous happened. Sam had filled an entire wall with photographs and newspaper clippings and his own handwritten notes, all pertaining to the Frank Hopkins case, or rather, as he thought of it, the List-of-Nine case. Since his trip to visit Frank Hopkins's sister, Cynthia, down in Florida, Sam had become consumed, not just in getting periodic updates from Mary Parkinson of the state police, but in researching the two incidents that had taken place at the Windward Resort that Cynthia had told him about. And now he'd finally found something that seemed like it might be the key to everything that was happening.

At first, he had focused on the murder/suicide that had occurred in 1961. A man named Bart Knapp from Portland, Maine, had committed suicide in one of the Windward's rooms after murdering his mistress, a woman named Betsy Sturnevan. Both were married, and both worked at the same accounting office in Portland, Maine.

297

Details about this particular story were not too hard to find, since the case had made national news. Because there had appeared to be no significant struggle in the room, and because both of the deceased had been found with sedatives and alcohol in their bloodstreams, the official verdict had been a double suicide, the assumption being that Betsy had slit her own wrists while she was in the bed, then Bart had gone to the tub and used the razor on himself. Betsy Sturnevan's family had rejected that verdict, claiming that not only had Bart murdered Betsy Sturnevan, he had taken her to the Windward Resort against her will, keeping her drugged with sedatives.

It was a sensational story, and Sam had dug up a number of articles to read, most from a local paper at the time, the *Kennewick Star*. None of the police officers involved in the case were still alive. But both Bart Knapp and Betsy Sturnevan had had young children at the time of their deaths, and Sam had considered seeing if he could find them now. They'd be in their early or middle sixties. He might have done it except for the fact that he wasn't able to find any connection whatsoever between either of the lovers and anyone on the list. Ultimately, he decided that it was a dead end.

That had left him with the young girl who had drowned out by the stone jetty. When he put "Windward Resort" and "drowning" into a search engine, all that came up was the story of a teenager named Duane Wozniak who had drowned while swimming off the jetty in 2000.

He read what he could about that incident, but it was clear it had been an accident, and he couldn't find any connection between Duane Wozniak's family and any of the people on the list. For whatever reason he was much more interested in the story that Frank's sister had told him. Cynthia had said that she thought she was fourteen or fifteen years old when the girl had drowned, and since she'd also said she'd been eighteen in 1961, that meant the drowning most likely occurred in either 1957 or 1958. It made sense to Sam that he hadn't been able to find any mention of a drowning at the Windward Resort in those years using online searches. A young girl's accidental drowning at a beach in Maine would not necessarily have made it into a national publication, one that had been archived online. But the story would certainly have been mentioned in local papers. So for the past three days Sam had sat bleary-eyed at the Kennewick public library going through microfilm from both the *Kennewick Star* and the *Southern Maine Forecaster*, two local papers that were active in the mid-1950s. He had been close to giving up when he decided to expand the time frame, look for articles in 1956 and 1959, as well. He'd hit the jackpot just three hours earlier, finding a story in the *Star* about the tragic drowning of Faye Grant in July of 1956. She'd been ten years old, staying at the Windward for the summer with her mother and brother. A police detective by the name of William Cable was quoted as saying that the drowning was accidental, that Faye Grant had probably climbed into the crevice at the foot of the jetty, then been unable to get out when the tide came in.

In one of the articles, the names of Faye's immediate family were mentioned. The father was John Grant, an insurance executive from Hartford, Connecticut. Faye's older brother had probably been named after his father, since the newspaper referred to him as "little Jack Grant," and the mother was Lily Grant, née Lily Radebaugh, originally from Baltimore.

When Sam had read those words, an electric shiver had passed over the skin of his arms and the back of his neck. "Little Jack Grant" could be going under the name of Jack Radebaugh. If Faye had been his sister, then the List of Nine would have something to do with her death. Probably revenge. Frank Hopkins, who would have been at the Windward Resort when Faye had died, had been drowned by the jetty. The other names on the list, all people too young to have been present for Faye's death . . . well, Sam had no idea why they had been targeted. His best guess was that they were somehow related to someone that Jack believed to be guilty. Maybe one of their parents. The dates would work.

After sending an email to both Detective Mary Parkinson of the state police and to Agent Ruth Jackson of the FBI with JPEGs of all the relevant articles, Sam was now studying the notes he'd taken on the victim's families. And it was all starting to fall into place—there were more similarities between the parents of the victims than the victims themselves. They were all white, all middle- or upper-middle class, all clustered around New England. And there was something else, something Sam had noticed a week earlier. On the list of nine names there were six men and three women. He'd wondered about that. If Jack Radebaugh, or someone else (it was possible), was murdering the children of people he considered complicit in the death of his sister, then not only would he try to make their deaths painless, but maybe he'd also pick sons to murder and not daughters. Jessica Winslow was targeted, of course, but she was an only child. And Caroline Geddes, while not an only child, had one brother who lived outside of the country. Mind racing, Sam went and got another beer from the fridge, not even bothering to look at the football game on television.

When he returned to his study he thought about Alison Horne, who had never been found. Was she dead already? Probably not, he thought, because if she'd died there would have been a police report, a death notice, something to alert the FBI. Maybe she was dead, and her body hadn't been discovered yet. But someone surely would have reported her missing. No, Sam assumed she was still alive, and he wondered where she was, and if she knew how much danger she was in.

2

MONDAY, OCTOBER 31, 3:03 P. M.

Jonathan Grant was going to text Alison from the airport to let her know he was back in Bermuda and would be at the house in thirty minutes, but decided not to. He thought he'd surprise her, despite the fact that he knew her well enough to know she was not big on surprises.

He let himself into the house on Church Folly Lane and shouted a "hello" as he wiped his shoes on the inside mat. The house was quiet, and he wondered if Alison was down at Tobacco Bay or out for a walk. But then she appeared on the stairwell in a long white nightgown, and for a strange moment, Jonathan felt like he was looking at a ghost.

"I'm back," he said.

She came down the stairs and embraced him, saying, "I'm glad," followed immediately with, "You could've called first."

"I thought I'd surprise you. You seem thin."

"Oh," she said, and looked down at herself in the sheer nightgown. "Living on yogurt and fruit, I guess. I really am glad you're back."

"Let me unpack and shower and then we can go out for a big meal."

They went to the Swizzle Inn, Jonathan complaining, as he did every time they'd gone there, that it was now a tourist trap that sold T-shirts and specialty glasses. But still, he had a favorite table that they had managed to get, and he ordered the chowder as an appetizer and then the liver and onions. Alison ordered a salad.

"Tell me about your trip," she said.

"I'm done with all that, now."

"What do you mean?"

"Commitments. Money. All that. Tell me about Bermuda. What's it like without me here?"

Alison took a sip of her rosé, and said, "I thought I'd like it, but I'm not sure I do. Did I ever tell you how I have ESP?"

He lowered his brows. "No, I don't think so."

"It's no big deal but ever since I was girl, I've gotten feelings, almost like a cold chill goes through me, whenever bad things are going to happen. Or sometimes when they have happened."

"Tell me more. I'm interested."

She told him about how she knew her grandmother was going to die before it happened, and about the time in high school when she'd passed Missy Talbot in the hall on a Friday afternoon and she'd felt as though all the warmth had been sucked from her. Missy died that Saturday night, thrown from a car when her boyfriend careened off Pope Road coming home from Brian Sherzinger's party. She didn't tell him that she'd had the same feeling of coldness on the night that Jonathan had asked her if she wanted to get a glass of wine with him after her shift. But she did tell him that after he left Bermuda, and she was alone in his house, she'd been swamped with bad feelings, cold feelings.

"It wasn't like a premonition, exactly. At first, I thought it might be, but I think it's maybe the house, that being alone there . . . maybe I was picking up on some things that happened in the past . . ."

"You're preaching to the choir," Jonathan said, and he took a long sip of his gin martini. "There's some history there. Not just my family, but probably from before that."

"Or maybe I was just lonely."

The waitress came to clear their plates, calling Jonathan "hon."

"How long have you been coming here?" Alison asked him after the waitress had left.

"My whole life. Since I was a kid. This is an old restaurant. It's been here about a hundred years."

"Can I ask you a personal question?"

"Sure."

"I've been poking around the house, as you know, digging through closets, and I found some more pictures you might be interested in. And I noticed, not that it's any of my business, but the only pictures I've found of your sister are when she was very young."

"She died very young," Jonathan said. "I didn't tell you that?"

"You told me she was dead, but, no, I didn't know when or how it happened."

"She died when she was ten years old and I was twelve. That was a long time ago."

"Still, I'm sorry to hear that, Jonathan. What was her name?"

"Faye."

"How did she die?"

"She drowned. In Maine. We'd gone as a family for one month to a resort in Kennewick. There was this stone jetty at the beach, like a breakwater, and at low tide there were all these tide pools to explore, little caves where the granite blocks didn't perfectly meet up. She got trapped in one when the tide was coming back and that's how she drowned."

"Oh, that's terrible."

"It was," Jonathan said, and something in his voice made Alison think that he was done talking about this particular subject.

Back at the house they had a nightcap in the living room, and Alison stood looking at the oil paintings of Faye and Jonathan above the fireplace.

"She was pretty," Alison said, almost to herself.

"She was," Jonathan said. He was standing by the drinks table, a carafe of whiskey in one hand.

"Where did you pose for those pictures?"

"Not here, I'm pretty sure. In West Hartford, where we grew up. I don't remember much except that my mother insisted on the sailor suits, and I was old enough to be mortified by that."

"Well, you both look cute in your sailor suits. Little Jonathan, or little Johnnie . . . What were you called then?"

"Jack, mostly."

"Oh. When did that change?"

"When I changed it, I guess."

"When I was growing up everyone called me Ali. Everyone but my father, who always called me Alison, which made me feel grown-up and sophisticated. When I got to college, I told everyone that I was an Alison, and now that's who I am."

"That's similar to what happened to me," he said, "but I actually made it legal. After my sister died, neither of my parents handled it well at all, but my father, in particular, decided that the best thing would be to pretend she never existed. I never really forgave him for that, for his weakness, so as soon as I was able I actually changed my last name to Radebaugh, my mother's maiden name. These days some people know me as Jack Radebaugh, and some, like you, as Jonathan Grant. I don't care about my name anymore. I guess enough water has passed under that bridge." Jonathan put the carafe down on the table. He hadn't filled his glass.

"Blood under the bridge," Alison said.

"Huh?"

"It was something my father used to say. 'That's all just blood under the bridge.'"

"Well, he was right. That's all it is, now."

"That name is so familiar to me," Alison said, her eyes off to the side.

"What, my name?"

"Yes, the last name. No, the whole name. Jack Radebaugh."

"I did write a book once. And it was published under that name."

"What kind of book?"

"A business book. It did very well, but—"

"No, that probably wasn't it." She sat down on the closest chair, upholstered in a blue fabric with tiny white anchors.

He watched her, wondering if she was going to remember where she'd seen the name Radebaugh, wondering if she even remembered the list she'd received, but after taking a sip of her wine, she smiled and said, "It's Halloween."

"I know. Do you like my outfit?"

"What are you?"

"A man in the winter of my years."

She jutted out her lower lip. "Autumn, maybe, but not winter. God, I'm exhausted. Should we go to bed?"

"Yes, let's go to bed."

3

TUESDAY, NOVEMBER 1, 1:10 A. M.

Jack Radebaugh—known by Alison Horne, and a few other people, as Jonathan Grant, the name he'd been given at birth—walked carefully down the creaky hall to the bedroom that used to be his father's, so many years ago now. He stepped into the narrow closet that smelled of cedar and dust and reached up to where the .22 rifle was held in place by two nails. He pulled the rifle down, checked to make sure that it was loaded, then walked back to the bedroom. Alison was asleep on her side, a hand tucked up under her cheek. He stood over her, a little concerned that even at point-blank range, the bullet might hurt her before it killed her. He'd heard of bullets ricocheting off skulls, but that was certainly rare. He doubted it would happen if he aimed the gun correctly.

Maybe I should have drugged her drink just to make sure she didn't suddenly wake up, he thought, the way he'd drugged Caroline Geddes and Ethan Dart. But he told himself not to worry about it. He'd gotten to know Alison Horne, and one thing he knew about her was that she was a deep sleeper. He braced himself, the barrel of the gun two inches from Alison. He didn't love her—he wasn't sure he truly loved anyone, at least no one currently alive on the planet—but he did like Alison quite a bit.

He thought back to a year ago, when he'd first walked into that awful steak house she was hostessing at, just to get a look at her. At that point he had fully planned everything but was still not entirely sure he was going to go through with it. He'd already written the list of nine names—nine potential victims, unaware that they'd been marked for death. The private investigator he'd hired to provide biographical information had handed him extensive files on all of them. In a way, going to see Alison Horne in the flesh had been a way for him to test himself, to see how he felt about playing the role of God. He sat at the bar in his best suit and watched her at her hostess stand, trying to imagine what it would feel like to end her life. He thought of Grace, his only child, who would be around Alison's age right now if she hadn't been hit by a drunk driver the year after she'd graduated from college. She'd been driving home after working the dinner shift at a swank French restaurant. She hadn't needed to be a waitress, especially since she'd landed an entry-level job at the Ithaca newspaper she'd interned at her senior year at Cornell, and, besides, if she'd needed extra money Jack would have been happy to give it to her. But she'd always been independent, and she loved being a waitress, ever since she'd gotten her first job at a catering company in New Jersey her junior year of high school. And he remembered her telling him that she made more in one night of waitressing than she made for the whole week at the paper.

She'd been inordinately pretty, his daughter, and Jack had imagined the way that men dining at Salt Bistro would've noticed her. And he worried about her leaving the restaurant late at night and walking to her car. But the things we worry about are not the things that eventually happen. The drunk driver who hit her crossed four lanes of traffic, missing other cars, then ramming Grace's GTI so hard that it went through a guardrail, flipped over twice, and landed upside down in the parking lot of a strip mall. She had been less than a minute from her own apartment complex.

Watching Alison at the steak house Jack had wondered if, like his own daughter, she loved working there. Somehow, he doubted it. She was nearing forty, he knew, but still sexy enough to get away with the cropped top and tight leather skirt. She caught him looking at her and smiled brightly at him. Maybe he should get to know her more intimately, if that was possible. I'm thinking of killing this woman, he'd thought, so getting to know her first would be the right thing to do, both logistically, but also maybe morally. He realized, of course, that he had no intentions of getting to know his other victims, but they weren't right in front of him, in smiling distance.

He'd returned several times to the steak house, eventually asking her to join him for a glass of wine. And then he'd suggested the idea of her becoming his mistress. It had been easy, and except for her prettiness, and her job at a restaurant, there had been nothing else that reminded Jack of his daughter. She was just a random human being alone in the world like we all are. Not particularly good, and not particularly bad. He didn't want to hurt her, but he did want to kill her. She was a small piece of machinery in an incredibly complex system, and he needed to make an adjustment. He was restoring karma to the universe.

He carefully aimed the barrel of the rifle at the back of her skull and pulled the trigger.

ONE

Matthew Beaumont

Jay Coates

Ethan Dart

Caroline Geddes

Frank Hopkins

Alison Horne

Arthur Kruse

Jack Radebaugh

Jessica Winslow

I

TUESDAY, NOVEMBER 1, 3:45 P. M.

Instead of flying from St. George's Airport in Bermuda to Portland, Maine, as he'd planned, Jack Radebaugh had changed his ticket and was now descending in a half-filled Airbus A320 toward Bradley International Airport. He knew it was a potentially disastrous mistake, especially when he was so near to the end, but suddenly he didn't care. He had decided to return to West Hartford for one hour, two at the most, then head to Maine. At least this way, he'd be able to take his own car.

Jack's mind these days was like a slideshow he had no control over. Images and thoughts and fixations ran rampant, but he'd learned to live with it, to control it for the most part. It also helped knowing that soon he'd be snuffing out those thoughts like blowing out the candles on a birthday cake.

A taxi took him from the airport to West Hartford. He moved rapidly through his house, changing his clothes so that he was wearing something more appropriate for the cold, blustery weather. He pulled a few items from his travel bag that had come with him from Bermuda, and went downstairs to the basement, where he added a few more items that would help him deal with his next-door neighbor. That was the real reason he had come back to West Hartford. Since having dinner over a month ago with his lovely neighbor Margaret and her smug, son-of-a-bitch husband Eric, he'd kept thinking about them, kept fantasizing about what he wanted to do to Eric. Maybe it was simply that Margaret, with her long hair and slender neck, and her timid wit, reminded him of his sister. Or maybe it was that she was simply a good person, and Eric wasn't. And maybe since he was now so close to completing his life's work, he thought that he might as well do one last favor for Margaret. Did he even know her last name? He couldn't remember ever hearing it. He did, however, remember talking with her about her part-time job at the library. "I work evenings Monday through Wednesday," she'd said, "and then all day on Saturday. Just about the worst schedule." Maybe he'd remembered her schedule because he'd been planning this all along.

After locking up his childhood home for the final time, Jack crossed to his neighbor's house, and rang the doorbell. What would he do if Margaret answered the door? He supposed that he would simply let her know that he was going away for a while and he'd come to say goodbye. And then he'd be off. It would look strange, but what did that matter in the big scheme of things?

As it was, Eric answered the door. He was dressed in loose shorts and a sleeveless T-shirt. His skin glistened with sweat, like he'd been working out, but he was also holding a can of beer.

"Sorry to bother you, Eric, but is Margaret home?"

Eric blinked several times and Jack surmised that Eric was trying to remember his name. Then, apparently remembering, he quickly said, "Sorry, Jack, she's at work, at the library."

"Oh, never mind," Jack said. "I just had a question for her, but . . ." He paused, then said, "Maybe you can answer it for me. Do you mind if I come in for a few minutes?"

Eric hesitated, and Jack waited, not changing his expression or his position on the front stoop, not offering up an apology, and Eric finally said, "Come on in, man. Can I get you a beer?"

Stepping into the foyer Jack said, "No, thank you. As I said, five minutes of your time is all I need."

Eric led Jack to the living room and indicated a chair. Jack sat, rearranging his jacket so that he had access to the right-hand pocket. After putting his can of beer on the coffee table between them, Eric sat too, an odd expression on his face. It took Jack a moment to figure out what the expression meant, but then he had it. It was that Eric didn't know how to feel about his neighbor yet. Was Jack a washed-up old man, or was he still someone influential, a best-selling author, a man who still had connections? Eric was trying to categorize him, so that he could know how to act with him.

"I'll come right to the point, Eric," Jack said. "I don't want to waste your time, and I don't know when Margaret will be coming back."

"Not for a while," Eric said.

"So here is the question I was going to ask her, but I will ask you instead. How is it that a decent, kind person like Margaret ended up with a fucking asshole like you?"

An awkward, slowly forming grin creased Eric's face, as he tried to absorb the question. "Are you serious?" he said, at last.

"Am I serious? Yes. I want to know. I mean, my guess is that she reminds you of your mother, who was probably bullied by your father, and vice versa maybe, or else I don't see why she puts up with your shit."

A deep flush of color was rising from Eric's neck up toward his face. "Hey, Jack," he said. "I thought you might have some sort of pathetic crush on my wife, and now I know for sure. Why don't you get the fuck out of my house, before I throw you out myself."

Jack smiled. He reached into the pocket of his goose-down parka and pulled out his Taurus .44 magnum revolver, the same gun he'd used to kill Matthew Beaumont what felt like years ago in a suburban town outside of Boston. He pointed the barrel of the gun at Eric's chest.

"What's your last name, Eric? I don't think I know it."

Eric was frozen, his eyes on the revolver, his jaw moving as though he were chewing on something. "Um," he said, at last.

"I'm going to kill you, Eric, and it doesn't matter whether I know your last name or not, but I was curious."

Eric moved his eyes from the revolver to Jack's face. "Why?" he said.

"Why am I going to kill you, or why do I want to know your last name? I'm going to kill you because you're a bully and a coward and I don't like you. You also happen to be married to someone that I do like. So killing you will make her life better, and it will probably make a whole lot of other people's lives better as well. I'm also killing you because I've gotten good at killing people, so I thought I'd use this new skill I've acquired late in life. I can tell by the expression on your face that you're confused, so I'll make it simple: You are going to die because I want you to die."

"Look, Jack. If this has to do with Margaret . . . if you're in love with her, or something, we can work this out. I mean, Jesus . . ."

Jack had been briefly tempted to extend the conversation, to tell this man the full story of what he'd been planning over the past two years of his life. And what he'd achieved. The thought of it was tempting, like some supervillain in a James Bond film monologuing away about his plan, but Eric would not have really listened. He was already trying to figure out how to save his own life, his body probably coursing with adrenaline. So Jack shot him in the chest, dead center, and watched as he slumped back onto the pristine white couch, a perplexed and pained expression on his face.

After standing up and looking out the front bay

windows to see if anyone had been walking by on the street and heard the gunshot, Jack crouched over Eric's body and pressed two fingers to his neck to feel for a pulse. There was none. On the table next to Eric's can of beer was his cell phone. It was locked but that didn't matter. You could always call 911 on a locked phone. He put the phone into his front pocket, then put the gun into his travel bag, and exited the house, stopping briefly to look at a pile of unopened mail on a waist-high table in the foyer. The first envelope was addressed to Margaret Hutchinson, and the one below it to Eric Miles. He wondered if Margaret had kept her maiden name. It would make it easier for her if she had, not having to change her driver's license and her bank accounts.

When he was a mile from his neighborhood in West Hartford, and stopped at a red light, Jack called 911, gave them the address of Margaret Hutchinson and Eric Miles, and said that a man had been shot there. The least he could do was to spare Margaret the sight of her dead husband when she returned home from her library shift. He threw Eric's phone out the window of his car as he merged onto Interstate 84, heading north.

It was just a regular Tuesday in November for most of the world. He thought of his wife, wondering what she'd be doing right now. Drinking chardonnay and watching one of the early evening shows she liked. Either *Jeopardy!* or the *PBS NewsHour*. They'd come to her, wouldn't they, after they figured out what he'd done? Interview her, maybe even try to find out if she had assisted him in anyway. At the very least they'd ask her why he'd done it. He thought that maybe she'd mention the glioblastoma and how his personality had changed after the diagnosis and treatment. She'd mentioned it enough to him, convinced that something had altered in him. He thought she was probably right. He *had* changed a little after that particular ordeal. He'd realized not just his own insignificance, but the insignificance of everyone else in the world. And, yes, that had been around the time he'd begun to fantasize about killing the children of the Pirate Society, about setting the world to rights.

And he wondered if his wife would mention their only daughter, and how she'd died the year she'd graduated from college. He'd changed then, too, but that was to be expected. It was the second time he'd learned that the world would happily rid itself of its young and beautiful inhabitants. There was no order, only chaos. He'd created the list to bring back order, but his wife would never make that connection, and he doubted that anyone else would either.

It was late by the time he pulled the car into the half-empty parking lot of the Windward Resort. He stepped out into the cold, briny air, and was flooded with the weight of sadness that always accompanied the smell of the seashore.

The young woman at the reception desk took his information and smiled at him with an empty look that made Jack feel pretty certain she hadn't been told to be on the lookout for anyone checking in under the name Jonathan Grant. He asked if she had a tide table, and she dug around in her desk drawer, finally finding one.

"Are you going fishing, Mr. Grant?" she said.

"No. Just going to the beach."

"It's nice this time of year. Empty." She was looking directly at him, but he clocked her eyes darting to the side of his head. Normally he combed his hair in such a way as to cover up the raised white scar from his brain surgery three years ago, but he'd forgotten to do it before entering the hotel.

He took the stairs to the second floor, and went down the dingy hallway to his room. As a child at this resort he'd been dazzled by the luxury, or maybe it was just the freedom that at such a young age he'd been given the run of the place, with its cavernous dining room, and darkly lit lounge, and endless hallways. Now it just seemed worn-out and sad. The hallways smelled of canned soup and disinfectant.

In his room, where the smell was worse, he studied the tide table, confirming that low tide was going to be at 1:49 a.m., and high tide was at 7:53 a.m. It was perfect. It didn't give him a lot of time to do what he'd come here to do, but it was enough. He cracked the seal on a bottle of Macallan 25 and poured some into the water glass he'd taken from the bathroom. Then he sat at the desk and wrote his letter.

At just past midnight he poured the remainder of the scotch into a sterling silver flask he'd had since college and left the resort, going out the back entrance that led to the rear parking lot. The cold wind was still whistling over the empty asphalt. Jonathan wore waterproof boots and flannel-lined jeans, plus a thick fisherman's sweater under his parka. He'd always hated the cold, and despite what he planned to do, was nervous about the temperature outside. He dug the woolen cap out of his pocket and put it on his head, then walked purposefully across Micmac Avenue and down toward the stone jetty.

The night was clear, the sky peppered with stars, and with a three-quarters moon. He had no trouble making his way across the dark beach, despite the damp wind that tugged at his parka. When he got to the jetty, he risked using his flashlight briefly to locate what he believed was the place where his sister had been left to die over fifty years ago. He'd scouted the spot earlier, back when he'd waited out here for Frank Hopkins. He couldn't be one hundred percent positive that it was the exact location, but it was close enough, a crevice in the base of the stone wall just large enough for an adult to squeeze into. He studied it now, a tidal pool reflecting the moon, something scuttling away as he pressed his boot into the damp sand.

He dug the pills out of the front pocket of his jeans and washed them down with the rest of the scotch. Then he lowered himself to his knees and wriggled his way under the seaweed-blanketed rocks, finding a position that wasn't exactly comfortable, but that wasn't painful. It was actually okay nestled in the blackness of the rocks, even as the icy water began to rush in, then out again, occasionally splashing up against his face. He could taste the saltwater on his lips. There was a roaring in his ears, the water filling every available cavity around him. Something, maybe a crab, touched the back of his neck. He closed his eyes and thought of Faye. He was very tired, actually. There was something almost soothing about the sound of the water shushing into the cave, then shushing out again. Shushing in. Shushing out.

He thought he'd be colder, but he wasn't. Maybe it was because he was out of the wind. Or maybe it was the pills and the scotch starting to kick in. It was cheating, of course, to have ensured that he would be unconscious as the tide rose. Faye hadn't had that luxury. But he wasn't a perfect man. He never had been.

NONE

Matthew Beaumont

Jay Coates

Ethan Dart

Caroline Geddes

Frank Hopkins

Alison Horne

Arthur Kruse

Jack Radebaugh

Jessica Winslow

I

FRIDAY, DECEMBER 2, 5:13 P. M.

Sam Hamilton settled onto a stool at the bar at the Windward Lounge and ordered a Shipyard IPA.

"Oh, hey, Sam," Shelly said, looking up at him as she poured his beer. "Nice to see a familiar face. It's tourist season in December this year."

"Oh, yeah?"

"The lookie-loos are out in force."

"What do you tell them?"

"Depends on my mood. Usually I tell them the truth—that I never saw him the night he was here. But just for the fun of it I did tell a couple of folks that he was in here buying drinks for the whole bar. I mean, you think he might've done that, considering he was going to walk down to the jetty and drown himself."

"It would've been generous."

"Right. That's what I'm saying. You can't take it with you, you might as well buy a few drinks for your fellow man. You staying for dinner tonight?"

"I haven't decided yet," Sam said.

"Well, no rush. The special is striped bass and Thomas tells me it's pretty good."

Shelly went down the bar and poured two glasses of

wine for a middle-aged couple. When she came back, Sam said, "Shelly, correct me if I'm wrong, but there's still a library here, right?"

"A library?"

"Yeah, like a help-yourself lending library."

"Oh, right. Of course. On the third floor."

He took a long pull of his beer, suddenly eager to go upstairs and look through the library. He'd just remembered it existed, a room with floor-to-ceiling bookshelves, all filled with donated books. It had been started way back when by Frank Hopkins's father, Murray, the original owner of the Windward Resort—there was a faded handmade sign that called the library something like "Uncle Murray's Book Nook." He only knew about it because two or three years ago he used to spend an occasional night at the Windward with a divorced real estate agent from York. She refused to come to his apartment—for reasons he never understood— but she'd meet him at the hotel, stay for only an hour, and then leave him with a room for the night that he didn't really need. He'd discovered Uncle Murray's library, a collection that had been started when the Windward was more of a resort, back when families would come for a month, or a whole summer.

On the last night of Jack Radebaugh's life, after he'd checked into room 207, it was clear that he'd written some sort of note or letter. There was a pen on the desk and a few sheets of blank paper. But they'd yet to find whatever it was that he had written. The current theory was that he brought it down with him to the jetty and it had washed out to sea with the tide. But Sam had given that theory a lot of thought and it hadn't made sense to him. If he'd written some sort of letter—a confession, maybe—then why not just leave it in his hotel room. Unless, of course, like the killer in *And Then There Were None*, he felt the need to write a letter explaining why and how he did what he did, but then he hid it somehow. In the book the killer put the letter in a bottle and threw it into the sea. Had Jack Radebaugh done the same thing? Or had he hidden it some other way?

Sam, having reread the Christie novel twice in recent weeks, remembered that the killer was torn between wanting to leave behind a perfect mystery and also wanting the world to acknowledge his artistry. He thought about that constantly. He'd learned a lot about Jack Radebaugh since his body had been found wedged into the base of the jetty on Kennewick beach. All of his victims, with the exception of Frank Hopkins, had been children of previous guests at the Windward Resort, and although the dates hadn't been entirely confirmed, the parents had all been guests when they'd been children themselves, back when Jack's sister Faye had drowned. It was Daniel Horne, father of Alison Horne, who'd had the best memory of the drowning of Faye. He had told the investigating FBI detectives that there was a group of children who called themselves the Pirate Society and that both Jack and Faye had been part of it.

"Same again?" Shelly said, her hand on the beer pull.

"Not right now, but I'll be back. I need to go check out the library. Is it unlocked?"

"Should be. What's someone gonna steal? A book?"

The door to the library was unlocked, and Sam had to search the wall just inside the door for a light switch. The room flickered into being, a windowless space not much larger than a typical hotel room. A few vinyl club chairs were scattered around on the burgundy wall-to-wall carpeting. The room smelled of musty books and mustier carpet.

He decided to work clockwise, scanning the shelves. He wasn't exactly sure what he was looking for but was hoping he'd know it when he saw it. A book about drowning, maybe, or about pirates. It was a long shot, he knew, but maybe Jack Radebaugh did write that confession, but then decided to hide it somewhere it was unlikely to be found. The first section was hardcover fiction, indicated by a faded handwritten sign. The books were alphabetical by author, mostly fiction that had been popular about forty or fifty years ago. Lots of Michener and Leon Uris. A whole row of Catherine Cookson books. Here and there was something a little more modern. There were quite a few John Grisham novels, and a ton of Stephen King hardcovers.

He moved on from fiction into history, then biography. Then there was a large section of paperback novels, mostly thrillers and romances. In the Ross Macdonald section he spotted a paperback called *The Drowning Pool* and pulled it out to flip through the pages. Nothing there.

Then he thought of Agatha Christie. It took him a while, but he found a high-up shelf that contained about twelve of her books. And there it was: *Ten Little Indians*. He pulled the pocket-sized book off the shelf. It had a blue cover and showed a wooden statue of an Indian getting chopped in the neck with an ax. He shook the book out, then flipped through its pages. Nothing there either.

The last section was kids' books, at least on the lower shelves. Sam crouched and scanned the titles. Lots of Nancy Drew and Hardy Boys, plus even a few Bobbsey Twins. The picture books had such narrow spines that it was hard to read all the titles, and Sam found himself simply skimming through them. Many of the books were familiar to him from his own childhood, including an Enid Blyton book, *Five on a Treasure Island*, that transported him back to his grandmother's house in Yorkshire, which had an enormous collection of Blyton. He pulled it out—wondering how it had ever ended up in Maine—and started to flip through it, getting caught up in the story before telling himself that he needed to keep looking through the shelves. For whatever reason Sam thought that his chances of finding the note, now that he hadn't found it in the Christie book, were best here in the kids' section. If Faye Grant's drowning was the event that sparked the entire murder spree, then that had happened when her brother Jack was only twelve years old. Sam kept looking.

He'd pulled out several books, anything that looked as though it might have been here in 1956, and was about to give up, when he spotted the spine of a book that was familiar to him. *Walt Disney's Peter Pan*, it read. One of his cousins from Alabama had it when he was a kid. It was the companion book to the animated film, and Sam had loved anything Peter Pan-related when he'd been young. And it was about pirates. Not only that, but one of the things Sam always remembered was the part where Captain Hook tried to kill Tiger Lily by drowning her in a rising tide. Sam's heart beat a little faster as he recalled that detail.

He pulled the book off the shelf and opened it. Three folded-up pieces of paper slid from the book and landed at his feet.

To Whom It May Concern,

I suppose that someone, someday, will read this letter. Maybe that first reader will be an astute police officer or federal agent, or maybe it will be someone many years from now, a mother, maybe, who has picked up this book at a tag sale and found this piece of forgotten history.

Whoever you are, I apologize in advance for both my handwriting and for the subject at hand. But I did want to explain why I did what I did. Maybe I want to explain to help in the understanding, or maybe I simply want to explain it to myself in writing. I suppose I hope that someday someone will read these words, but if they don't, I'll never know about it.

Let me begin.

In 1956, my mother took my sister, Faye, and me to the Windward Resort for the months of July and August. We lived in Hartford at the time, and my father came up most weekends to join us. Back then a few families still did this type of extended vacation, but it was a custom that was soon to go out of fashion. Nowadays, you can't take a two-month vacation if both parents are trying to hold down jobs.

Faye and I were in heaven that summer. The resort was right on the beach, and we were free to roam, just so long as we met our mother for lunch and then for dinner. There were multiple other kids staying for the summer as well, and we soon formed a tight-knit group. I remember that time of my life more for the feelings it evoked than the actual specifics of the day-to-day. I was a twelve-year-old boy who had never had that many friends. Now I had about ten of them.

We were quite the gang. I'd have never remembered their names, of course, not all of them, but as a bookish boy, I had taken to keeping a journal. More of a notebook, really—filled with drawings and lists and blueprints and plans. And that summer I must have brought the notebook with me to the third-floor library at the Windward, where the members of the newly formed Pirate Society would meet after dinner, because it was there that I wrote down all their names under the heading "Windward Resort Pirate Society."

Jack Grant

Meg Gauthier

Danny Horne

Gary Winslow

Deborah MacReady

Wayne Coates

Art Kruse

Paula Shepherd

Frank Hopkins

Under that list of names I had skipped a line and then written my sister's name, Faye Grant, followed by the word apprentice. The members of the Pirate Society weren't quite ready to afford a ten-year-old full member-ship in our group.

I don't remember if we named ourselves the Pirate Society before or after someone had pulled out the Peter Pan book to look at. I do remember that we all felt a little old to be calling ourselves pirates, so we added "society" in order to make it sound more sophisticated. And I also remember a bunch of us flipping through that book, Wayne lying and telling us he'd seen the movie the summer before, even though we all knew it hadn't played in a movie theater for years.

What I don't remember is who got the idea that we should initiate Faye into our society by tying her up and putting her into the secret cave at the base of the jetty during low tide. Someone must have come up with it while we were looking at the Peter Pan book, because it was the way Captain Hook tried to kill Tiger Lily. I'll never forget the illustration of Tiger Lily just barely holding her head above the water as Peter Pan and Captain Hook fight with swords. It is an image forever burned into my subconscious.

But someone did come up with the idea.

If Faye could survive the rising tide, as Tiger Lily had, she would become a full-fledged member of the Pirate Society.

And we all, every last one of us, agreed that it was a perfect plan. We told it to her during one of our secret meetings in the library, and she immediately agreed to take the test. I think, or rather I know, that she would have agreed to anything to be made a full member of our group.

In my mind this all happened during the course of a single day, but I can't be sure of that. What I do know is that Wayne Coates had a tide chart and told us all that there would be a low tide in the middle of the afternoon, when we were all free to be on the beach between lunch and dinner. In my memory it was an overcast day, spitting rain, and we had the beach practically to ourselves. Danny had brought a length of rope that he'd found snarled up in a half-submerged lobster trap, but Faye initially refused to be tied up. One of the girls, and I want to say it was Meg, told Faye that she didn't have to be tied up but in order to pass the initiation test, she had to stay in the cave until the very last moment, until the water went over her head, and only then would she be allowed to leave.

"If you come out one minute before, we'll know, and you'll never get to be a pirate."

Those are the words I remember, and I also remember all of us saying it again and again to Faye, who stood there in her loose one-piece bathing suit, wide-eyed, stick-limbed, long hair plastered to her frail shoulders, nodding ferociously, desperate to please the older kids.

We formed a circle around her, all chiming in to let her know that if she emerged too early, if she panicked and left the cave before the tide reached her, we wouldn't even talk to her for the rest of the summer.

Not one of us said something different.

No one told her it was just a game.

No one, in my recollection, even smiled at her, or winked to let her know it wasn't real.

We all watched her crawl into the cave, the water already starting to fill up the crevices and tidepools at the foot of the wall. She lay down on her back with her hands down by her sides.

And then we forgot about her, running off, laughing. It had started to really rain at that point, so we went to the game room at the resort and played board games all afternoon.

It was only around cocktail hour that my mother asked me if I knew where Faye was. I told her I didn't, of course, then quickly spread word around to the other

Pirates that no one should mention what we had done to my sister. I must have been worried at that point, worried about Faye I mean, but for some reason I thought she'd be just fine, and that maybe she was hiding somewhere else to get us all into trouble.

Word spread fast that Faye was missing, and several of the adults fanned through the resort grounds and the beach to look for her. My group all met together in the half-filled dining room and pledged to never say a word.

It was after dark by the time they found her body, still in that little cave. The tide was already going out again.

That was sixty years ago, and I've never forgotten what I and those eight other kids did to her. We might not have tied her hands behind her back, as we'd planned, but our words did the trick just as well.

My whole life I've thought about Faye in her final moments, and what it must have been like for her to die alone in the rising tide. I wonder if she tried to get out from under the rocks, or had she been determined to wait until the last possible moment, hoping to impress the older kids who'd already forgotten about her. Or maybe she'd gotten so cold lying there in the frigid water of the Atlantic Ocean that her muscles could no longer move. And I wonder who she thought about as she died. Our parents, I imagine. Our mum. Or maybe it was me she was thinking of, her big brother who knew where she was. Maybe she was waiting for me to come back and rescue her.

Two years ago, I hired a private detective to find the members of the Pirate Society. Surprisingly, they were all still alive, and except for Frank Hopkins, they had all had children. At that point, I had begun to form a plan. I was old enough to know that there is no justice in the world. Bad people go unpunished all the time. And innocent people suffer outrageously. My own parents were never the same, not even remotely, after Faye's death. They lost faith in the world, and I'm not sure either of them ever truly felt joy again. I decided that the best punishment— the only punishment—for the people responsible for my sister's death was for them to lose a child as well.

It wasn't simply revenge. It felt like something much more than that. Karma, maybe. I had the money, and I had the will, to do what the natural world would never do. I could set the world to rights, in one small way.

Was it fair that these people would lose a child because of a single careless act they did at the age of ten or eleven? Of course it's not. But life is seldom fair to anyone. It wasn't fair to my parents, having their beloved daughter taken from them, and life hasn't been fair to me, either. I lost my own daughter when she was on the cusp of a happy life, and now my brain has turned against me in multiple ways. My ex-wife, I am sure, will tell you all about it.

I didn't like killing those eight innocent people, but I decided that it was the only thing to do. In the long history of humans inhabiting this planet, my small act of retribution was minuscule, I know, but it was some-thing. And for those of you who say that two wrongs don't make a right, then I suspect you're a person who has never been wronged.

My hand is cramping up, and it is past midnight, so I'll be quick with the rest. When you've made a million dollars many times over, a lot of doors open up for you. I won't name names, but my money bought me not just information, but surveillance on all of my targets. I knew where they'd be, and when they'd be there. I knew their weaknesses, and strengths. And I was able to buy them painless deaths. All except for Frank Hopkins. I drowned him right near Faye's watery grave, and I even whispered her name into his ear as he died.

Matthew Beaumont was Debbie MacReady's son. She'd been a mousy thing who barely talked, although I remember her almost hysterical giggle, especially as Faye slid underneath the rock that would be her final resting place.

Matthew was quite wealthy himself, and it made me wonder if he'd hire a private security detail to protect himself after receiving the list. For that reason I took him out quite early. That was me in the woods in Dartford, shooting him in the back. He looked quite peaceful on the orange mat of fallen pine needles.

Arthur Kruse Junior was Art Kruse's boy, and I heard through my sources that Art had already abandoned his son because he was gay. Not surprising since I remember the young Art as the most enthusiastically fascistic of the pirate society. He'd been sorely disappointed when we decided as a group to not tie Faye up. His son, Arthur, by all accounts, seemed to be a decent man. I almost considered killing the father and not the son, but that would have gone against my plan. And if there's one thing I like in my life, it is order. Still, I made sure Arthur would have a painless death, dying in his sleep while the police watched his house. A source who shall remain nameless provided me with the canister of carbon monoxide and the ingenious timing mechanism.

After killing Arthur Kruse, I traveled to Albany, where I planned on attaching an explosive device to Jessica Winslow's car. But as soon as I got there it was clear to me that her townhouse and her vehicle as well were being very carefully watched. She was an FBI agent, after all. I'd made a mistake, I realized, and should have killed her earlier.

Jessica was the adopted daughter of Gary Winslow, who was the oldest member of the Pirate Society, and I had often thought that he should have been the one to stop us from doing what we did. Either him or me, of course. But we all listened to Gary, and I remember him saying once—and maybe this is a false memory—that although we were pirates, we were the good kind of pirates.

A lifetime as a successful businessman and consultant has taught me many lessons, one of them being that you can't do everything yourself, and that sometimes you need to hire experts. That is what I did in order to dispatch Jessica. I'm a little ashamed to admit that I subcontracted that particular death, but I knew that she had left town, and that my chances of finding her and killing her without getting stopped or caught were slim. I paid a lot of money to have it done right.

Killing Jay Coates was comparatively easy, and I did that one myself. I'd learned enough about him to know that he hadn't fallen far from the tree that was his psychopath of a father. I remember just how much glee Wayne Coates had taken in the initiation rite of making my sister survive the tide. And I also remember that he stayed joyful even later on that terrible day when it became apparent to all of us that something had gone very wrong.

The FBI never located the real Jay Coates. I wonder if he even got the list in the mail, because I did hear that a Jay Coates in Georgia had stepped forward to say that he had received one. It doesn't matter either way, but it did make Jay's death one of my easier tasks. I followed him around Los Angeles on a Saturday night, just waiting for an opportunity, and unless I imagined it, he was stalking someone as well. A young inebriated woman that he'd followed from a bar. I wonder if my killing Jay prevented something terrible from happening to that girl. Maybe the karma I was returning to the world was already paying off in dividends?

Caroline Geddes was the daughter of Meg Gauthier (my first kiss, also that summer), and Ethan Dart was the son of Paula Shepherd, the quietest of our bunch. How odd that the list brought Caroline and Ethan together just before the end.

Arranging their deaths was not easy. But I knew in advance that they would be together in Makanda, Illinois, and then it was just a matter of two very large bribes, one to a local police officer and one to an employee at the Rolling Brook Cabins who provided me with a master key. The hardest part was lying underneath their bed and listening to their final moments together. But as in the killing of Arthur Kruse, I made sure that neither Ethan nor Caroline suffered any pain. And I do know for a fact just how happy they were in their final moments. Maybe I'd done them a favor, ending their lives then. I wonder what I saved them from: A crushing breakup? A bitter divorce? A loss of a child? I certainly saved them from something. Happiness is always a temporary state.

And Alison Horne, of course, was the daughter of Danny Horne. Not only had Danny helped orchestrate Faye's death when he was twelve years old, he would eventually abandon his own family for a tawdry love affair. I wonder what Danny'll think of all this if it comes out that his old childhood friend had an affair with his daughter before murdering her in Bermuda.

I felt bad about Alison, of course. It was a pleasure to spend time with her in Bermuda. I'd been wanting to go back there for years, and it was nice to see the old haunted place through her eyes. And it was nice to be *able to tell her about my sister, about what happened to her. I suppose the psychologists out there will say that was what I was doing all along, that my entire plan was an elaborate way to tell the world about my sister. They'll say I wanted to get caught, and maybe that is true as well.*

I know that I've left some questions behind that have not been answered in this letter. Like why did I even bother to mail the letter to myself and then give the FBI information about the Windward Resort? I don't really have the answer to that question except that it felt like the right thing to do. I am guilty, as well, in the death of my sister, and I deserved to be on the list, just as I deserve what is about to happen to me.

Maybe you will wonder why I even wrote the list in the first place, sending it to the victims. It made my job harder, and it made their final moments more filled with dread, but, again, all I can tell you is that it felt like the right thing to do. Their deaths were an attempt to add order back to a chaotic world, and the list itself was just part of that order. And being on that list only told them something that they should already have known. That death is coming for us all.

And what about Eric Miles, my neighbor in Hartford? All I will say about him is that he deserved to die, more than most of us. Think of me as a garbage man, just out doing my job of picking up the bagged garbage left along the side of the road. Eric was just a piece of trash that floated into my path at random. It wasn't a whole lot of effort for me to throw him into my truck, as well.

My time is up, I think, and I won't bore you any more with self-reflection. I'll hide this letter in an appropriate place, then take my remaining whiskey out to the jetty. I'll be joining Faye soon. I don't mean in heaven, because I don't believe that such a place exists. I mean that other place. The cold nothing that awaits all of us when we finally leave this world.

May your gods have mercy on all your souls.

    Sincerely,
    Jack Radebaugh né Jonathan Borland Grant
    June 21, 1944—NOVEMBER 2, 2014

ONE

Matthew Beaumont

Jay Coates

Ethan Dart

Caroline Geddes

Frank Hopkins

Alison Horne

Arthur Kruse

Jack Radebaugh

Jessica Winslow

I

SUNDAY, MARCH 19, 5:14 A. M.

She'd been hearing voices for so long—some she recognized and some she didn't—that they had begun to mean nothing to her. But then some of the voices began to break through, and one of them said, "Her eyes just opened."

Or maybe she'd dreamed it.

She was in the darkness again, but there had been a flicker of light.

One of the things she liked about the darkness was that there was no pain.

But then she heard a voice she recognized—her mother's voice—the words floating in her head, and she remembered that once upon a time she had opened her eyes. So she tried to open them again, and this time there was nothing but darkness, and the sound of machines. The sound of the room she was in, doing whatever it was that rooms do.

When she next heard voices, and felt a hand on her arm, she opened her eyes again and this time a face looked back at her. She didn't recognize it, but it smiled. A woman's face, dark freckles along the hairline, a razor-thin scar on her chin. "Why, hello, you," she said.

Later, there were so many faces around her hospital bed that just looking at them made her happy and tired all at once. Her mother was by her side, holding her hand.

"Am I dead?" she asked. Her voice was scratchy and didn't sound like hers. Everyone in the room laughed, although some were also crying.

"Well, you came close." This was from her doctor. "What do you remember about it?"

She slowly shook her head back and forth, trying to find the words that would explain her memory. Eventually, she said, "I work for the FBI."

"That's right, honey," her mom said.

Much later, two people she remembered from working at the FBI came to visit her. It was a good afternoon, her mind swimming with memories, and a bar of summer light lying across her legs and warming them.

The woman's name was Ruth Jackson and she had a round face and a deep voice. The man's name was Aaron Levin, and he kept bouncing up and down on his toes. She knew that she and the man had been more than co-workers. Her memories kept throwing a few random slides at her—the two of them untwisting themselves from bedsheets, and laughing uproariously; the man outside her door, thumping at it, trying to be let in.

"You look good," Ruth Jackson said.

A few sarcastic thoughts went through her head, but she dismissed them, and said, "Thank you. So do you. I like your suit."

Ruth smiled, and next to her Aaron went up and down on his toes, his hands in his pockets.

"Your doctor tells us you're remembering more and more these days."

"Just this morning I remembered all of seventh grade in a rush. It was terrible."

Ruth laughed, and she remembered how much she liked making other people laugh. "I'm sorry about that," Ruth said. "Are all your memories old ones?"

"Can you both sit down?" she said. "I'm happy to talk, but Aaron, you're driving me crazy bouncing up and down like that."

Both the agents laughed, and she thought that part of their laughter was relief. Then they both sat down on molded plastic chairs, Ruth still closest to her.

"What do you remember about being here?"

"I know that I was shot. I don't know why."

"Uh-huh." Ruth frowned and cast her eyes at the ceiling, as though she were deciding what to ask next.

"Do you remember anything about a list?"

"I remember being asked about a list, but that was here in this bed. Someone else asked me, but now I can't remember who that was."

"Probably me. Probably I asked you about it when you weren't ready. But the list has to do with why you're here."

"Oh, then please tell me. No one says anything. I keep thinking that I did something horribly wrong."

"You did nothing wrong."

She pushed herself up a little in her bed, the movement causing her to blink rapidly. "So tell me the story of the list, and why I'm here. I want to hear it."

"Are you sure?"

"Yes, I'm sure."

"Okay. I'll tell you the basics, and please let me know if you get tired, or if it gets too much for you."

Her arms tingled, and she took a deep breath. "Just start. I need to hear it. What kind of story is it?"

"Not a good one, I suppose," Ruth said.

"Not completely bad," Aaron blurted out, scooting forward on his chair.

Her eyes went back and forth between them both, wanting to hear the story, but also not wanting to hear it.

"Right," Ruth said. "It's not completely bad. But I'm going to stop talking about it, and just tell it, okay, Jessica? And that way, you can be the judge."

ACKNOWLEDGMENTS

Martin Amis, Jane Austen, Danielle Bartlett, Lawrence Block, Angus Cargill, Agatha Christie, Caspian Dennis, Victoria Dillman (thanks for the title), T. S. Eliot, Bianca Flores, Joel Gotler, John Grindrod, Kaitlin Harri, David Headley, David Highfill, Tessa James, Weldon Kees, Philip Larkin, John D. MacDonald, Louis MacNeice, Sara Paolozzi, Sophie Portas, Josh Smith, Nat Sobel, Muriel Spark, Virginia Stanley, Sandy Violette, Judith Weber, Dave Woodhouse, Adia Wright, and Charlene Sawyer.

*Now read the exclusive
first chapter of*

THE KIND WORTH SAVING

PETER SWANSON

Publishing March 2023

I

Kimball

"Do you remember me?" she asked, after stepping into my office.

"I do," I said, before I could actually place her. But she *was* familiar, and for a terrible moment I wondered if she was a cousin of mine, or a long-ago girlfriend I'd entirely forgotten.

She took a step inside the room. She was short and built like an ex-gymnast, with wide shoulders and strong-looking legs. Her face was a circle, her features—blue eyes, pert nose, round mouth—bunched into the middle. She wore dark jeans and a tweedy brown blazer, which made her look as though she'd just dismounted a horse. Her shoulder-length hair was black and glossy and parted on one side. "Senior honors English," she said.

"Joan," I said, as though the name had just come to me, but of course she'd made this appointment, and given me her name.

"I'm Joan Whalen now, but I was Joan Grieve when you were my teacher."

"Yes, Joan Grieve," I said. "Of course, I remember you."

"And you're Mr. Kimball," she said, smiling for the first time since she'd entered the room, showing a row of tiny teeth, and that was when I truly remembered her. She *had* been a gymnast, a popular, flirtatious, above-average student, who'd always made me vaguely uncomfortable, just by the way she'd said my name, as though she had something on me. She was making me vaguely uncomfortable, now, as well. My time as a teacher at Dartford-Middleham High School was a time I was happy to forget.

"You can call me Henry," I said.

"You don't seem like a Henry to me. You still seem like a Mr. Kimball."

"I don't think anyone has called me Mr. Kimball since the day I left that job. Did you know who I was when you made this appointment?"

"I didn't know, but I guess I assumed. I knew that you'd been a police officer, and then I heard about . . . you know, all that happened . . . and it made sense that you were now a private detective."

"Well, come in. It's nice to see you, Joan, despite the circumstances. Can I get you anything? Coffee or tea? Water?"

"I'm good. Actually, no, I'll have a water, if you're offering."

While I pulled a bottle of water from the mini fridge that sat in the south corner of my two-hundred-square-foot office, Joan wandered over to the one picture I had on my wall, a framed print of a watercolor of Grantchester Meadows near Cambridge in England. I'd bought

it on a trip a number of years ago not because I'd particularly liked the artwork but because one of my favorite
poems by Sylvia Plath was called "Watercolor of Grantchester Meadows," so I thought it would be a clever thing
to own. After I'd rented this office space, I dug out the
print because I wanted a calming image on my wall, the
way dentists' offices and divorce lawyers' always display
soothing art so their clients might forget where they are.

Joan cracked open the bottle of water and took a seat
as I moved around my desk. I adjusted the blinds because
the late-afternoon sun was slanting into the room, and
Joan was squinting as she took a long sip. Before I sat
down myself I had a brief but vivid recollection of standing in front of my English students a dozen years ago, my
armpits damp with anxiety, their bored, judgmental eyes
staring up at me. I could almost smell the chalk dust in
the air.

I lowered myself into my leather swivel chair, and
asked Joan Whalen what I could help her with.

"Ugh," she said, and rolled her eyes a little. "It's so
pedestrian."

I could tell she wanted me to guess why she'd come,
but I kept quiet.

"It's about my husband," she said at last.

"Uh-huh."

"Like I said, it's probably something you hear all the
time, but I'm pretty sure . . . no, I *know* that he's cheating
on me. The thing is, I don't really care all that much—he

can do whatever he wants as far as I'm concerned—but even though I know he's doing it, I don't have proof yet. I don't *really* know."

"Are you thinking of filing for divorce once you know for sure?"

She shrugged, and that childish gesture made me smell chalk again. "I don't even know. Probably. What really bothers me is that he's getting away with it, getting away with having an affair, and I tried following him myself, but he knows my car, of course, and I just want to know for sure. I want details. Who he's with. Well, I'm pretty sure I know that, too. Where they go. How often. Like I said, I don't give a shit, except that he's getting away with it." She looked over my shoulder through the office's sole window. When the light hit it in the late afternoon you could see just how dusty it was, and I reminded myself to wipe down the panes when I had some spare time.

I slid my notebook toward me and uncapped a pen. "What's your husband's name, and what does he do?" I said.

"His name is Richard Whalen and he's a real estate broker. He owns a company called Blackburn Properties. They have offices in Dartford and Concord, but he mainly works out of the Dartford one. Pam O'Neil is the Dartford office manager, and that's who he's sleeping with."

"How do you know it's her?"

She held up a fist and stuck out her thumb. "First, she's the only really pretty employee in his office. Well, pretty *and* young, which is the way Richard likes them. Second, Richard is a liar but he's not great at it, and I accused him of having an affair with Pam and he couldn't even look me in the eye."

"Have you accused him of having affairs in the past?"

"The thing is, I don't think he *has* had an affair in the past, not a real one anyway. He does go to this bullshit conference every year for real estate brokers in Las Vegas, and I'm sure he's hooked up with a stripper there or something, but that's not really the same as an affair. And I'm kind of friends with Pam, that's the thing. When she first got the job at Blackburn I invited her to my book club, which she came to a bunch of times, although none of us thought she really read the books.

"I was nice to her. I even introduced her to the guy who does my husband's investments, and they went out for a while. I took her out for drinks at least three times."

"When do you think the affair started?"

"I think it started around the time Pam stopped texting me, which was about three months ago. They've made it so obvious it's like they want to get caught. You must see this stuff all the time?"

It was the second time she'd mentioned that, and I decided not to tell her that it wasn't something I saw all the time because my only regular clients were a temp agency that employed me to do background checks, and an octogenarian just down the street from my office who was always losing her cats.

"My guess is," I said, "that they are trying to be secretive and failing at it. Which probably means that your husband, and Pam, as well, haven't had affairs before. The people who are good at hiding secrets are the people who have practice at it."

She frowned, thinking about what I'd just said. "You're probably right, but I guess I don't particularly care one way or another if my husband is cheating on me for the first time. I don't know why I feel this way but, honestly, it's Pam that is pissing me off a little more than he is. I don't know what game she thinks she's playing. Hey, did you keep teaching after the seniors graduated early that year? I know you didn't come back the next year."

It was an abrupt change of topic and for that reason it made me answer honestly. "Oh, God, no," I said. "I don't think I could've ever walked back into that school. I felt bad about it, but there was only about two weeks left anyway."

"You never taught again?"

"No, not high school. I do occasionally teach an adult ed class in poetry, but it's not the same thing."

"The basketball player," she said, and her face brightened as though she'd just won a trivia contest.

I must have looked confused because she added, "It's all coming back to me, now. For the last month of classes you had us read poetry because you knew we wouldn't be able to focus on full books."

"Right," I said.

"And we read this poem about a kid who used to be—"

"Oh, right. John Updike. The poem was called 'Ex-Basketball Player.' I haven't thought of that for—"

"And you got in a fight with Ally Eisenkopf because she said you were making up all the symbolism in it."

"I wouldn't call it a fight. More like a spirited intellectual debate." And now I was remembering that day in class, when the lesson plan was to dissect that poem line by line, and I'd drawn a map on the chalkboard that located the gas station described in the poem, and the street it was on. I was trying to show how a relatively simple poem such as "Ex-Basketball Player" by John Updike could be as carefully constructed as a clock, that every word was a deliberate choice for both the text and the subtext of the poem. The students that were paying attention had rebelled, convinced I was reading things into the poem that didn't exist. I'd told them I found it interesting they could believe that someone could go to the moon, or invent computer coding, yet they couldn't quite believe that the described location of the gas station in a poem was a metaphor for the stalled life of a high school basketball champion.

Ally Eisenkopf, one of my more vocal students, had gotten visibly upset, claiming I was just making stuff up, as though I'd told her that the sky wasn't blue. I was very surprised that Joan remembered that particular class. I told her that.

"I have a good memory, and you were a good teacher. You really made an impression on me that year."

"Well," I said. "You and no one else."

"You know that Richard, my cheating husband, went to DM too."

It took me a moment to remember that DM was what the kids called Dartford-Middleham High School. "No, I didn't know that. Did I have him in a class?"

"No, you didn't have him in one of your classes. No way did he do honors English."

I was surprised that Joan had married a high school boyfriend. The towns of Dartford and Middleham might not be as ritzy as some of the other towns around them, like Concord, or Lincoln, but most of the kids from the public high school went on to four-year colleges, and I doubt many of them married their high school sweethearts.

"Were you dating him back then, in high school?"

"Richard? No, hardly. I knew him, of course, because he was a really good soccer player, but it was just random that we got together. We met in Boston, actually. I lived there for a year after college, and he was still at BU and bartending in Alston. That's where I lived."

"Where do you both live now?"

"In Dartford, I'm sorry to say. We actually live in Rich's parents' house. Not with them. They live in Florida now, but they sold us the house and it was such a good deal that we couldn't really pass it up. I suppose you'll need to know our address and everything if you're going to be following Rich?" She pulled her shoulders back a fraction and raised her head. It was a gesture I remembered.

"You sure you want me to do this for you? If you already know that he's cheating—"

"I am definitely sure. He's just going to deny it unless I have proof."

So we talked terms, and I gave her a rate that was slightly less than I should have, but she was a former student, and it wasn't as though I didn't have the time. And she told me the details about Richard's real estate office, and how she was convinced that the affair was only taking place during work hours. "You know it's the easiest profession for having affairs," she said.

"Empty houses," I said.

"Yep. Lots of empty houses, lots of excuses to go visit them. He told me that, a while ago, when two of the agents in his company were sleeping with one another, and he had to put an end to it."

I got more details from her, then let her know I'd work up a contract and email it to her to sign. And as soon as I had her signature and a deposit I would go to work.

"Keep an eye on Pam," she said. "That's who he's with, I know it."

After Joan left my office, I stood at my window with its view of Oxford Street and watched as she plucked fallen ginkgo leaves off her Acura before getting inside. It was a nice day outside, that time of year when half the leaves are still on the trees, and half are blowing around in the wind. I returned to my desk, opened up a Word document, and took notes on my new case. It had been strange to see Joan again, grown-up but somehow still the same. I could feel myself starting to go over that period of time when I'd last known her but I tried to focus instead on what she'd told me about her husband. I'd tailed a wife once before, but never a husband. In that previous case, just over a year ago, it turned out the wife wasn't cheating, that she was a secret gambler, driving up to New Hampshire to visit poker rooms. Somehow, this time, I thought that Joan's husband was probably exactly who she thought he was. But I told myself to not make assumptions. Being at the beginning of a case was like beginning a novel or sitting down to watch a movie. It was best to go in with zero expectations.

After locking up my office and leaving the building I was surprised to find it was dusk already. I walked home along the leaf-strewn streets of Cambridge, excited to have a paying job, but feeling just a little haunted by having seen Joan again after so many years.

It was mid-October and every third house or so was bedecked with Halloween decorations: pumpkins, fake cobwebs, plastic tombstones. One of the houses I passed regularly was swarmed with giant fake spiders, and a mother had brought her two children, one still in a stroller, to look at the spectacle. The older of the two kids, a girl, was pointing to one of the spiders with genuine alarm and said to her mother that someone should smush it.

"Not me," the mom said. "We'd need a giant to do that."

"So, let's get a giant," the girl said.

The mother caught my eye as I was passing and smiled at me. "Not me either," I said. "I'm tall, but I'm not a giant."

"Then let's get out of here," the girl said, her voice very serious. I kept walking, thinking ominous thoughts, then disregarding them, the way I'd taught myself to do.